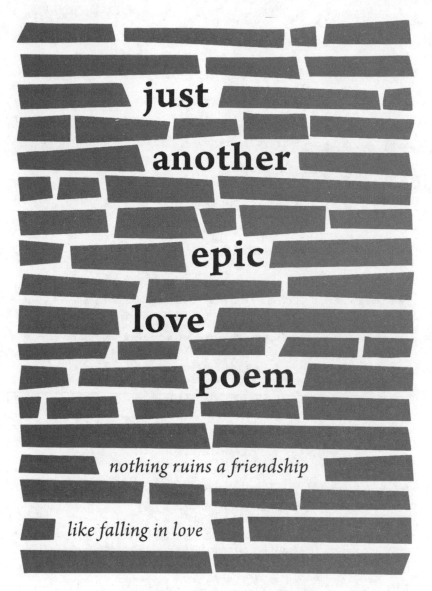

just another epic love poem

nothing ruins a friendship

like falling in love

PARISA AKHBARI

Dial Books

DIAL BOOKS
An imprint of Penguin Random House LLC, New York

First published in the United States of America by Dial Books,
an imprint of Penguin Random House LLC, 2024

Visit us online at PenguinRandomHouse.com.

Library of Congress Cataloging-in-Publication Data is available.

Printed in the United States of America

ISBN 9780593530498

1st Printing

LSCH

Design by Cerise Steel
Text set in Yoga Pro

*To my big sister, Taraneh, who came out at age sixteen
and dyed her hair blue on her last day of Catholic school:
You set an amazing example for me. They say nothing can
"turn" you gay, but I'm pretty sure that Gossip concert you took me
to for my fourteenth birthday did the trick. This book is for you.*

There are treasures within you.
Split the melon. Hand them out.

—Rumi (translated by Haleh Liza Gafori)

The Never-Ending Poem

WHENEVER SHE GOT nostalgic, Bea would ask me, "Do you remember how it started?"

And I wouldn't need to ask her *What?* because I already knew what she was talking about. But she'd coax me on anyway: "The first thing I ever wrote to you."

I remember how the poem started, I want to tell Bea now. *I remember, I remember.* But I think she'd rather we both forgot.

The Beginning

BEA AND I were thirteen when we met, when I transferred into her eighth-grade classroom at Holy Trinity. Bea would fight me on this part, but our friendship—and everything after—began with her pelting me in the back of the head with a wad of paper.

Not that I was a stranger to fielding other people's spitwads. But my first day had already been off to a miserable start, mainly because of the uniform jumper. It hung in this thick, carpet-like fabric down my body, a pleated headache of red and gold plaid.

This is the first day of the rest of your life, I thought. I looked like a human Christmas tree ornament. And maybe that was the point of Catholic school. How would I know?

We had just moved to Crossroads, the one almost-affordable pocket in the uber-rich city of Bellevue, Washington. I loved our new neighborhood because of its proximity to the Crossroads Shopping Center, home of the only Iranian-owned pizza parlor I had ever heard of. I also loved it because we were surrounded by other brown people. Crossroads felt like a little belly button of familiarity in a giant and strange new city.

But our new school wasn't in Crossroads. It was in Medina, where everyone had a home tennis court or a pool. And it wasn't like my old school, which my dad referred to as a "crunchy hippie place" when he found out I spent science class sifting through trash bins to start a composting system. Holy Trinity was a private Catholic school.

Which was a weird choice, given that my dad was raised Muslim.

Dad had ushered my eleven-year-old sister, Azar, and me into our new student orientation with a pep talk about how Catholics valued education above all else, and how the teachers would only care that we studied hard. I guess he believed that good grades would shield us—like nobody would notice that we were clearly Iranian American, and didn't know a thing about Catholicism, because intellect would render us into amorphous orbs of knowledge.

The idea of Catholic school had me convinced I'd be transported into a staging of *The Sound of Music,* nuns and all. From the brochures, the entire student body of Holy Trinity looked like a beaming sea of von Trapp children. I half expected them to twirl around in their matching jumpers and suit coats and serenade me with "Do-Re-Mi" on my arrival.

Turns out, didn't happen.

Dad pulled up to the school grounds that first day, sneak-attack kissing my and Azar's foreheads. "Make it a good day," he shouted as we slipped out of the car, his accent snagging the attention of some tall boys in blazers. "Make it the best day of your life!"

That's how Dad said goodbye to us every day since we left Mom—a charge to make the best of crappy times.

Azar and I headed toward the complex of brick buildings, and she immediately broke away from me, flocking toward a gaggle of sixth-grade girls on the lawn. I kept my eyes on the scattered leaves in front of me, not looking up until I reached the arch at the school's entrance, which was engraved with the words: *May God Hold You in the Palm of His Hand.*

Each building on campus was named after a Jesuit priest or saint, their faces embossed above the doors so that some old, dead white guy was always scowling down at you upon entry.

Xavier—or Creepy Goatee Dude, as I came to think of him—was cavernous, with a long, dark hallway parting two rows of lockers. The space was packed with students huddling by their respective lockers, every single one of them glued to a phone. The front door thudded behind me, and some of the kids looked up, glaring, before going back to sending their last messages before first period. I didn't even have my own phone; Azar and I shared my dad's old Galaxy, which meant she was constantly wresting it out of my hands so she could play Pet Rescue Saga or video chat the gazillion friends she left behind in Sacramento. I didn't need my own phone, because I didn't have anyone to talk to.

As I worked my way toward the classroom, I snuck glances of the Holy Trinity girls. They all looked so shiny and *wholesome*,, like they ate apple pie every night and said prayers and flossed their teeth before bed. Some of them had cross necklaces over their jumpers, and they were all wearing knee-high socks, not the crew-cut ones my dad had picked out for me at the sporting goods store. I'd have to ask my dad for a cross necklace so I could go incognito for as long as humanly possible. I wondered how soon it would be before everyone found out that Azar and I weren't Catholic.

Behind the door of Ms. Byrne's eighth-grade classroom, thirty-three sets of eyes zeroed in on me. This was the problem with transferring to a new school in October: Everyone had already established a routine, and here I was, shattering their normalcy with my unfamiliar face and my weird crew-cut socks. I tucked into a desk in the corner of the classroom and stared at the crucifix by the doorway. Jesus, blue-eyed and bleeding, hung stretched out on the cross. Beads of red paint circled the nails in his palms and feet. His head lolled to one side under a crown of thorns. It struck me as pretty graphic for a school where you weren't allowed to expose your collarbones or wear nail polish.

"Jesus was a nice guy," my dad had told me when I asked him why we were going to Catholic school. Lots of Christians don't know this, but Jesus was revered as a prophet in Islam, and there is even a whole chapter in the Qur'an named after Mary. But I had never seen a dead body like this before, sculpture or otherwise. It made me rethink the cross necklace idea.

"Peace be with you, class." A light-skinned woman with smooth brown hair broke my focus. She wore a gold blazer and knee-length skirt with a red-and-gold tie. Going off her outfit alone, I could tell she was nothing like my old teacher Edgar. He smelled like pipe smoke and his jeans were chronically mud-stained from helping us collect earthworms for our compost project. Anytime one of us shoveled up a worm from the garden patch, he'd say something ridiculous like "Ya dig it?"

Ms. Byrne pulled out a clipboard for roll call, and I allowed myself to peek at the other students as their names were read aloud. *Tristan? Leah? Savannah? Matthew? Spencer?* All of them wore red jumpers or blazers, and they all whirred together in my brain like one of Azar's berry smoothie blender experiments.

"Beatrice?"

My eyes wheeled to the row behind me. Beatrice teetered on the back legs of her chair, the metal frame creaking beneath her. She wore round glasses, her knee-highs were mismatched, and her haircut was definitely of the DIY variety. And still, somehow, I knew she was cooler than me. Not *popular*, I guessed, but memorable. Other kids looked to her when her name was called.

She met my eyes. "Bea," she said to Ms. Byrne—and also, it seemed, to me.

"We don't use nicknames at school, Beatrice," Ms. Byrne said, returning to her list. "Oh yes, that's right. We have a new student joining us today." The teacher scanned the back of the class and landed on me. "Mitra . . ." She stalled. "How do you say this?"

My voice was stuck in my gut somewhere beneath the shir berenj I'd had for breakfast. "Esfahani."

Bea was still watching me. Her skin was amber-brown like mine, but with dark freckles dusting her nose.

"Es-fa-*ha*-ni." Ms. Byrne jotted down a pronunciation note on the roll call sheet. She was trying to be helpful but had already spent ten more seconds focused on me than I could handle. "What kind of name is that?"

As she asked, it occurred to me that I should've practiced answering these kinds of questions at home. Then I'd be a pro at deflecting any inquiries into my background. Like Wonder Woman, when she used her bracelets to deflect hundreds of whizzing bullets.

But I didn't have magic Amazonian bracelets, so I winged it. "It's, um, a last name?"

Bea laughed so hard that it verged on inappropriate.

"Okay," Ms. Byrne said, mercifully choosing to move on. "Welcome, Mitra."

She set down her roll call sheet and faced the class. "Today we're going to continue our unit on poetry. Page one eighty-one, Billy Collins's 'Litany.'"

Everyone except me pulled out thick textbooks and flipped through the pages. I glanced at the girl next to me, who had red ringlets over her eyes. I could make out some of the poem on the page of her open book, but when she caught me looking, she blocked my sight with her elbow.

"Follow along with me," Ms. Byrne said.

I dug my thumbnail into the wood of my desk. The poem started like this:

> You are the bread and the knife,
> the crystal goblet and the wine.

It continued describing its subject through metaphors like that, bringing images of birds and bakers and bright sunshine clear into my mind. And it named what the subject is *not*: not the plums on the counter, *certainly not the pine-scented air*.

When she finished the poem, Ms. Byrne lifted her eyebrows at us. "Reactions?"

Bea's hand shot up.

"Yes, Beatrice."

"I like the images. I like the 'burning wheel of the sun.' But, who does this guy think he is?"

"Pardon?"

"He keeps saying 'You're *this*, you're *that*, you're *definitely not that*,'" she said. "What if I *am* the pine-scented air? Where does he get off thinking he can tell me what I am? He doesn't know my life!"

A boy behind me chuckled.

"All right, Ms. Ortega. Calm down," Ms. Byrne said, pinching the bridge of her nose. "Time for small group discussions. Pair up with your partners and share your responses to 'Litany.' I want you to identify how Billy Collins uses the elements of poetry we've been learning about: form, sound, imagery, metaphor." A teacher's aide knocked at the door, and Ms. Byrne stepped out of the room.

Everyone turned toward the kid next to them, and I just sat there, not sure who my partner was supposed to be.

"I have to work with the new girl," the redhead beside me whispered loudly to a girl across the aisle from her.

Her friend groaned. "Don't work with the *new girl,*" she whined. "Work with *me.*"

My chin sunk toward my chest, and my eyes locked on the crucifix again. It would be a lot easier to blend in if I at least had a textbook to look through. I kept hearing my dad's voice in my head: *Jesus was a nice guy.*

Then, *flick.* Something soft bounced off the back of my head. *Excellent.* My first day at Holy Trinity, and my head was already serving as the backboard for someone's private game of basketball. The kids around me stopped chattering, and I took in a slow breath. Then I twisted around in my seat and found it: a wad of crumpled paper. I kept it closed in my palms and slumped back into my chair.

"Hrrm," someone coughed. "*Hrrrm!*"

It was Bea. When I looked at her, clueless, she rolled her eyes and then made a gesture with her hands, like she was unfurling a scroll.

I stared back at her for a moment too long. Then I opened my hand and smoothed out the paper against the edge of my desk. Tiny purple writing emerged from the inside of the page.

> They say you're just the new girl
> but they should know better,
> you're really the jelly
> holding the sandwich together,
> I'm a thunderclap
> not some goblet of wine,
> Holy Trinity sucks
> but at least my poem rhymed.
> —Bea-lly Collins

Ms. Byrne came back, and I hid Bea's note in a pleat of my jumper. Nobody had ever written me a poem before. Unless you counted the improvised rhymes Azar liked to scream at me whenever she was mad, like *Mitra's alone sitting in a tree, F-A-R-T-I-N-G!* But those were more spoken word performances than actual poems. When I finally worked up the courage to look back at her, Bea tilted her head to one side and lifted an invisible pen in her hand, scrawling imaginary cursive in the air.

She wanted me to write back.

When Ms. Byrne turned to the whiteboard, I inched Bea's poem out of the pleat in my skirt and scribbled something down. When my moment arrived, I chucked the paper ball back at Bea.

She unfolded it immediately.

You're the thunderclap
and the flash of bright light,
I'm the bunny down below
watching the sight,
I'm sorry to tell you
but I think we're outmanned—
we are both held hostage
in The Palm of God's Hand.

A grin broke across her face, lifting the rims of her glasses.

There was a flicker, even back then—one tiny flash of feeling in the empty shell of my chest. I called it relief.

I didn't know to call it love.

Senior Year

Mitra: you're late

Bea: always

Mitra: you're not sorry?

Bea: never sorry

Bea: important business

Mitra: mass is mandatory.

Mitra: so is not abandoning your best friend

Mitra: on the first day of our LAST SEMESTER OF SENIOR YEAR

Bea: YOU KNOW HOW I FEEL ABOUT ALL CAPS

Bea: THEY'RE CONTAGIOUS

Mitra: stop

Bea: I CAN'T MITRA, I'VE BEEN INFECTED!!

Mitra: . . .

Bea: THIS IS GOING TO BE A LONG DAY FOR YOU

Mitra: I'm walking into chapel now

Mitra: putting my phone away

Mitra: if you get here before communion I'll forgive you

Bea: PRAISE TO YOU

11

Mass

IT'S THE FIRST day back at school after winter break and I'm stuck in chapel packed with the red-and-gold student body of Holy Trinity, with "Alleluia! Sing to Jesus" ringing in my ears. Mass feels nightmarish without Bea, especially after she coaxed me into that Catholic horror movie marathon over winter break. This is not how I wanted to start the last semester: friendless, my eyes whirling between the statue faces of the saints, trying to detect any signs of demonic possession.

"You having flashbacks to *The Devil's Doorway*?" Bea's voice slinks into my ear from the pew behind me.

"Flashbacks would suggest I actually watched any of it," I say. "Most of my view was obscured by your crochet blanket."

"Fair point," she whispers.

If Bea were a witch, her magic would be coiled up in her voice. She can broadcast it loud and low when she wants to, like when she used to ward off middle school mean girls with just a word. Those growls I could handle. It's when her voice turns quiet that I get restless: It's so soft, too close. It sprouts a wave of goose bumps along my neck.

Bea must notice them, because a tiny breath of her laughter hits my skin. "I didn't mean to traumatize you," she says.

I'll let her believe it's fear that lights the hairs on my neck. "Next time, I pick the movie," I say. "Something with kittens and rainbows. Fun for the whole family."

Father Mitchell's voice scrambles toward the high notes of the hymn, teetering around off-key. "What he lacks in vocal training, he makes up for in sheer conviction," Bea says solemnly. "But could he sing to Jesus a little softer?"

"Quiet," I whisper. Bea hates the hymns and psalms and stuff, but I don't mind them. If I look at them the right way, it's easy to find poems in them.

He who dwells in the shelter of the Most High will rest in the shadow of the Almighty. I will say of the LORD, "He is my refuge and my fortress, my God, in whom I trust."

Surely he will save you from the fowler's snare and from the deadly pestilence. He will cover you with his feathers, and under his wings you will find refuge; his faithfulness will be your shield and rampart.

You will not fear the terror of night nor the arrow that flies by day, nor the pestilence that stalks in the darkness, nor the plague that destroys at midday. A thousand may fall at your side, ten thousand at your right hand, but it will not come near you. You will only observe with your eyes and see the punishment of the wicked.

If you make the Most High your dwelling—even the LORD, who is my refuge—then no harm will befall you, no disaster will come near your tent. For he will command his angels concerning you to guard you in all your ways; they will lift you up in their hands, so that you will not strike your foot against a stone.

You will tread upon the lion and the cobra; you will trample the great lion and the serpent. "Because he loves me," says the LORD, "I will rescue him; I will protect him, for he acknowledges my name. He will call upon me, and I will answer him; I will be with him in trouble, I will deliver him and honor him. With long life will I satisfy him and show him my salvation."

you
shelter thousands
under the fortress
of your feathers

you
command night
and make refuge,
shield me from

my snared
fear, come delivering
arrows, guard my
name in your hand

Bea slips one of her wireless buds into my ear before I can argue with her about church etiquette. "It's not auditorily possible for anyone to hear us over that pipe organ," she says. "I can feel it in my bones."

Auditorily? I mouth. She must be desperate for escape if she's resorting to made-up-sounding words. My messy morning hair does a decent job of concealing the earbud, but Bea always insists on blasting music at eardrum-bursting volume, because "if it's not loud, we're not *really listening.*"

The church is at capacity this morning because this Mass is not optional—in honor of our first day back in school, we get our cells rattled by the death groan of the pipe organ. The chapel is divided by grade, with seniors occupying the last few pews, maybe a nod to the fact that we're on our way out. Our bodies are here, but our souls are caught in some timeless dimension waiting for our college admission letters.

When I first started at Holy Trinity, my sole mission was to survive long enough to work my way back through these pews. Study hard, stay quiet, and get out. The *getting out* part glued Bea and me together from the start. To Bea, Catholic school feels like one prolonged slap on the wrist from her parents. But staying quiet is my own rule. Silence has never been Bea's style. She starts humming along to the King Princess song blaring in her earbuds, and this kid Jason from French class turns his head to glare at her.

"Do you want to get stuck on bathroom duty again?" I whisper over my shoulder. There are no detentions at Holy Trinity; here, it's Service Work. Not that I've ever been put in Service Work. But Bea's shenanigans have led her to scrub out more than her share of toilets.

Before winter break, she got a week of Service Work for "defacing school property" after she covered the gendered bathroom signs around campus with rainbow duct tape.

"Music is a healthy distraction," she tells me.

She's needed a lot of distractions lately.

Across the aisle, Cara Liu thumbs through a hymnal, her black hair blocking her tan face from our view. But that doesn't stop Bea from looking, because she's a glutton for self-punishment. Cara was Bea's first real love and most brutal heartbreak. I watch as all traces of church-mischief glee drain from Bea's face.

Down the pew from Cara are Max Jasinski and Ellie O'Reilly. Ellie's head bobs with imminent sleep, and Max jostles her with a free hand, the Bible flopped open in Max's lap.

We never used to need an aisle to separate us in church. The five of us used to sit together at every mandatory Mass. Ellie and Bea groaned their way through the sermons, Max and Cara sung dutifully along to all the hymns and refrains, and I tried not to sneeze when Father Mitchell waved around his pungent incense. But that was before the breakup.

I rap my fingers on the wooden back rest of my pew, trying to break Bea out of her daze, and she wrenches her head back to me, forcing a smile.

"Just hold on," I whisper. "As soon as Mass is over, we're ascending this purgatory."

"Poetry seminar!" Bea hisses back at me with a smile.

Bea told me about the seminar in eighth grade, and we've been holding it out like a carrot in front of each other for four years, a prize that will make all the Holy Trinity nonsense worthwhile. It's open only to seniors, and the teacher, Ms. Acosta, makes everyone submit a portfolio of writing samples to even be considered. We have our first class right after church. Assuming Bea doesn't get kicked out of Holy Trinity for blaring gay music during Mass.

When we stand for Communion, she reaches under my hair to take the earbud back, pocketing both of them.

"We'll be good. If you'd really rather listen to Father Mitchell, I'm not gonna get in your way. You know he's probably gearing up for 'Come, Holy Ghost' next." She slips into step with me as we march down the aisle in the procession of students, casting one last glance at Cara.

Nobody questions Bea cutting in line. People here act like we're interchangeable humans, probably because we're two queer brown girls in this conservative bastion, and the uniform coordination isn't helping. But her family is from Mexico, not Iran, and she's the social kind of introvert, whereas I still think "hanging out" over lunch break means simultaneous silent reading time in the empty chapel.

"So." Bea sneaks her words in between the organ chords. "You don't want to know why I was late?"

A smile rises across my face immediately, a flashlight beaming down the dark aisle. I already know.

"I brought you something," Bea says, pulling something from her backpack.

The Book.

The Book

NOT THE BIBLE, but our book—the thirteenth one in a line of notebooks we've been writing back and forth in, ever since that impromptu poetry swap on my first day of eighth grade. One long poem, a neverending thing. My hands itch to open it. But I won't allow myself to read it yet. Whenever it's my turn with The Book, I want to devour Bea's writing and somehow also savor it, like the too-sweet last bite of cake. Every single one of her poems is a shiny little gift.

Even when they're laced with heartbreak.

The Rules of the Never-Ending Poem

Why would you try to put a stop to this poem??

I wouldn't!!

1. For *our eyes only*!! ☠

Never.
How could I?!

2. Each new verse has to start with the ~~line~~ word the last person ended on.

!!!

3. Terminal punctuation is hereby BANNED. No question marks, exclamation points, periods, or anything else that signals an ending—because this is an endless thing.

4. Say what you ~~gotta~~ say, and don't ~~tell~~ take it back! No rewriting, no ~~tearing~~ out pages, no apologizing for your writing.

5. No criticizing each other's writing—or each other. The Book is for building each other up.

6. Total honesty—because what's the point of The Book (or our friendship) if we don't tell each other the truth?

And then one unwritten rule, just for me:

7. You can be honest about everything, except the one thing that would destroy your friendship. No letting your love for Bea show.

Confession

LOVING BEA ISN'T a choice. Love is the reflex to Bea existing at all. Like squinting at the sun, or shivering when she touches the back of my neck. My body just knows to do it. I can't control a reflex, and that petrifies me.

In the past, Bea was off-limits. She's always had some kind of romantic possibility in the works. There was Cara, and before Cara there was Harper, and before Harper there was Natalie, whom she sort of dated at the same time as Harper.

Bea attracts romantic entanglements like cat hair to a lint roller. She can't help it, it's just how she is. And because she was always taken, I could seal her off behind a brick wall of *Best Friend* in my mind. I made watertight boundaries. But now that she's single, all my feelings are starting to leak through.

If I had to pinpoint a beginning, it's this: The summer after sophomore year, Bea came over for one of our marathon nights of chatter and reading and snacks, which she'd just started calling wake-overs, because we were terrible at remembering to sleep. Around eleven, Bea pointed out my bedroom window. "Up for stargazing?"

The window formed a perfect portal to a flat section of rooftop; we'd only ever gone out there for daytime sun-soaking. But it was a gorgeous night, and Bea put on her begging eyes.

We dragged blankets, books, and a thermos of chai through the mouth of the window and made a nest on the rooftop. The June air filled my nose with earthy, after-storm smells. Bea in the blanket was soft and cozy, and the night around us sighed with breeze.

The darkness gave me permission to ask Bea the question that had camped in the back of my brain since we were thirteen.

"Why did you single me out that first day?"

I homed in on her face. Bea's curls expanded in proportion to how late we stayed up. The tip of her nose flushed warm from chai, and her chestnut eyes lit with the glow from my bedroom lamp.

"I could've been literally anyone," I said. "You didn't know what you were getting into."

"You looked like a reader." She shrugged. Like it was so easy for her to choose me. That first choice catalyzed a thousand others, and there we were, still bobbing in the ripple of her paper scrap.

"I thought . . ." Her eyes tracked mine. "I guess I thought we'd understand each other. And we did." She reached into the blanket tangle and brandished The Book. It was our first one, with a tattered black cover and red-ribbon bookmark. "Thought we could read some together."

She shed her glasses and brought her face close to our thirteen-year-old handwriting. I expected her to cringe at our dorky rhymes, but instead she smiled this private smile and huddled closer to me in the blankets. I leaned into her side and rested my head on her shoulder while she read, my cheek nuzzled into her collarbone.

Maybe I was the only person who got to see this Bea: the wee-hour Bea, starry and bound up in wonder.

"Look at us," she said.

When she read the passages to me, her mouth carried everything. All the awkwardness, all the treasures. Her voice wrapped around me.

In that moment, I knew it: I loved Bea. And not in the way I should've loved her, if she were only my best friend. This was a whole new layer of feeling, like that night had stripped the haze off everything around me.

And swirled up in the rich darkness of that night, loving her felt possible. Like I'd found some way to stretch beyond friendship and reach something deeper. Like maybe, just maybe, she could love me too.

But then she put The Book down and started analyzing a thirty-second conversation she'd had with the popcorn girl at the Crossroads movie theater who she'd always suspected was gay.

"I think there's something there," she said. "You know? Maybe I should go for it."

And just like that, the possibility burned away.

When we crawled back into my room, evidence of our friendship was everywhere: pictures of us with Azar in our uniforms on the last day of school; ticket stubs from our trip to the Butterfly Exhibit; a tragically ugly teacup we made at Paint the Town. Panic iced up my spine. Bea was everything to me. Without her, I'd have no one.

I couldn't gamble our friendship on the improbability that it could become something more. Love meant something different to Bea than it did to me: She fell hard and fast for crushes, like tripping face-first on pavement. My feelings were a slow, sinking sort of love. Like easing into a hot bath that leaves you dizzy and slack. If I let myself sink in further, I would never come out again. I couldn't allow any more space to that unruly feeling. I had to be okay with the fact that Bea didn't feel the same way about me.

That night, I lay with my arms and legs stiff against me, while Bea flopped around in the bed beside me. Her fingers twitched against my arm when she dreamed.

Everything had changed for me. But nothing had changed for Bea.

After that, I didn't let myself wish for anything when it came to Bea. Except one thing: I wished I could love her even a little bit less.

Mitra

our church took root
years ago, founded
in that paper scrap

you flung at my hair—
a never-ending chorus
ignited in the

space between
our minds, a thread
of endless prayer

that always finds
its answer, a ritual
of yeses

warmer than any
hymn—a ministry
of seeing and

being seen, this thing
built beyond ourselves,
sanctuary of words

Bea

words in our hands are bricks, watch
us shape clay soft and steady for our
feet to land on, one step, then two

'til we span the whole of that unknown road from here to the stars
embedded in our eyes—sharp

and too bright, a reflection we hold
impossibly—tell them we're
coming, Mitra, tell them

our plans could steal the gleam
from their static, star-faces,
tell them everything we've shouldered—

the swallowed words that couldn't be
spoken, the fang tooth of heartache
gnawing at my heels—all that, braved

to escape the fist of god's hand, tell them
our lives sparkle already from the
dust of things we haven't yet touched

Girl Plans, God Laughs

INSIDE BALD MAN with Halo, the building formerly known as Loyola, Bea and I brace ourselves as we step into the elevator. When we emerge on the bottom floor, I have to take a breath before reaching for the poetry classroom doorknob. I'm trying to hide my jitters. *We made it.* I know Bea will never feel the way I feel about her, but at least we can have this one precious thing together: poetry seminar.

We step inside the classroom, which looks like a habitat for ancient armchairs. Columns of books balance on end tables, and notepads and pens are strewn in the shaggy carpet. Baldie is set into a steep hillside, so even this basement room has a huge window overlooking the edge of Meydenbauer Bay. The space is cramped and bright, and it smells like rain. It's everything.

Poetry has lived in my back pocket for a long time now—first reading it, then writing it too. It's this perfect, slippery, secret thing that my fingers keep reaching for. Like a wriggly fish or an ember, it's alive and changing, a surprise every time.

Whenever things got hard with my mom when I was little, I'd hide out with Azar in a blanket pile in our bedroom and read her ancient Persian poets like Hafez, whom my dad recited on holidays. His poems were a kind of incantation, casting a spell with colors and sounds, drawing up a reality better than the one we were in.

If I reach back far enough, before my mom's car accident, before the painkillers turned her into someone else, I can remember my mom reading us poetry too. She'd pull me into her lap and let me ask a question about the future, and then she'd flip the pages of Hafez's *Divān* until an answer would reveal itself under her fingertips.

It's been years since I've talked to her, but I still seek answers from Hafez. And I write my own reality: words that curl up with me, block out the noise, pluck me out of my own head, and plant me in one cherished image.

"Take a seat, everyone," Ms. Acosta says.

We've never had Ms. Acosta as a teacher before, but she's notorious around campus. She's in her late seventies now, but when she was in her twenties, she was one of those radical nuns who rode around the country on a bus advocating for prison reform and women's rights.

A globe of snowy hair rings Ms. Acosta's fair face, and her reading glasses dangle from a silver chain around her neck. Her thin lips part in a sort of endlessly amused smile. She's dressed in all black: turtleneck, sweater vest, slacks. Teachers are supposed to dress in uniform colors like the rest of us, but the only school colors on her person are her red Keds. The absence of gold and tartan is like a vacation for my eyes.

I grin at Bea as we dive into adjacent armchairs by the window.

Next to me, Max takes a seat. They unwind a scarf from their pink-flushed neck and shake a few raindrops from their sandy hair.

"Hey!" Max squeezes my hand and waves at Bea. "I was hoping you'd be here." We haven't really talked since before winter break. I should've messaged Max when I found out Bea and I got into poetry seminar, but our group chat has been dead silent since Bea and Cara broke up.

I miss Max. Bea and I met them freshman year, when Bea got a bit part in *Little Women*. Max assisted with sound design, Ellie was one of the junior light techs, and Cara played Amy. I was in charge of moral support and rehearsed lines with Cara. We all started eating lunch together every day in the empty auditorium, trying on the weird prop hats and messing around with the plastic food. When we weren't together, we were sending each other inside-joke memes in our group chat.

As painful as it was for me to watch Bea fall for Cara, I miss what the five of us had. But Cara got Max and Ellie in the divorce—she was friends with them first, and I guess that's contractually binding when it comes to friendship custody—and I hardly ever get time with them now.

"Bea made us spend winter break perfecting our writing portfolios so we'd get in," I say. "Considering you hate Holy Trinity with the fire of a thousand suns, you can be a real homework taskmaster when you want to be," I tell Bea.

"I *made* you?" Bea scoffs. "You're the one who wanted to email that teacher's aide to see if we could get our hands on the syllabus early."

I roll my eyes and turn back to Max. "She says that like she doesn't already have the reading list tattooed on her bicep."

"It's impossible for you two to out-nerd each other," Max says. "You might as well quit now."

"Let's begin." Ms. Acosta clears her throat and stands in front of her desk. "You made it to the senior poetry seminar. That's no small feat! You have a lot to be proud of."

As she talks, I scan the small classroom. There are only ten of us here, and I recognize everyone—if not by name, then at least by face. There's Tala, who suffered silently with me in the volleyball unit of gym junior year; Rashad, who is Holy Trinity's reigning Quiz Bowl champion; and Lilith, who I'm pretty sure is goth when she's not forced into Holy Trinity's red and gold. There are a handful of other students who I don't know very well, but from the looks of them, they're all exactly the kinds of bookworms you'd expect to self-select into a poetry seminar.

"Let me share with you my vision for this seminar," Ms. Acosta continues. "I plan to push each of you to carve out your own paths toward truth, toward a better and more just world. Faith and community are your tools. Poetry is your vehicle. Okay?"

I don't exactly understand what she's saying, but I'm in.

"To show you what I mean, let's start with a reading." Ms. Acosta pulls out a book with a familiar cover and reads aloud.

> *Before you know what kindness really is*
> *you must lose things,*
> *feel the future dissolve in a moment*
> *like salt in a weakened broth.*
> *What you held in your hand,*
> *what you counted and carefully saved,*
> *all this must go so you know*
> *how desolate the landscape can be*
> *between the regions of kindness.*

I know the poem before she finishes the first line, and I'm reciting the verses along with her in my mind. The author, Naomi Shihab Nye, is one of my favorites. She said language "will find you and wrap its little syllables around you and suddenly there will be a story to live in." That's exactly how I felt when Bea and I began our never-ending poem. Like together, we were building this world I could live in forever.

When Ms. Acosta finishes the poem, she's silent for a moment, savoring the last words. She sits down on the armrest of a burgundy chair. "'Kindness,'" she says. "Naomi Shihab Nye."

Bea taps her elbow against my side at the sound of the name.

"How desolate the landscape can be!" Ms. Acosta says. "That's why your voices are needed in this world. Your poetry is needed." She passes small red notebooks around the circle.

"These are your journals for the rest of class. You'll write poetry on a variety of prompts each week and turn them into me, and I'll respond with feedback for you." She brandishes the last red journal. "Writing the truth is not easy, but it's worth the struggle. In the words of Pope Francis, *realities are more important than ideas.* Opening our hearts to truth—to the pain, the sorrow, the messy beauty of reality— and choosing to respond with compassion and kindness? That's what our Catholic faith is all about."

I've never heard someone at Holy Trinity talk about faith like that. Most people here are so focused on sin and sacrifice and penance that *compassion* doesn't really factor into the conversation. But I'm not brave or honest like the speaker in Naomi's poem. I'm not holding or saving anything. If something can be lost, I'd rather never hold it in the first place. I've lost enough already to know that counting on anything isn't worth the pain.

"I agree with Ms. Nye," Ms. Acosta says. "Loss is with us always, even when we're happy, just on the other side of the curtain. So let's peel back that curtain. What have you lost? When did you feel the future dissolve?"

My mom's face rises up from somewhere, lit in Sacramento sun, charcoal curls shaking with her laugh. When I was really little, I loved touching the gold hoop in her nose, all warm from the sun and from her breath.

As I work to uproot the image from my mind, the classroom door claps open. Bea's face blanches. I follow her gaze, my hands gripping my armchair when I see who is framed in the door.

Cara.

"I'm so sorry." She brushes the hair from her eyes, handing Ms. Acosta a piece of paper. "There was a mix-up with the registrar. I just got my schedule sorted out."

Bea's breath quickens. There's a gnawing high up in my stomach. Meanwhile, Max wiggles their fingers at Cara, apparently oblivious to the mini-volcano of panic that just erupted all over Bea and me.

"Not to worry." Ms. Acosta directs Cara to the empty armchair next to Bea. "Can you help our new classmate get up to speed?"

Bea's eyes link with mine. The words of Ms. Byrne, our eighth-grade teacher, dance into my ears: *If you want to make God laugh, tell him your plans.*

Cara

WHEN MY MIND is in the mood for some extreme self-sabotage, it circles back to Halloween.

Halloween is Bea's favorite holiday, and we had gone to Cara's for our annual HolyHorror costume party. It had started as your standard screening of *The Rocky Horror Picture Show,* this 1970s cult classic gender-bending musical. We were four years deep into the tradition by now, and we had our roles down: Cara made the living room hazy with dry ice, Bea coordinated our character costumes, Ellie did our stage makeup, and Max took snack duty. I did lots of dollar store runs to secure the water guns and party poppers for the audience participation props. Cara's parents were good sports about the whole thing, and her dad periodically burst into the living room to shout out lines.

When the movie was gearing up for *Time Warp,* I got up for a bathroom break. I hadn't even registered that Bea and Cara were missing from the living room until I heard Bea crying.

Right down the hall from the bathroom, Cara's door was open wide, with Bea slumped on the bed in her sequined Columbia costume. Tears smudged her black eyeliner.

I went in after Bea like some kind of novice medic running into a disaster. No idea what I was supposed to do, but I knew I needed to be there. The only thing that seemed to calm Bea's cries was my hand on her back, and that's the only reason I allowed myself to keep it there. I tried to piece together what had happened. The one word I could make out was *over.*

I used to think Bea was untouchable—loud, brilliant, sure of herself. If Holy Trinity didn't dull her shine, nothing could. But Cara changed that.

When Bea finally told me what happened, it sounded so pragmatic. Cara said she was just trying to preempt the inevitable heartache when they'd part ways for different colleges. She didn't want to be saddled with an expiration-dated relationship for the rest of senior year.

"She thinks I'm great"—Bea dragged her hands down her face—"but I'm a distraction. She said she didn't think we were that serious anyway."

From the second they'd started dating, Bea fell hard for Cara, and worried that Cara wouldn't take her seriously or see her as take-home-to-Mom girlfriend material because she'd cheated on someone in the past. Like Bea was just someone to kiss and have fun with, not someone to love.

I didn't hate Cara then, and I don't now. We had been friends, and in a place like Holy Trinity, we'd learned to lock tight around each other. But I will never understand what she did.

Cara won a cosmic lottery that granted her the full force of Bea's love, and she walked away from it.

Confession

FOR THE BETTER part of November, I lay on my bedroom floor with Bea eating our weight in frozen desserts. She swore the numbing cold of our Mango Icys had an anesthetic effect on her pain. I think she was self-punishing via brain freeze.

I felt like human garbage watching her claw her way out of that heartbreak. All the comforting words and late nights and Mango Icys in the universe couldn't blot out the truth: I wanted them to break up.

This deep-down part of me hoped for it, and it happened.

Thursday

Bea: what do you think of Mr. Frederich?

              Mitra: are we playing Gay or Nay?

              Mitra: he owns a lot of bow ties

              Mitra: like an ungodly amount

              Mitra: signs all point to gay

Bea: noted

Bea: but I mean generally

Bea: like what do you think of him as a
teacher

              Mitra: ?

Bea: he's teaching the open creative writing
elective

              Mitra: you wanna take two writing
              electives?

              Mitra: thought your schedule was
              full?

Bea: it is

Bea: but if we had to drop poetry seminar we
could switch to his class

              Mitra: what are you talking about??

              Mitra: BEA.

              Mitra: you've waited years for this

              ~~**Mitra:** Don't let her take this from us.~~

              Mitra: don't let her take this from
              you.

Something You've Never Done Before

ON THURSDAY AFTER poetry seminar, Bea and I slump on a bench next to a statue of St. Ignatius on the plaza. The rosebushes behind us have been pruned down to stalks, and they stand out like prickly fingers in the dirt. Bea leans back against the statue, tucking her knees into her body, molding herself into the metal. Some runaway raindrop lands on her cheek. Light obscures the lenses of her glasses, so for a moment I can't tell if she's still awake. Until she curses.

"Fuck!" She brings her thumb between her teeth, chomping at the confetti polish left over from New Year's Eve. Nail polish is banned here, but she's always waging these mini rebellions for bodily autonomy.

I want to believe the *fuck* she's giving is about me. But as loud as my wanting is, the truth is louder. All her *fucks* are about Cara.

For class today, Ms. Acosta asked us to each bring in a poem that evokes an emotion in us, and we took turns reading them aloud. Cara picked a poem by Pablo Neruda. Bea should've been pissed—she got Cara that Neruda book for her birthday. It takes some next-level lesbian passive aggression to serenade your ex-girlfriend with the love poems she once gave you, all the while pretending it's for a homework assignment. But judging by her face, Bea was too busy holding back tears to muster up the energy to be mad.

It's been like this all week. Cara sits across the circle of armchairs from us, perfectly aligned in Bea's view. And she's always doing something that snares Bea's attention—laughing with Max, drumming her pen during freewrite, spouting smart answers to Ms. Acosta's questions. Back when we were friends, Bea and I would've been laughing along with Cara, and her smart comments would've sparked us into nerd hyperdrive. I used to love spiraling out with Cara when she was reading scripts. We'd get deep into analyzing a character's motivation or backstory together. These days it just feels like she's showing off, rubbing salt in Bea's raw heartbreak.

This was supposed to be the space where Bea and I could just *be*. Now Bea's body is taut as a guitar string every class. Like she's waiting for Cara to pluck some sad melody out of her. Bea feels further from herself than I've ever seen her, and that breaks my heart even more than my trampled dreams about the class.

Our next assignment is to do something we've never done before and write a poem about it. I'm already bracing myself for Cara's next poem, and Bea's reaction.

"How am I going to do this?" Bea lifts herself from the foot of the St. Ignatius statue, resting her head in the lap of my skirt. Sun blazes her brown eyes. "I can't be in that seminar with her every day until graduation."

I bring my hand to her forehead with my heartbeat thudding in my throat, brushing stray locks of hair back from her face. She leaves her eyes on mine, beat after beat. I'm pushing past everything inside myself to stay there with her. Whenever she looks at me that way, it's like holding a lit match in my fingertips. I know I should let go, but there's something in me that wants to watch it burn down.

"Holy Trinity owed us this *one* kindness," she says. I hold my arms stiff against my sides to keep myself from playing with her hair.

I can't tell her what I already know: It's my fault. I wanted to live with Bea and poetry in a cocoon forever. This is the universe's swift remedy for my selfishness, and her pulverizing heartache is collateral damage.

My voice buries itself below my throat. "Sorry."

"What are we gonna do?" She says it like a prayer, and it pulls the ground out from under me. She's never been the uncertain one.

I want to trace my hand across her cheek and promise to unmake every awful thing that's happening.

"What do you want to do?" I ask instead.

Bea's eyes latch onto mine again. "You really think we shouldn't switch to Frederich's elective?"

Poetry is the place inside me that makes sense. It's a web linking everything—the ancient Persian poets, the beautiful chaos of Bea's brain, little me and little Azar curled up in the shelter of a book.

And now Cara could demolish all of that.

"No." This hot, urgent feeling forms under my skin. Instead of tamping it down like every other feeling, I let it take over. *This is ours.* I shift Bea's head out of my lap and get up from the bench, facing her.

"What?" She looks up at me.

"You're not giving up. Come on." I hold my palm open for Bea. Waiting for her hand pins my heart to my ribs.

Bea pokes my hand, her smile breaking me open in the best way. "What's happening?"

"We're not going to hide out and waste our last semester. You really want to just surrender to someone else's choices?" I say.

"No?" She's grinning now.

"Then let's make our own. Let's *do* something."

She finally slips her hand into mine. My spine turns electric when our skin meets.

"What do you wanna do?" She's on her feet now, game for whatever.

A part of my brain surges on the freedom of being the one calling the shots. Not waiting for Bea to carve out a path, not waiting for Cara to hurl a wrench at our hopes.

The rest of my brain is dolphin-jumping around the instant before Bea drops my hand, when her fingers are locked with mine.

"Our homework," I tell her.

Miracle Adjacent

THE BELL FOR second period rings as we make it into the athletics complex. For once, it's me leading the way, Bea following. We pass the basketball court, surrounded by the thunder of dozens of gym sneakers.

"You know you're late for French?" Bea glances at me. "And that's in the other direction."

"C'est la vie." I push open the back door to the girls' locker room. "Not going. But we can practice while we ditch, if you want."

There's a trace of pride in the way her eyebrows lift and her lips twist. Bea could make a scrapbook out of her tardy slips, but I've never cut class before. We dodge the open lockers and abandoned shoes and then, finally, I'm standing at the doorway to the pool.

"No!" Her face ignites with her grin. Whatever punishment might come of this, I already know down to my toes that it's worth it to see the earlier hesitation drop from Bea's face.

"It doesn't open for swim practice until three," I tell her. Only the blue light of the pool glows through the foggy window. "I'm going in."

Bea pauses, just watching me.

"What?" I ask.

She's seeing something in me. I want her to see, and yet I know I can't let her.

"You gotta admit"—she gestures around my body like she's feeling for my aura or something—"this is a new look for you. You've made it clear that you're categorically opposed to water. Even on the holiest of occasions."

"Last time I checked, the day you got your driver's license wasn't deemed a miracle by the pope."

"It's miracle-adjacent, though, right?" She wrinkles her nose at me.

The summer after sophomore year, when Bea finally wore down the DMV and they issued her license, she took me on a victory drive to Lake Sammamish. It was the breezy end of a late-August day, after all the kids and runners and picnickers had packed up and left. She pulled up to the lakefront and cut the ignition. I should've spotted trouble from the look in her eye alone: She gets kind of winky when she's about to pull something. But I didn't gauge just what we were in for until she started wriggling out of her green romper.

Here's the thing: Bea is a naked person. I am not. If she lived alone, she'd probably be lounging around in nothing but boyshorts and fuzzy socks all day long. I wear undershirts beneath my school uniform so that my belly button might never in its life be exposed to air. So, for Bea, whipping off her romper and hopping in the lake was a totally valid choice. And staying inside the car to make sure nobody stole her clothes was my way of living my best life.

I never forgot what she looked like, though—soft brown skin, decorated with her glasses and a collection of rings on her right hand, and nothing else. The freckles from her cheeks echoed on her chest and shoulders and the tops of her knees. She didn't even wear sandals. She just waved goodbye to me through the windshield, then sprinted toward the lake, and sunk in. Like she was at home.

That image catches me sometimes, when my brain is too tired to do the work of pushing it away, her smile glinting brighter than the water.

Now, Bea steps forward, opening the door to the pool room. I've never been in here before. It's humid and dark, alive with the smell of warm chlorine and the humming of the water heater. Jets bubble in streams under the surface of the pool, fracturing blue lights that bounce over Bea's glasses.

Fear grips my stomach as soon as I step out of my loafers.

"Scared of getting caught?" Bea looks to me.

Yes, I want to say. Terrified. I'm pitching myself into something I can't take back, and I know it. But I shake my head at her and let my skirt puddle on the tile. When I peel off the red blazer, Bea follows suit.

"Just to clarify," she says, "in four years I've never once succeeded in convincing you to get into a body of water." She hops around on one foot, tugging off a shoe. "And now you're stripping down in the middle of the school day because I said we should quit poetry?"

"It's a writing assignment." I work my way down the buttons on my blouse. "And remember that pope quote Ms. Acosta told us? Something like 'Be real and stop overthinking so goddamn much.' That's what we're doing."

She folds up her glasses and nestles them into one of her shoes. "I think the pope would be scandalized by your radical interpretation of the text."

I'm down to the gray undershirt and briefs that Bea calls my *regulation underwear*—it's not my fault that the military also has an appreciation for practical basics—when Bea slips out of her plaid skirt. All the tiny hairs on my arms lift toward her skin. And then I'm caught in this polar pull between looking and not looking at her.

I've seen Bea naked three times before. Once on a camping trip when we were fourteen; once when she dragged me swimsuit shopping at Crossroads; and that day at Lake Sammamish. Three times, but never like this. And it's not her comfortable, naked-person presence that's changed. It's me. My cheeks draw all the heat from my body.

Her skin chameleons with the wavering pool glow, amber-brown painted over with bits of moving light. Her skin looks so much like my own, but it's new and beautiful.

Something deepens in her face when she takes off her blouse and unclasps her bright yellow bra. "I know what you're thinking."

My fingernails dig into the hem of my tank top. "Yeah?"

"It's not going to happen." She's undressed now. My bare feet on the tile are the only things holding me up, and suddenly that doesn't feel like enough. Bea crooks her finger at the empty pool. *"You're going in first, Mitra."*

"Me?"

"What's that thing Mrs. Fournier always says when someone complains?" Bea tosses her bra at me. "Ce n'est pas la mer à boire." *It's not as if you have to drink the sea.*

I lift the tank and sports bra over my head and dash to the pool, plunging in ahead of any conscious thought. I'm swallowed immediately. Before I can surface, before my brain catches up to the shock, Bea leaps in beside me. My eyes blink open underwater to find her. She sinks like a capsule, and then her arms and legs fan out, reaching toward me. A train of bubbles travels up from her mouth, tangling in her hair.

Bea comes up for air first. "Warmer than the lake!" She's squinting through the water trickling from her hair. Keeping my eyes from drifting away from her face is the hardest thing. "You got off easy, girl."

Her swishing arms displace water, and the water rushes across my collarbone. Everything she touches ripples toward me. I thought water was supposed to dilute, but it amplifies the wanting coiled in my limbs.

Bea treads beside me. "How's your belly button?" she asks. "Will it survive this freezing torture?"

My belly hasn't stopped backflipping since she undressed. "Can you please remember that it's a Californian belly button? It's not adjusted to freakishly cold environments like yours."

"Give it time." Her hand skims my waist when she lowers her arms in the water. I don't know if I've ever been touched there before. My skin stirs up, like it's been waiting for her.

That was an accident, I scold my own skin as I back away.

"Hey." Bea registers something in me again. "What's going on with you?"

No, no, no. I'm scrambling to rebuild whatever walls I just let down. "What do you mean?" My heart rams against my ribs.

She holds my gaze and stretches it longer than I can stand. "You're acting different." Her eyes turn serious, like she's puzzling something out.

She wades an inch closer to me in the water, and I float another inch away. "I'm not different," I say.

And technically, it's true. I loved her for years. That hasn't changed. It's just gotten harder to hide it.

"Whatever it is, you know you can tell me." Her voice is so warm that it fills up the whole room.

"There's nothing to tell."

"You can't lie to save your life, Mitra."

Bea draws her wet hair back from her face, and the gesture smatters droplets across her cheeks. Water-freckles. "You can't hide from me." She flicks her wet fingers at me. "I'll figure it out one of these days."

You won't, I vow, then slip under the water where she can't see the telltale flush in my cheeks.

Pool Rules

All persons must shower before entering pool or spa.

(Swim) at your own (risk.)

No (person) may use the pool alone.

Swim (only) when lifeguard is on duty.

No (jumping,) running, or horseplay.

No food, drink, or glass (containers) allowed near the pool.

No (unsupervised) visitors or children may use the pool.

If (you) suffer from (heart) disease, low blood pressure, or another medical condition, do not use the spa without first consulting (a) medical provider.

Do not (stay) in spa longer than 15 minutes at a time.

(Overexposure) to hot water may cause (dizziness) or fainting.

heart swims dizzy
unsupervised
you: only a person
overexposed
risk jumping
or stay contained

Mom

I'M AWAKE BEFORE my alarm on Friday morning. Apparently my body doesn't require rest anymore. Obsessing about Bea is the new sleep.

Whenever I close my eyes, I'm caught with Bea in the pool again, honed on her skin and the droplets sparkling down her cheeks. I turn the moment over and over in my memory, imagining all the ways it could have gone. Like, what if I hadn't backed away from her when she came toward me? And what if I had been real with her when she asked what was going on? And what is it that she's seeing in me now?

Can she see that I love her? Does it scare her?

My stomach churns. I'm playing with fire and I know it.

I'm turning into the worst type of trope: the one that says queer girls always fall in love with their best friends. I don't want to live out the stereotype. I want to be smarter than that.

"Mitra joon!" My dad's voice rattles me out of the Bea-memory-loop and I bury all thoughts of her. "Breakfast."

Joon is not my middle name. It's one of those Farsi words with a zillion meanings: *soul* and *spirit* and *life* and *dear*. I am all of those things to my dad.

A turmeric-tomato smell reaches me before I even make it halfway down the stairs. Dad's cooking has always been bold, with thick steam and the kind of fragrant spices that leave a ghost behind. Those scents were the only things that could pull me out of bed when we first moved to our Crossroads house: butter in a saucepan warming rosewater for shir berenj, or oil toasting black pepper and turmeric awake. Azar and I used to flop down at the dining room table for breakfast before the sun had even risen, and then Dad would drop us off at school on his way to work at the start-up that brought us to Bellevue. The company—developing a planet identification app for amateur astronomers—went belly-up, but our morning ritual of Dad's concoctions survived.

Turmeric and tomatoes means it's an omelette Irani morning: fried onions and Roma tomatoes held together in a net of scrambled eggs. Azar has a major sweet tooth, so she's all about Dad's rice pudding or sour cherry preserves on flatbread, but omelette is my favorite. Maybe Dad's buttering me up for yet another college pep talk. It's still eight months away, but he's already started interjecting bits of wisdom about the college life into our conversations. Some of it's understandable, like *always read the syllabus for your classes*. But some of it comes out of left field, like when we were driving to school last week and he made me swear I'd wear flip-flops in the dorm showers. *You don't want to get a fungus!*

Bea and I cemented our college escape plan years ago. We're going to the University of Washington together, where she'll take all the creative writing classes she can juggle, and I'll have an excuse to read my favorite poets like it's my job. We both applied to a few backup options—Western Washington University and the University of Oregon—and I applied to a small private college, Reed, on a lark. But we're both set on heading to UW in Seattle. That's assuming we both get in—and assuming I don't blow up our future with my feelings.

When I reach the dining room, Dad and Azar are already gathered around a mounded pan of tomato eggs, but neither of them have dished up. They're both leaning on their elbows at the table, Dad whispering something through the steam to Azar. He cuts the conversation when they spot me.

For a second, I wonder if he got a call from someone at Holy Trinity about my truancy, but that would be out of character for a school that likes to shame students directly to their faces. I already got a pink slip and a ton of weird looks from my French teacher when I showed up late and damp-haired. Bea insisted on saving my slip and taped it to the inside of her locker.

"Morning," I say.

Dad scratches his beard, eyeing me. He's had the same thick beard since before I can remember, only now it's highlighted by two white streaks. His wavy brown hair hangs long enough to obscure the tops of his ears. "Sit." He pats the empty chair between him and Azar. He looks tired today. Dark circles hug his eyes, shading his olive-brown skin.

Azar scoops a heap of omelette onto each of our plates without saying anything. She's wearing her uniform already, her black curls fanning out against her red jumper.

"What's going on?" The first bite melts into a swirl of salt and acidic tang on my tongue.

"We have some changes coming that I want to talk to you both about," Dad says. His tone takes me back to the breakfast three years ago when he told us the start-up was folding, and he was taking a job at a local smartphone company.

I keep funneling eggs into my mouth, trying to delay whatever family discussion we're about to be flung into. Azar is suddenly fixated on her tablet. She got super into editing and doodling on photos last summer, so Dad bought her a tablet with starter digital art software over winter break. Now all of her IG posts show her friends with neon lasers beaming out of their eyes, or trippy geometric stripes swirling behind them. I peek over her shoulder at the tablet screen, where she's drawing a megaphone into the hand of one of her blond friends I recognize from our pep assemblies.

"You should tint the background in green," I say. "It'll look cool with her outfit." Azar scowls at me. She never willingly shows me what she's working on, and she always ignores my input.

I watch her add text in a cartoon bubble coming out of the megaphone that says "OBEY THE NOODLE." I won't even ask.

"I spoke with your mother yesterday," Dad says.

Calls from our mom are nothing new. It's been a while, but middle-of-the-night messages were a common occurrence when we first left Sacramento. They were usually slurred nonsense at best, and hostile toward my dad at worst.

"You shouldn't answer next time," I tell him. "Just let it go to voice mail."

Azar's eyes dart up from her tablet to meet mine. "They've been talking," she says.

I set down my fork and stare at my dad. "Talking? Like, before yesterday?"

He takes a long sip from his chai. A classic Iranian parent stalling strategy.

"She finished a very good treatment program," he says after he swallows. "She has been doing well for a while now. I wanted to keep checking in to make sure things were stable before I told you both."

"How long have you been talking?" I ask.

"Only a few calls, joon. Just to be sure that she's really doing well."

"But how long?"

He closes his hand over mine on the table. "Since the end of July."

"Six months?" My brain clamps down around that fact, but Dad keeps speaking, and I can't absorb any of it.

"She'll be visiting Washington soon for a job interview in Renton. She said she would like to see you both again, maybe take you out to breakfast when she's here."

"Seriously?" I try to picture Azar and me sitting down to brunch at The Waffler with our mother. But I just draw up a jumble of memories of her sleeping through breakfast, forgetting to help me pack the lunches, yelling at Azar when she couldn't figure out how to tie her shoelaces. "On what planet would that be a good idea?"

Dad deliberates on his words, sipping chai in the silence. "I think you should consider it," he says.

My dad encouraging a reunion feels as far-fetched as the likelihood that my mom is actually clean this time. He and I used to tag-team the repair after her catastrophes, like we were our own disaster relief squad. He'd put the pieces back together: pick me up from school when she didn't show, call and apologize to whomever she burned bridges with when she was high. And my job was Azar. I read her *Charlotte's Web* at bedtime; I helped with math homework; I put her favorite Robyn song on when our mom yelled.

Azar reaches for another scoop of omelette. "What job?"

Dad lifts his eyebrows at her. Not the follow-up question I expected from her, either.

"Grant writing. At a nonprofit organization, I think. It sounded like a good opportunity for her," he adds. "Structure, but also flexibility."

I can't figure out why Dad would entertain inviting chaos back into our lives. Like he's opening the door for a tornado. "Can't she find some other *good opportunity* in Sacramento?"

"I think her intention is to find a job in Washington," he says. "She's hoping to be closer to you both."

All the moisture in my mouth evaporates. "No. Dad, no. Come on."

Azar's eyes land on me for a moment, and then she's back to her eggs.

Dad inhales through his nose. "It's her decision to look at jobs here. And it's your decision if you would like to see her again. But things have changed for her, Mitra. That means things can change for all of you. I think this is a good thing."

I push back from the table before he can say any more. "We have to finish getting ready," I tell Azar.

I shove my socks on and brush my teeth upstairs, and then I head for Azar's room. She's at the mirror tying her hair back—it's the same shade of black our mom's is—and she's got earbuds in.

"Hey, Aziz." I don't even know where to start. Usually when we're talking, it's to sort out rides and schedules, or figure out whose ridiculous plaid thing is whose. And at school, the main variety of interaction she permits with me is accidental.

Azar pulls out her earbuds and peers back at me. "Yeah?"

"Um. So. Mom's visit. I'm not sure what's gotten into Dad, but obviously I'll tell him we don't want to see her."

Her mouth flies open, but instead of speaking, she sinks her teeth down into her lip. "*You* don't want to see her," she says.

"You *do?*" I can't help the jump in my tone.

Azar finishes looping the hairband around her locks. "She's our mom, Mitra."

It's like a rock lodges in my throat, burrowing down into my body. Maybe Dad and I did too good of a job hiding Mom's drug problem from Azar. I never wanted Azar to remember what it was like.

But I remember.

Not-Mom

TWO DAYS INTO Azar's first week of sixth grade, she woke up clammy and nauseated. Dad had already left for work, but our mom had been doing well, so she was back in the house with us. When I went to ask her for help with Azar, Mom was still in bed, her pupils blown and eyes smudged with yesterday's makeup. She had the kind of faraway voice that I'd somehow already catalogued as *not-mom*. When she was slurry and distant like that, I knew better than to expect her to show up in any real way.

I went back to Azar, who was red-cheeked and burning up, vomiting in her sheets. She'd never gotten a flu this bad before, and I'd never seen her so sick, and we were both panicked. All she wanted was our mom. She kept chanting it: *Mom, Mom, Mom,* like it was a buoy she could cling to.

I didn't know how to tell her Mom wasn't there.

Lies We All Believed

I'll pick you up at three thirty, okay? Be ready for me.

We'll make bademjan for dinner, just the two of us.

I'll bring Azar's project to school.

I forgot, I had a meeting.

I caught a cold.

I have a headache.

I have an appointment.

I'll be back to tuck you in.

I'll be back by the time you wake up.

It's just too much stress.

It was only a little.

Just to take the edge off.

So we don't have to tell Dad, okay?

That isn't my medication, anyway.

I'm holding on to it for your grandmother.

I wouldn't do that.

I won't do that again.

It's just this once.

I promise.

I'm done.

Bashful as a Sunflower

WHEN WE MAKE it to school on Friday, rain bats the windows of our poetry classroom, drumming under the scuttle of feet and backpacks dropping to the floor. Bea and Cara sit a couple seats apart, Max and me forming a human barrier between them. While everyone else chats as they settle in, the four of us stay silent.

"This is awkward," Max says, ruffling their bangs nervously. We've both been caught in the middle of Cara and Bea's breakup, but poetry seminar puts that awkwardness under a spotlight.

Lilith, the closet goth, looks up at us from her Edgar Allan Poe book. Cara and Bea turn to Max, admonishing them with glares.

"What?" Max says. "I thought saying it out loud would help! Just trying to ease the tension."

"Points for trying," I whisper. "But they're beyond help."

Cara used to be my friend. Not the kind of friend I'd hang out with alone, but the kind who would be my default group project partner in any class we had together. We were in the same circle. We ate lunch together, and went to animated Miyazaki movie marathons at the Crossroads theater with Bea, and Cara always invited me to her birthday parties.

We weren't super tight, but we did have our own text thread, just the two of us, where we aired our grievances about all the things our immigrant parents did that nobody else would understand. It didn't matter that hers came from Taiwan and mine were from Iran—our parents still managed to share a textbook on *how to annoy your children with your old-world ways.* She'd text me at six a.m. with no context, and it would read something like: *There are eight giant yogurt containers in my fridge. Not one of them contains yogurt.* And two days later I'd write back: *My dad just made me talk on the phone to four people I've never met before in my life. Apparently they're all my cousins.*

We haven't texted since Halloween.

Now I watch Cara looking over at Bea, tucking her hair behind one ear. Cara didn't even like poetry when Bea first tried to get her into it, sharing from our treasure trove of chapbook collections. She said it was too elitist and that theater was way more accessible. And Bea would shout back, *It's not elitist! It's economical! It's the language of the people!*

I can't for the life of me figure out why Cara would sign up for this seminar. Bea said it's because Cara wanted to try something new before graduation, round out her laundry list of experiences before college. Diversify.

If she wanted to diversify, she could've learned to play the tuba or taken up needlepoint. Maybe she just wants to be closer to Bea. Regrets ending things.

Whatever her reasons, I can't live up to my job as a human buffer between the two of them today. Half of me is here in class, but half of me is rooted back in my dining room, as my dad drops the bomb that my mom is coming back.

Bea stretches her arm out on the armrest between us. She's wearing a short-sleeved white blouse with a red-and-gold tie today, and the soft hairs on her forearm tickle my hand. The contact makes her flinch. A stressed exhale peters out from her lungs.

"You okay?" I whisper.

She gives me a full-mouth grin, the kind that's proving something—to herself, to me, to Cara. "I'm fine. Are *you* okay?"

In the time it takes me to formulate a coherent answer, Ms. Acosta begins our lesson for the day.

"We've been looking at the poetry that moves you," Ms. Acosta says. "Poetry is at its most evocative when it reveals to us some core truth about our experiences. For today's prompt, I was inspired by the second epistle of John: *We ought to walk and practice truth.* That's a tough task! Let's see if we can pinpoint this radical honesty in a poem you love. What does the writer make you feel? What do they reveal within you? Take some time to freewrite on the subject in your poetry journals."

There's this poem by Naomi Shihab Nye called "Making a Fist." Naomi is a little girl in the poem, driving across the desert with her mom, asking her questions about death. The poem always reminds me of my mom—all the questions I have for her, still unasked, living right under my tongue. But the thing about "Making a Fist" is that I never really have to look at my mom head-on when I read the poem. Naomi's words build a kind of muscle for the things I can't carry. I don't have to face the truth about my mom when I'm reading about hers.

So maybe it's not what poetry makes me feel. It's that poetry does the feeling for me, so I don't have to.

I don't have to feel the pain of my mom choosing pills.

I don't have to feel the pain of Bea not choosing me.

The pain of her still wanting Cara.

But now my mom is about to burst into this world we've built here in Washington, and I don't have a say in it. And I have to watch Bea agonize over Cara five days a week, and I don't have a say in that, either. There are things even the shelter of poetry can't guard me from.

Two seats down from me, Cara stands to stretch and stare out at the rain. Her eyes pass right over Bea's head and toward the corner of Meydenbauer Bay out the window. Bea's shoulders creep upward as she traces Cara's movements, and then she pulls off her glasses and cleans the lenses against her skirt just to give herself something to do. When her hand drops to her lap, I'm rushed with the memory of her hand grazing my waist in the pool. Suddenly the air is too heavy on me. Like my skin is too tight for my body.

A line from "Making a Fist" wears a path through my thoughts: *The borders we must cross separately/stamped with our unanswerable woes.*

I don't know about unanswerable woes, but I'm swamped in more unanswerable questions. And these are ones I don't even want to own up to, because they're too cliché. Like, how many times has Cara seen Bea naked? Does Cara's brain serve up regular reminders of every time she touched Bea, like mine does? What's it like to have feelings for Bea without getting snared in gut-twisting guilt? And why do I have to be living, breathing proof of why you should never fall in love with your best friend?

Bea drums her fingers on my thigh. At first I'm not sure which one of us she's trying to comfort. When she stops drumming, I realize she's tucked a note into the pleat of my skirt.

Don't worry about your mom. You're a fierce and beautiful human. You got this. And I got you, okay?

I didn't think it would be possible to make me smile today. But Bea is always doing impossible things. When I look up at her, she meets my gaze again. I expect her to look away, but she doesn't. Her eyes are warm and searching.

For the first time I catch a glimmer of something more there—a layer underneath her intensity. Like inside, she's asking her own unanswerable questions. Then Bea shifts her eyes away and picks at the rim of her glasses. Her ears pink up, and I catalog the few times I've seen her blush like that before: when her mom said something awkward; on the rare day she got called on in class and didn't know the answer; when we had to make free-throws in gym and everyone stared.

Embarrassment. Or—bashfulness?

Bea's usually about as bashful as a sunflower at high noon. She basks in attention—so I don't know why she'd shirk it now.

I bottle the air in my chest and let myself think one last unanswerable question: Could her feelings for me ever change?

Mitra

touch the bruise of an
old wound, Azar wants to
face the person who made

us, I'll call her *Jaleh*, a
name I can touch bare-
handed, safer and farther

away than *mom*—that
word looks so soft but
barbs round its corners

every gentle swoop ready
to prick open old memories
until they breathe again

and *mom* is a word she
lost the right to: it hauls
meaning we don't have

a gentle title she
gambled away, now I don't
owe her anything at all

Bea

all the world upside down, no sense to be made
in those rearview disasters, too busy clawing
your way free—fleeing chaos you never

deserved and darling, life owes only beautiful
moments now, days of sparkling champagne
you toast with hands stained—skin

an organ that breaks and repairs and
remembers, the shelter you've shed and
created a thousand times over—remember

this: there should be better words to lift
and carry and kiss and bandage you
through disaster-days come and gone

but words and mothers both fail, and you'll
keep casting hope from the iron of your own
skin, a cellular strength your body designed

Kiss

all the world upside-down, no sense to be made
in those rearview disasters, too busy clawing
your way free-fleeing-chaos you never

kiss

deserved and darling, life owes only beautiful
moments now, days of sparkling champagne
you toast with hands stained-skin

kiss

kiss

an organ that breaks and repairs and
<u>remembers</u>, the shelter you've shed and
created a thousand times over-remember

kiss

this: there should be better words to lift
and carry and **kiss** and bandage you
through disaster-days come and gone

kiss

but words and mothers both fail, and you'll
keep casting hope from the iron of your own
skin, a cellular strength your body designed

kiss

kiss

I didn't know kiss could land on me with such force and gentle-ness, as if the word actually carried her lips.

That's What Friends Are For

AFTER BEA HANDS off The Book to me on Friday afternoon, I spend a full twenty-four hours cradling and incubating the word *kiss* like a penguin with its egg. I'm cartwheeling around the sweet note she slipped me in class: I am *fierce* and *beautiful* and held by her words. And that moment when she kept her eyes fixed on me, like I was the answer to some labyrinthine riddle—in four years of friendship, she's *never* looked at me like that before.

But I know I'm chasing nothing. Spinning out over one word in her poem, a note she passed, a look in her eye? *You're seeing what you want to see, Mitra.* Every time my heart blasts me into outer space, my brain boomerangs me back to reality. I'm confusing the type of love Bea feels for me—the comforting, familiar, friendly kind—for the way I love her.

By the time Bea and I meet up at her house on Saturday for Sadeh, I'm exhausted from the whiplash.

"Get the lighter," Bea says, kneeling in front of her living room fireplace, waving her hand at me like a surgeon waiting for her scalpel.

"We don't have to do this," I tell her.

"Come on!" Her head snaps back toward me. "People have been building fires since the dawn of time. If cave people made it happen with flint, we can pull it together enough to light this fire log."

Sadeh is the Iranian festival honoring the discovery of fire by this ancient mythological guy Hushang. But my dad doesn't really get into celebrating it. It was a bigger thing for my mom, who was raised Zoroastrian. She'd cook up a pot of ash-e reshteh, an herby soup with sour kashk and a tangle of noodles, strings of crunchy fried onion and mint, and read us stories about Hushang from the epic poem *Shahnameh*. I wonder if she eats ash-e reshteh alone now.

I wonder if she knows we don't eat it without her.

I join Bea on the floor, handing over the lighter. She marries the lighter flame to some crumpled-up junk paper. A white light races across the surface of the log, and we hold our breath, watching it tremble. Then it fizzles. Smoke puffs in its absence, billowing out from the fireplace at our faces.

"Did you open the flue?" I cough.

"Flue? What even *is* that?"

I snatch back the lighter. "Okay. Sadeh has officially been marked. We can say this was a tribute to Hushang's undocumented, failed attempts at discovering fire. Solid effort, but we're not burning down your parents' house. And we don't want a reenactment of freshman year Día de los Muertos."

Bea was showing me her family's altar honoring her grandparents who had died, and she'd learned this trick where she could flick her finger back and forth through the candle flames without burning herself. Or so she said. She lost an eyebrow trying.

"Never forget," Bea chuckles, sweeping her hand over her brow. Her mom got so mad that we almost set the ofrenda on fire. I learned three new Spanish swear words that night.

I flop back onto the carpet. "Where are your parents?"

"Secret spy mission in Austria?"

"So you have no idea."

"Out of town, working late, international espionage . . . what's the difference?" She shrugs.

Bea has what she calls *minimalist parents.* They have enough money to outsource things like gardening and housekeeping, and when it comes to Bea, they subscribe to the hands-off school of parenting. She rarely knows where they are or when they'll be home. But whenever they do show up, they arrive with a lot of opinions about Bea's life. I get why Bea loathes Catholic school even more than I do. When your home *and* your school are perpetually disappointed in you, you have nowhere to go to be yourself. It's why she's so desperate to get out, to get to college, where she'll finally be able to breathe.

"Anyway, we've got important things to do in their absence," she says. "Formal dress time!"

Bea's repulsion for Holy Trinity is such that in the four-plus years I've known her, she has never once wanted to attend a school-sanctioned event. We've managed to avoid every school dance since I moved to Bellevue, which feels noteworthy in a Catholic school where most kids are foaming at the mouth for a chance to ditch the uniform and listen to something other than Father Mitchell's "Immaculate Mary." Instead, we manifested our own alternative to school dances: Anti-Formal Fridays, where we've fulfilled pretty much every anti-dance agenda we could dream up since eighth grade—pinball tournament at 8-Bit Arcade, nature documentary night in our onesies, always culminating in a sleepover—and it's been perfect.

Which is why I can't wrap my head around why Bea is suddenly dead set on going to Winter Formal. She keeps insisting that *it's our senior year, and our last opportunity to have this formative high school experience.* I could go without the experience of getting locked in a sweaty gym, with chaperones breaking apart couples and demanding they "make room for the Holy Spirit." But we've done everything together, so now I guess we're doing this.

I try not to believe there's another reason she wants to go to Winter Formal with me now. It's a glint of hope that started in the pool room, and flickered with that note she wrote, and turned firecracker-red when I read her latest verses in the never-ending poem. The hope that says: Maybe she has her own internal buzzer shouting *It's senior year and the stars have aligned and we're both single and this could be our chance to be something more.* The hope that maybe, just maybe, she wants to dance with me.

"Let's put on our fancy clothes and raid my parents' leftover wine." Bea stretches out on her back beside me, the warm space between our arms buzzing. I hold very still so as not to scare that feeling away. "We could write an ode to fire. Keep the spirit of Sadeh alive. Want to spend the night?"

The distance between *want* and *should* forms a canyon in me.

I sidestep the offer. "If we drink all the wine and I stay over without your mom knowing, she's gonna have even more reasons to hate me."

"She doesn't hate you!" Bea's answer is so reflexive and loud that we both bust out laughing.

"I mean, your parents are aggressively polite around me. But they've never *loved* us hanging out."

"They still don't believe we're not dating." She laughs again, like it's ridiculous.

Because, of course, it would be ridiculous for us to date.

I make myself laugh too, that tiny hope faltering.

Bea shakes her head. "Every freaking time you sleep over, my mom pulls out the rosary."

"Did you at least tell her my family thinks Jesus was a nice guy?" I turn my head toward her, my cheek resting on the carpet, and my eyes follow the light down her face. "I want your mom to like me."

"You don't need her approval." Bea pats my cheek with her sooty fingertips. "You're the only person I care about."

She rests her thumb there on my jaw, and I'm waiting for her to break the moment, crack a joke, but she just holds my face, her mouth lifting in a soft smile.

I'm strung on one of her words again.

Only.

The word unveils all its sounds in the echo chamber of my head. *Only one. Lonely. Known, holy. Own,* like to belong to someone. I belong to Bea more than anyone else.

My skin catalyzes its own flame, and it sparks that hope in me again, a little miracle. I pull back.

"I brought outfit options," I say. "Want to help me pick?"

That pivots her attention. She leads us up to her bedroom, which resembles the aftermath of a Black Friday stampede at a feminist book-store. Poetry zines and used books pave the floor. Gloria Anzaldúa's face presides over the mess from a giant poster on the wall, and a colony of half-dead succulents inhabits any extra space.

Bea says the mess is *part of her process* because the rest of the house looks like it's perpetually staged for one of her dad's real estate open houses. So all her queer paraphernalia is relegated to the bedroom too—which kind of mirrors her parents' response to Bea's coming out. They swore they had no problem with Bea dating girls, as long as they didn't have to hear about it. My dad had a different reaction—he still uses PFLAG brochures as bookmarks for all his science-y books. I'll be trying to look up something on the Milky Way and then end up with a pamphlet on *Loving our LGBTQ Children* instead.

The only place to reliably fit my body in the disaster zone of Bea's room is on her bed. Which would be fine, except it's saturated with that cozy Bea-smell: coconut from her shampoo, and rosemary from her weird natural deodorant.

"Do what you will." I surrender my bag of formal options to Bea, who is more fashionably inclined than me. She rifles through the contents: a gray dress, a black dress, another black dress. It's an Iranian thing. Black is our color, occasionally accented with gold bangles or a necklace. Going to an Iranian party is like going to a slightly glammed-up funeral.

"Um, *hello*." Bea pulls my suit jacket and pants from the tote bag. "What's this little number?"

Okay, so the suit actually *was* for a funeral. But I won't tell her that. "That's your vote?" I ask.

"I have to see it on." She tosses it to me.

Bea saw me naked last week, but I still feel exposed tugging off my jeans. When I'm down to my sports bra and briefs, Bea grabs a blue button-up shirt from her closet for me to try with the suit. She drops her eyes to the floor when she hands it over. Looking away is something I would do—not her. Her formality throws me off.

"I get it, you hate the utilitarian undies." I try to shake us out of the weirdness. "But they're not that terrible."

She pauses a beat. "I don't hate them."

I slip into the black pants and Bea's shirt. It takes me forever to work my way up the buttons, and she's silent until I reach the last one. My heart rebounds around my throat. This doesn't feel like our old shopping trips at Crossroads. It feels like she's dressing me up for a date.

"You still thinking about it?" She finally raises her eyes to mine.

If it *is kissing you, then yes.* My teeth touch down on my lip to keep myself from saying something too honest.

"Seeing your mom?"

Oh. "Azar wants to. She thinks I'm overreacting," I say. "Like I'm just shutting my mom out for no reason." I wait for Bea to jump to my defense, but she doesn't. Her silence churns more words out of me.

"I know what you're going to say," I tell her. She lifts her eyebrows at me. I love the way they pop out from behind her gold glasses like cartoon eyebrows. She has no poker face.

"That I'm too careful. That I should just go and see what happens. But I can't lie and pretend everything's fine with my mom, and I can't be honest with her, either."

"Okay," Bea says.

She's never one to cede a conversation with *okay.* I can't figure her out today.

I turn toward the mirror and pull on the suit jacket. "I'm not as brave as you," I say over my shoulder. She traces the edges of my suit with her gaze. "You always say what you're feeling."

Bea's eyes flare on mine in the mirror. Her parents have a big thing against words like *always* and *never,* even though Catholicism overflows with absolutes. She had a lot of fun turning that around on them: *I* might *be going to hell. It's a gray zone.*

She doesn't make a joke out of it now. Her lips turn up just a little, the most un-Bea-like of smiles. I turn back to face her.

"Let me get these." She reaches for the buttons on my sleeves. I hold my breath while she fumbles with the cuffs, like any movement could spook this instant into flight.

Her eyes dance around me, and she sweeps her hands across my shoulders, adjusting the suit. "This is your new uniform, okay?" she says. "Every day, from here on out."

I'm fighting back the flush in my cheeks. "Our teachers would lose their minds. Dress code violation *and* gender nonconformity? I'd get, like, an entire book of pink slips thrown at me."

"Totally worth it." Her hands slide down my arms. "Also. What you said? Not always true."

I allow myself a shallow inhale. "Huh?"

"I don't always say what I'm feeling." Her hands land on the hem of my jacket, and she tugs at the fabric. Maybe she's fixing the suit, or maybe she's tugging me closer.

"Yeah?"

"If saying something out loud could change things, or ruin things," she says, "then, yeah. It's scary to bring it up." Her hands drop from me, hovering in the air for a second. "Even if I really need to say it."

The air between us forms a power line, crackling. I want to shout that quote from the second epistle of John at her. *Own your truth, damn it!* The voltage of the moment jolts my tongue: "If you need to say something that bad, then maybe it's worth whatever could happen after."

Bea's mouth opens for some thought that doesn't materialize, and she bites the inside of her cheek. She's holding the moment between us, letting it grow. *Kiss,* that hidden egg of a word, becomes a thing I can reach out and touch. That tiny hope strikes dynamite inside me. I reach for her hand.

And then *Ping!* Bea's phone chimes. The sound knocks her heels back a step. She bolts over to her bed to dig around in the sheets for her phone.

"Is that your mom checking in? How's the weather in Vienna?" I try to distract from the boiling well of disappointment in my stomach.

"Um." Bea's eyes won't break from her phone. "It's actually Cara. I, um, heard that she's going to Formal with Max and Ellie. She's asking if I'm going too."

Shame curdles in my airway.

Of course. Bea didn't want to go to Formal with me. She wanted to go because she knew Cara was going too. Maybe she wanted to tell Cara about the fact that she's still knee-deep in feelings. And she wanted me there as her security blanket.

That's what *friends* are for, after all.

Passing Period

Sunday, 4:21 PM

    Bea: winter formal approaches!!!!

    Bea: watch out, nuns!

    Bea: Mitra's about to destroy your heteronormative mating ritual

    Bea: with her SUIT

Sunday, 7:48 PM

    Bea: you want to get dinner before?

    Bea: my mom said I better not spill anything on the new dress she bought me

    Bea: so, challenge accepted

    Bea: spaghetti? BBQ? shawarma?

Sunday, 11:11 PM

    Bea: anything??

Today, 11:52 AM

    Bea: lunch in the chapel.

Revelation

I HIDE OUT in the plaza at lunchtime on Monday, leaning back against the façade of Baldie. My hair smooshes into the brick, and it's this one sweet little moment of feeling held up.

I've spent the past thirty-seven hours stewing in my own ignorance. For one glowing moment, I actually believed Bea could want me. But it's been Cara for her this whole time. I can't erase the awkward look on her face, like she thought I was flirting with her. And *I was*. I did the one thing I said I'd never do.

But that's not the worst of it—it's everything I told myself in the two years before: that I could be her best friend and love her all at once. I thought I could split my heart in half. I can't. All I know how to do is hide. And, as it turns out, not particularly well.

"Hey." Bea spots me from across the plaza, and her hand hesitates when she waves at me. I can tell from ten yards away that she's uncomfortable.

Shit. She steps toward me and my eyelids seal shut for a moment, trying to shut out the image of her frown.

"Chapel?" she asks. I nod and trail beside her on the walkway. A group of seniors stops chatting as they watch us pass by with our grim faces. We probably look like we're leading a funeral procession.

"So." Bea talks into my silence. "Dinner before Formal? You didn't message me back."

"Dinner?" February sun pounds my eyes. Normally I love false spring in Bellevue; it's like Sacramento sun pops up north for a quick

76

reunion with me. Today I just want the forgettable gray skies back. "Not sure."

"I sent you ideas." Bea futzes with her glasses. The look of expectation on her face yanks my heart up my throat. "Or we could just skip dinner and do after-dance snacks and desserts when you sleep over. What do you want to do?"

"I don't know."

She's reading the change in me, only this time I don't have the capacity to misdirect her. "I'm not sure if I can do Formal. I'm . . . There's just a lot going on."

"What?" She twists her mouth around, never finding the right place for it.

I push in the clunky wooden door of the chapel with my shoulder. "I'm sorry."

We used to meet in the empty chapel for lunch all the time, before we started hanging out with the theater kids. It's left open for breaks and free periods purportedly so students can "find moments of quiet reflection and prayer," but honestly we never ran into a single student there.

After over four years, dipping my hand in the holy water font at the entrance to the church is muscle memory. We're supposed to make the sign of the cross with holy water whenever we enter this space for prayer. It's been a while since Bea and I hung out here during lunchtime, so my brain expects to be in Mass when I step inside, and my finger is already submerged before I remember why I'm here. Bea watches me try to decide what to do with myself. I end up wiping the water between my hands like some sort of blessed hand sanitizer.

Bea heads for the front of the chapel and I shrug out of my backpack, taking a seat in the first pew. Bea's blazer and scarf sit abandoned down the pew from me, twirled into a makeshift pillow next to an open copy of Anis Mojgani's poetry collection, *In the Pockets of Small Gods*. I forgot she borrowed the book from me last fall. Anis wrote the only poem I ever memorized, about loving someone with every bit of your heart.

"What's your stuff doing in here?" I look up at her.

"Missed last period." She paces along the crossing between the altar and the seats.

"You're gonna get in trouble," I say.

Bea stops and looks at me. "What's going on with you?"

"Nothing."

A part of me wants to name what happened. *Well, Bea, I almost kissed you in your bedroom on Saturday, and it nearly blew up our friendship. So swaying back and forth in the dark to the latest Taylor Swift ballad isn't going to do us any favors right now.* But I can't say that.

"Why don't you want to go to Formal anymore?"

"I didn't say I don't want to go." My fingers dig into my eyelids. *Wanting is the problem.* "I just . . . can't think about it right now."

Bea's reaching critical levels of exasperation with me. She hasn't been this annoyed with me since the time I refused to dive into Phantom Lake with her during an August heat wave.

"You're being weird."

"Don't I get to change my mind sometimes?" My voice bristles.

"But *why?*" She turns away from the crossing and steps toward me, closing the space between us so fast that I pop out of my seat. "Something obviously happened. You wanted to go. You were excited."

My fingertips press into my temples. "I don't know what you want me to say."

Bea huffs and looks up to the ceiling of the chapel, like, *Lord help me with this girl*. "You've been weird ever since Saturday. You're pulling away. Just talk to me."

My eyes sting, and my jaw clamps tight.

"It's me." Bea's voice is low and quiet. She reaches for my arm, her hand circling my wrist. "Come on. What's really going on with you?"

Her touch propels me forward. "It doesn't matter how I feel." My voice breaks, and my cheeks swarm with heat, and I know I'm reaching a brink I can't reel back from. "Because you want Cara, and maybe you always will. If you want to get back together with her, you should."

Bea's hand latches tight around my wrist. "I don't," she starts, but her voice frays. "I don't want Cara." Her eyes chase after mine, and they're brimming with that warmth I saw in class, swirled with a kind of stubborn certainty.

"No?" I swallow.

She squeezes my palm. "No."

She slides her fingers from my wrist to my palm, locking them into mine. We both freeze like the saints encased in glass above us.

I finally see it. In all the moments she's offered me her honesty, it was never effortless. She's been holding her heart out for me. Waiting for me to show up. Waiting to see if I'd hold mine out too.

I step forward into her, her breath warming my cheek when she exhales. A thread of questions laces the space between us: What are we doing? and *Do you want this?* and *Is this okay?*

Her *yes* surfaces in the smallest gestures: her nudge of my nose, the drifting of her eyelashes as they close.

Our lips find their way to each other, and it's like they always knew they would meet. Her mouth moves with mine, resolute. She tastes warm and familiar from the vanilla lip balm I thought I lost at her house. The surprise of her tongue splits me open.

In all my wanting of Bea, I never let myself believe her kiss could feel like this—a revelation.

I cup her face in my hand to shelter the spark, and for once, we find a way forward without words.

Mitra

designed: the shell
and the pearl, fractals
in flowers and galaxy

swirls, a continual
call and response of
shrieks and whispers

just to find each other
and align some ancient
dial, hear that universal

click of bridges latching
to close distance between
us, an artery forming

language for un-
speakable truths like
this one: you are my

home, the only holy
thing, and I'm held
in the palm of your hand

Bea

hands like ours reach and sift and
scrabble for hope hard in the teeth
like agates, like sea glass polished

in the grit of bitter scrapes, jewels
and bones slipped and stolen from the
soft valleys of our palms, the reaching

like a net cast with eyes closed, like
launching firecracker prayers in dark
wild night—and if hope is the design

you are the fabric, laced with every
answer in those shells and flowers and
stars, a truth I gather tight—you cast

and I'll cradle like glass halos held in high
blue windows, like minerals dreaming in
ocean floor, cherished thing worth reaching for

Reply Hazy, Try Again

THAT NIGHT, I hold The Book to my chest under my blue sheets. The house is silent and the sky pitch-dark. When I turn on my lamp, I feel like a kid caught with the lights on after bedtime. I shouldn't be allowed to be this happy while the world around me sleeps.

My room looks the same as it did this morning. The wooden bookshelf and desk from Goodwill sit stacked with columns of text-books and poetry chapbooks and a backlog of borrowed fiction from Bea. There's a neat grid of art on my wall: a screen print drawing of pomegranates from the Midtown farmers' market, a poster of Janelle Monáe that Bea got me for my birthday, and an ad for last year's Seattle Queer Film Festival. A framed photo of Bea and me at Lake Sammamish sits on my bedside table. Her eyes squint with her smile, barely open behind her gold-rimmed glasses. I tip the frame back and forth with my finger, dazed.

If everything looks the same, then it must be me that's changed. I feel like I just drank the sun through a straw. Everything inside and outside of me glows.

We kissed!

We kissed and now I've short-circuited like some old toaster. We kissed, and we scraped the haze from my world. Now everything is brighter and sharper and burning vivid. Including my skin.

I never realized how much energy it took to lock down my love for Bea—that some part of me was always folding inward around that feeling, like muscles in spasm. For the first time in years, I release that fist inside me, and it's like I'm floating. Nothing can ground me again.

I run my finger down the face of The Book, but instead of the smooth cotton cover, I feel the soft curve of Bea's cheek. I flip to the verses we wrote in between classes today and reread her handwriting. Each of her words shines under my lamplight like the treasures she wrote about. Jewels, stars, stained glass.

She left the poem to dangle at the end, mid-breath, and that's our rule—no terminal punctuation. But the open air after her words makes my chest tighten. I don't know what comes next for us.

We have no map for this.

I set down The Book and pick up my phone, using sheer willpower to try to summon a text message out of the ether like it's a Magic 8 Ball. *Reply hazy, try again.* Bea hasn't texted me since she told me to meet her in the chapel at lunch. We never have a night of radio silence like this. If she's not talking to me, maybe she's overthinking. Maybe she's slipping into her own sinkhole of delight and panic.

Or maybe she's changed her mind.

Post-Kiss Playbook

ON TUESDAY MORNING, Dad lets us stop at Third Culture for coffee before dropping Azar and me off at the Palm of God's Hand. I gulp my drink down before we make it to school, fueled by nervous energy. My lips and tongue and fingertips still tingle from yesterday. I don't know what I'm going to do when I see Bea. In the pre-kiss era, she'd greet me with a hug or a tousle of my hair and we'd gripe about our mornings and whatever fresh nonsense was happening at Holy Trinity. I'd make some joke about us escaping to form our own gay convent, and she'd laugh, and it would be easy.

Now I don't even know what to do with my hands, let alone the rest of me. I carry a coffee for Bea in one hand and stuff the other in my blazer pocket.

We're early, which isn't unusual when Dad takes us to school before work. What's weird is that *Bea* is early. I spot her on the plaza before she notices me, and I allow myself the pleasure of really seeing her. She's wearing her scuffed-up loafers from freshman year that she refuses to trash because I Sharpied a Pegasus on each of the outsoles. Her socks have a yellow thread rimming the cuff, technically prohibited, but I'm probably the only one paying attention to her knees. Her dark curls coil tight this morning. She's wearing a sweater I lent her over her uniform today. We swap clothes all the time, but it feels different to see her in my white cardigan the day after we kissed.

"Morning!" The word comes out of my mouth with obnoxious

levels of cheer, and Bea suppresses a smirk. I give her the Third Culture cup, and then I have *another* awkward empty hand to contend with. I brush my fingers through my hair.

Bea's lips part, and she looks like she wants to say something, but she holds back. She takes the coffee and tips it at me. "You're really doing the Lord's work, Mitra."

Everyone's filing by on their way to first period, and I feel a weird kind of exposure, my cheeks shocking red. Like that coffee cup is a feelings beacon—like everyone can *see* me.

I've had crushes on girls and guys and people since I was twelve. Before I came to Holy Trinity, before I knew Bea. I've been bi all this time, but that queerness nested in my mind and heart and in the pages of the never-ending poem, always out of view. I don't know how to hold it now that it's rippling out into the world. I don't know how to be queer in a place like this.

My skin prickles with the thought. I feel like I'm living out the nightmare where I show up to school naked.

"So . . . how are you?" I ask. It's strange not to know anymore. What Bea wants, what she's thinking.

She nods. "Come with me." My heart takes off. I follow her toward the underground parking lot from a safe distance.

We reach Gary, Bea's green Subaru, and she slides into the front seat. Bea has always been bitter about people naming inanimate objects like cars and sailboats after women, so when she got her car, she named it after a dude.

I climb into the passenger's side and Bea swivels to lean back against the driver's-side window, facing me. It feels like we're in a tiny, Japanese-engineered confessional booth.

Even with Bea pressed against the window, we're too close. I can hear her breathing, and when she crosses her legs in front of her, the red pleats of her skirt fan out over my knees.

"So. We kissed," I say.

Bea huffs an anxious laugh. "I know."

"Do you?" My voice squeaks. "Because you haven't said anything about it in the last twenty-four hours. And you always come to me to unpack your latest make-out session. This was, like, a record in secret keeping for you."

Bea runs a hand back and forth through her curls, making them dance with static electricity. "I don't know. It's different when it's you." She brings her thumbnail between her teeth, chewing at her yolk-yellow polish. "I kind of freaked out last night," she admits.

"Yeah?"

"Things got so real yesterday. *Fast.*"

"I know." My eyes widen. "We've . . . never done that before."

She leans forward, reaching her hand out but stopping short of touching my knee. Instead, she drops her hand to the seat of the car, her pinkie brushing mine. "And you mean everything to me, and I don't want to lose that with you."

I swallow the dread in my throat. I get it. I can't even be mad if she wants to pretend we never kissed and go back to the way things were before, when we were only best friends. We gambled with something precious yesterday. There's so much we could lose.

"But." She sighs through her nose, and then sweeps her hand over mine to wrap around my fingers. Her warm eyes focus on mine. "I think we could be something?"

Bea's words lift the starting gate around my heart, and it takes off, bounding through my whole body.

We could be something.

"What about Cara?" My hand tightens in my lap. After they reacclimated to each other in poetry seminar, Bea said things have gotten better, that she's not hung up on Cara anymore. But I can't let go of Bea's heartbreak after Halloween.

"I get that things have been intense this quarter," Bea says. "Being in class together with Cara . . . all of that. But it wasn't just about her." She rests her head back on the glass. "It was more than that. I was trying to get over her, but I was also trying to sort out how I felt about you, you know? It was a lot, all at once. And I had to take the time to make sure I was ready for something with you."

"Okay." I turn my palm up to hers. "Okay. So . . . we're something?" My face breaks into a grin. "I don't even know how to do this."

"You think I do?" She swats my hand.

I look out the windshield at the deserted parking garage. "You've had girlfriends. I haven't even made it past the *is-this-a-date* phase before. Or the awkward attempts at flirty texting. This is, like, brand-new territory for me."

"Wait. Awkward flirty texts? Who were those with? And why didn't I get to see them?" Bea cracks a smile.

"You will *never in your life* see them," I say.

"But if we're *something* now, shouldn't I get to be on the receiving end of some of these texts? Just because we had our first kiss already doesn't mean you get to stop putting in work to *romance* me."

"Oh my god." My hand clamps over my eyes. "I promise to *romance* you. Back to the point."

Bea wrenches the hand from my face and holds it tight. "Yeah, Mitra, I've dated girls before. But I haven't been with *you*. It's scary."

"Too scary?"

She fixes her eyes on me. "No. But it's a lot to process." She lets out a tiny laugh. "And normally you're the person I'd turn to when I'm panicking, and you'd know just the right thing to say, and you'd talk me down."

"Can't I still be that person?"

Bea brings her thumb to the hair at my temple, tucking some stray strands behind my ear. "Maybe." She's still smiling. "I guess we'll find out."

The New Never-Ending Poem Rules

8. We've seen each other through braces and bad haircuts and that time we both had a crush on Ms. Dalton in physical science. So we can survive basically anything together. Best friends first and forever.
9. If we have something to say, say it to our faces! No writing angry. No fighting with each other through The Book. We're classier than that.
10. Honesty, always. Tell the truth even when it's hard. Even when it feels impossible.

Wooing

Mitra: are you a college acceptance letter?

Mitra: because I just want to take you home and show you off to my family

Bea: um

Mitra: are you a catchy timeless Queen song?

Mitra: because I can't get you out of my head

Bea: WHAT IS HAPPENING

Mitra: are you flashcards for my world history test?

Mitra: because I could spend all day memorizing you

Bea: wait!! are these my awkward flirty texts???

Mitra: I always live up to my word

Mitra: do you feel sufficiently romanced

Mitra: or should I keep going

Bea: nope nope nope

Bea: that's plenty

Mitra: thank goddddd

Bea: so . . .

Bea: brunch with your mom is tomorrow?

                              Mitra: yeah

                              Mitra: whether I'm there or not

Bea: but Aziz is going

                              Mitra: she doesn't know what she's
                              walking into

Bea: you know what they say about the
Esfahani girls . . .

                              Mitra: "what are these Iranian
                              nonbelievers doing in Catholic
                              school??"

Bea: that they're smart!

Bea: brave

Bea: and they know how to handle
themselves

                              Mitra: nobody ever says that

Bea: I do, Mitra

Jaleh

IT'S BEEN FIVE days since Bea and I broke the space-time continuum with our kiss, and four days since we became *something*. I can't tell you one thing I learned in class this week, but I can tell you how Bea wore her honeycomb knee-high socks on Wednesday, and how the bright February sun lit up all the marbled shades of brown in her eyes. My week was a fuzz of school and home and trying to act normal, punctuated by a jolt every time she'd grin at me or touch my hand. We haven't told anyone. Not Max, not Azar, and we haven't sent Bea's mom running for her rosary yet. I don't want to jinx it. Naming what happened could shatter the bubble of magic surrounding this week.

The aftermath of Monday kept me so distracted that I almost forgot about brunch with our mom. We arranged to meet her at Sally's Kitchen in Highlands on Saturday morning. Highlands is a neighborhood just north of the Crossroads house and south of where Mom is staying in Bridle Trails, so it feels like some kind of no-man's-land between our respective territories.

Dad drives Azar and me into the parking lot, futzing with his beard as he pulls the emergency brake. He's been quiet the whole morning.

"Mitra." He leans in for the requisite forehead kiss. "Aziz." On another day she'd probably whine about him messing up her makeup or something, but today she unbuckles her seat belt and pops her forehead into the front seat with zero gripes.

He doesn't tell us to make it a great day. Instead, he says, "Take care of each other. Call me if you need anything."

Azar and I walk up to the restaurant's picture windows. The place bustles with the weekend brunch crowd. All these people enjoying nice, normal breakfast foods with their families.

"He's leaving." Azar nods to Dad's car crawling out of the parking lot. She keeps toggling the power switch on her headphones, and it's the first sign of nervousness I've noticed in her since we finalized this reunion.

"It's gonna be okay." When she was little, she always let me reassure her. It's been a while since she accepted any sort of comfort from me. So I tell her what I think a big sister should say, even though inside I'm twelve again and terrified.

"I know." She shoots her sassy eyes at me.

Dad's car travels about a hundred feet toward the Goodwill parking lot, and when he's almost completely out of sight, he pulls into a parking spot and turns off the car.

"Look." I point. "Bet he's going to stay there the whole time. He probably thinks he's being stealthy."

"It's not like we need a chaperone," Azar says, but her shoulders relax a little. We turn back toward the restaurant, and I wait for Azar to make the first move toward the door, but she just stands there.

"Do I look okay?" She stares down at her oversized PNW sweatshirt and floral-print Toms.

"You don't need to impress her." The words come with a bite. I regret them as soon as I see Azar's cheeks fizzle red. She pushes through the front door without waiting for me.

I step inside, all the chatter and background music and clinking dishes reaching me like in a dream, or a nightmare. I see our mom before she sees us, and there's this one frozen moment where I just get to look at her. She's got the same dark kohl eyeliner that Azar used to ink across my eyes when we did makeovers. Her nose, an older echo of Azar's, now has a gold stud instead of the hoop I remember.

When her eyes click on mine, the moment breaks. She smiles a half-open, expectant smile, and waggles her fingers at us. Azar dashes over to her. "Mom!"

I stand back and watch our mom take Azar's face in her hands, kissing her on both cheeks. Her eyes squeeze closed when they embrace.

And then she looks at me. I step forward, letting her take my hand. Tears bead up in the corners of her eyes. She pulls me into a hug without asking, and I harden in her arms. Maybe she thinks this meeting means that things are magically okay between us. I wish I could tell her: *I'm here for Azar. Not for you.* But old emotions already threaten to pull me under. She smells like honey and jasmine, how a mom might smell. Inside I'm clinging to her name, Jaleh-Jaleh-Jaleh, because even thinking *Mom* in this moment feels like claiming her. And I can't do that.

"It's so good to see you again," she says. Her voice is warm and heavy with emotion.

She looks happy. I can't remember the last time I saw her like that. And a part of me resents that she gets to be happy about this reunion, while I get a blitz of adrenaline and panic.

"We missed you," Azar says as we sit down across from her. "How did the interview go?"

"Really well," Jaleh says. "This was a second interview—we met over Skype a few weeks ago. They offered me the grant-writing position."

I stare blankly at the brunch section of the menu. She got the job. And we got no choice in the matter.

"Congrats," Azar says.

The waiter arrives at our table. She's curvy and not that much older than me, with a bun of brunette hair and a yellow daisy tattooed on her arm.

Jaleh watches me watch the waiter. Maybe Dad told her I'm into girls during one of their secret phone calls, or maybe she just has functioning eyes. The spark of insecurity flickering in my chest embarrasses me. I didn't give a second thought to her approval when I came out—at that point our mom was just a shapeless ghost in my mind, filled in with old photos and bad memories. I didn't need her approval then, and I'd give anything not to crave it now.

A tiny part of me imagines another reality where Jaleh is a mom to me, where this is a normal Saturday brunch, where I can tell her: *Guess what happened this week? Bea and I kissed!* And she'd understand what an epic deal that is.

But that isn't our reality. On this planet, Jaleh doesn't even know me, let alone Bea.

"Good morning!" The waiter snaps me back to the breakfast table. "What can I get started for y'all?"

What I'd really like is for her to conscript me into waitresshood so I can follow her back into the kitchen and hide out there making hash browns for the rest of time. But that's not on the menu, so I go for the cheese omelet. Azar gets blueberry pancakes and Jaleh gets a cheese omelet too, which bothers me in a completely irrational way.

"I would love . . ." Jaleh clears her throat. "I'd love to hear what's new in your lives."

What's new?

My fingers curl into my palms under the table. *It's been four and a half years since we've seen you,* I want to say. *So, you know, not much has happened.*

Azar looks to me, prodding me in the thigh with her thumb.

"Azar had her digital art in the freshman showcase last June," I say. "She has A's in History and Physical Science."

"Wow." Jaleh's eyes soften with her smile. "Proud of you, Aziz."

"Mitra's applying to colleges," Azar counters. "And she got into this super-advanced poetry class."

"Poetry?" Jaleh's expression brightens. "That's wonderful, Mitra joon. You've always been a writer. You get that from me."

Her words are too familiar. She doesn't get to call me joon. She doesn't get to take credit for the person I've become. But taking is what she's good at.

"It's not like what you do for work," I tell her, not willing to give her the comfort of feeling like she knows me.

Jaleh nods, parting her curls behind an ear. "I understand. Maybe sometime I can read a bit of what you've written."

I let her suggestion dangle in the air until the waiter returns, cutting the tension with platters of eggs and pancakes. The bites of omelet land like paperweights down my throat. Azar tells Mom all about Bellevue and the house and her friends at Holy Trinity. She's got four years of pent-up excitement and stories rocketing out of her.

The normalness of it all is what destroys me. We're occupying some alternate dimension filled with breakfast foods and fake smiles, where we talk about everything except the thing that actually matters.

Jaleh finishes her last bite of fried potato, and she puts her fork down with a finality that sets my heart on a spin cycle. "I wanted you both to know I signed a lease on an apartment this morning," she says. "It's in a complex northeast of the shopping center, close to your house."

My stomach twists around the omelet. She already made her mind up about inserting herself into our lives again. This brunch didn't really matter. What I think and want doesn't matter to her.

"No way!" Azar's face lights up with a grin that makes her look eight years old again. Her hopefulness claws into me.

"Your baba said it would be close enough for you to walk over." Jaleh meets my eyes. "If you wanted to. And it has an extra bedroom that I'll put twin beds in, so you both can stay over with me some weekends. If that's all okay with you."

If that's okay.

I drop my napkin on the table. "Why are you asking if it's okay? You've already made all these plans without us."

Azar's mouth puckers into nothingness.

"You've been talking to Dad behind our backs, you're taking a job here, and now you're moving in down the street from us."

Azar's hand slips over my knee.

"No. It's not okay. No."

In incremental bits, Jaleh's face transforms until she looks like the mom I remember: tired. Disappointed. Disconnected. This sick righteousness kicks up in me, like—*There*. I found her. I knew she hadn't changed. The confirmation feels hollow.

"Okay." Jaleh raises her hands in surrender. "I hear you, Mitra."

"You don't get to decide that for both of us," Azar mumbles to me before turning back to Jaleh. "I want to come over, Mom."

Heat toasts my skin and I glare at Azar. "You don't know what you're doing. And I'm not coming with you."

My legs lift me up from my chair, carrying me through the restaurant and out the door without looking back.

I should wait for Azar, and I should go find Dad in the Goodwill parking lot, but I don't want to see either of them. I walk on autopilot until I land outside Oskoo, an Iranian market down the street. Inside, the store smells like a bubble of cardamom pods and tart sumac powder. It smells like home: the Crossroads house, and our home before that too, in Sacramento.

Maybe I'm the only one who remembers the reason we left Sacramento. We were trying to start over. To get away from her.

After everything Jaleh put us through, I thought they'd be smarter than this. I can be pissed at her for traipsing into our lives again and acting like nothing happened, but I expect chaos from her. It's Dad and Azar who should know better.

The three of us built a life that was peaceful and predictable and secure. We fought for a balance that stitched our little family together. And now Azar and Dad are shattering it.

TOGETHER Together

WHEN I WAS fourteen and my dad lost the job that brought us to Washington, I melted down in panic on the phone with Bea. I was sure our lives in Bellevue were over and we'd have to move back to Sacramento. After we hung up, Bea spent forty-five minutes on two city buses in the dark just to get to my house. And when she got to our door, she tackled me in a hug so massive it knocked me backward.

Now I pull out my phone to text Bea and drop a pin with my location.

Mitra: Come find me?

While I wait for Bea, I buy a package of nan-e nokhodchi, tiny clover-shaped cardamom cookies, and take them across the street to the edge of Highlands Park, sitting under a tree in the parking lot. Azar is obsessed with these cookies. They're dry as hell because they're meant to be eaten with chai, and as a kid she'd eat them so fast that she choked on the chickpea flour. I feel like a jerk for buying myself a box and eating them without her. And for leaving her at the restaurant with Jaleh, when I only went along in the first place to look out for her.

But she's made it clear she doesn't want my help.

Bea pulls up in Gary just as rain starts to spit overhead. She's wearing her sleepy Saturday morning best: cat-print pajama pants and Birkenstocks, a roomy red sweatshirt that warms my cheek when I burrow my face into her shoulder. She constricts her arms around me in a hug, and I try to let myself soften into her. When we step apart, Bea opens the passenger door for me without a word and we sit side by side. I watch a train of children sprinting from the playground toward the sheltering canopy of evergreens.

"You wanna talk about it?" She straightens her glasses. "Or . . . you don't have to."

She understands I don't always know how to talk about things. But with Bea, I want to try.

"Jaleh and my dad have been making all these plans behind our backs." I can't look at Bea as I explain the rest. I've never figured out how to get eye contact right, especially when I'm having a Feeling. But she never seems to mind.

"They just want to pretend nothing happened." I pick at the plastic of the cookie package.

Bea places her hand on my knee, her warm fingers reaching my skin through the hole in my jeans. "I'm sorry," she says.

That night when we were fourteen, after she'd pounced on me with the biggest hug she could muster, she'd said: *I love you. I'm sorry this is happening.* Today, those other words float just under the surface, but she can't say them anymore. *I love you* means something different now.

I know Bea feels bad about what's happening with my mom, but she can't understand the looming panic I feel. I've never told her about everything we went through back in Sacramento. She knows about the addiction, but I never told Bea who my mom became when she was using.

Part of me wants to tell her about Jaleh's rages, the lies, the days we didn't even know where she'd gone. To let Bea all the way in. I want to be honest with her, but to talk about what happened with my mom feels like going back in time, to a place I never want to visit again.

I lean into her shoulder, watching rain spatter the windshield. "My dad was always so willing to welcome her back in the house with us at the *first* sign that she was taking recovery seriously again. When I was nine, she spent the summer at this residential treatment program in the Bay Area. It was hours away, but my dad would drive us out there *every* weekend to visit her because she was 'working so hard.'

"That's what he said. When she missed Azar's seventh birthday, or my science fair award, it was because she was 'busy working very hard to come home.' We did all this prep work with the counselors there to help her transition back—setting up therapy and a sponsor in Sacramento. She came home in September." I dig my fingernails into the rip in my jeans. "She didn't even make it to Halloween."

Bea presses a kiss to my temple. "I can tell she really hurt you. And—there's obviously a lot I don't know." She keeps her eyes on me. "What happened?"

I can't tell Bea everything. I can't tell her that when my mom had a choice between Azar and me or getting high, she chose pills every time. So I tell her a safer truth, instead: "I don't like talking about it."

I don't realize I'm crying until Bea lifts the sleeve of her sweatshirt to my cheeks, dabbing under my eyes. My face burns hot and all my breath feels trapped in my airway. "Can we talk about something else?"

"Okay." Our breath has steamed up the windows of Gary, and Bea doodles a heart in the steam with stick arms and legs jutting out of it.

"So, Formal is next weekend." She traces a top hat above the heart. "I know we're going to the dance together. But, do you want to go *together* together?"

"Like a date?" I swipe the last of the tears from under my eyelashes. "Like corsages and cheesy photos and all that?"

"Yeah, all of that." Bea adds a little smile to her heart doodle.

I can't believe the two of us. Formal was a hetero charade we used to scoff at while we were shooting pinball or crying over *Planet Earth* marathons on our Anti-Formal Fridays. I thought for sure we'd escape Holy Trinity without being swayed by the whole spectacle: the dressing up, the DJ playing Cha-Cha Slide, the nervous *Will I have someone to slow dance with?* energy. But the mental image of holding Bea close at the dance washes me clean of all skepticism.

"Sounds perfect," I say.

I guess it's true what they say: Love changes you.

Poetry Journal:
In the Time Since I Saw You

In the time since I saw my mother,

her curly hair streaked silver.

In the time since I saw my mother,

each hair on her head that I knew
and felt with my hands fell away,
and something different grew in its place.

The skin of hers that touched my face and
tied my shoes and contained all of her, that skin

became particles of nothing-dust for other
faraway people to breathe into their lungs.
And she grew lines around her lips and new
curves in her cheek, and wrinkles folded
to hug eyes

that stayed the same.

Thank you for sharing this, Mitra. As the reader, I imagine a sense
of longing and tremendous loss here, but these emotions aren't
expressly named. How does the speaker feel about the reunion? Is
there grief, sweetness, bitterness, resentment, etc? —Ms. Acosta

Very Big, Shocking News!

THE NEXT FRIDAY, Dad gets off work early, and he takes Azar and me to Aria, the Iranian bakery in Kirkland. Time for our semi-regular dose of sangak flatbread and saffron rice pudding.

Azar and I have been tiptoeing around each other since the disastrous ending at brunch with Jaleh. Dad made good-faith attempts to ask us how Saturday went, but when I shot him gamma rays of *DON'T GO THERE* energy from my eyes, he backed off. I want things to return to how they were between the three of us before Jaleh thundered into our lives again, but I can't shake the knowledge that she's out there. Somewhere a few blocks away from us in Highlands, she's installing a new set of twin beds in her second bedroom.

"I can't believe you're actually coming to Formal tonight," Azar says as we drive toward Kirkland. "You never go to dances."

As unbelievable as it may be that I'm voluntarily attending a Holy Trinity social function, the real bombshell is that I'm going with *Bea*. On a date.

I haven't told Azar or my dad about everything yet. Azar has a penchant for nosiness when it comes to anything dating related, and my dad would probably want to sit me down and *talk* about it, so we've kept things under the radar for the past week and a half. The fact that they haven't detected my explosive levels of glee lately is on them.

Dad's gaze leaves the road for a moment and he gives me an approving nod. "Going to the dance? That *is* different for you."

I cross my arms over my chest. "Last year at Holy Trinity. Just trying to soak up the ridiculous traditions before we miss out on them entirely."

My dad turns to me at a red light. "You can give Azar and Gigi a ride, then."

"Wait," I scramble. "No. Bea's taking me." It's our first real date since becoming something, and I've pictured the night a thousand times in my head. None of those fantasies include my sister and her hype girl in the back seat of Bea's car, shouting Doja Cat lyrics the whole way to school.

"So?" Azar bobs her head into the front seat space. "Gigi's coming over to our house to get ready beforehand. And we're all going to the same place."

"I can't." I tug at my Peter Pan collar. Dad's blasting the heater to combat the cold, and it's suffocating me. I feel bad about keeping my relationship from my dad and Azar. It's big news, and I want to break it to them in the right way. Part of my hesitation is knowing how they'll respond. Bea has been my friend for long enough now that my dad sees her as a bonus kid. He'll freak out when he learns this extra layer has been brewing under our friendship.

Azar is another story, because she *loves* Bea. They're close enough that they text on the regular, so she's going to lose her mind when she finds out we've been keeping this from her. And even though she's never cared that I'm bi, she might resent it if I attract any more attention to our otherness at school. She somehow mastered the ability to blend in at Holy Trinity and craft a functioning social circle for herself. Maybe she'll think my being out will sabotage all that.

"Mitra, there are five seats in Beatrice's vehicle. Plenty of room. Take your sister and her friend."

"It's not about the car," Aziz grumbles. "She's punishing me for what happened at brunch. You can't just trap me at home and refuse to give me rides because you're mad at me."

"I'm not," I say.

"It's going to happen, Mitra. I gave Mom my phone number, and I'm going to see her new apartment this weekend. Dad's fine with it. You don't have to come, but I want to keep seeing her."

"If your mother is really doing well," Dad adds, "she has a right to spend time with Azar."

"Whatever." Azar pulls out her phone. "I'll just ask Bea. *She's* never annoyed when I ask for a ride."

"It's not about that!" I'm about ready to jump out of the car and jog the rest of the way to the bakery. I'd rather walk on the shoulder of the 405 for another six miles than see this conversation through.

They're both going to flip out. And I get it. It's a lot. Speeding down the highway toward our favorite sangak bakery might not be an ideal moment to spring this revelation on them, but here goes.

I steady myself with a sharp inhale. "I can't take you because we're going together. Like, on a date."

"Wait, what?" Azar's eyes transform into full moons. *Here it comes.* "You two are *dating*?" she shouts like she's calling into a dark cave, but that cave happens to be my ear.

I tip my head back against the headrest, preparing myself for the onslaught of their shock. Then Azar jabs her finger into our dad's shoulder. "Called it."

"What do you mean, *Called it?*" I scoff. "You did *not* call it."

Dad smacks his hand on the steering wheel, grinning and shaking his head. "We had our suspicions," he says. "Congratulations, joon. She's a very smart, very nice girl."

Suspicions? I want to ask Dad where the hell these suspicions came from. This revelation should blow their minds, but they're both acting totally unsurprised. I thought I was announcing some jaw-dropping news like a spokesperson at a press conference, but they're acting like I took the mic and said *Listen. I've given it a lot of thought, and I know you won't believe this, but I've decided I want to be a librarian when I grow up.*

"How long?" Azar demands.

"Like, a week?"

"Just a week?" Azar quirks an eyebrow at me. The Iranian I'm-Judging-You Face. "Huh. Thought you'd been dating way longer."

"What?" I pivot in my seat toward her. "What are you talking about?"

Dad's eyes find Azar's in the rearview mirror. "I told you, Aziz. Sometimes it takes *time* for friendship to grow into romance."

"I can't believe this!" I blow up at them. "You're being way too chill. We're *dating*. It's a big deal!"

We pull up to Aria and my hands scratch at the car door handle, praying for an escape. *Damn child safety locks.*

"Of course." My dad tries to wipe the grin from his face. "It's very big, shocking news. We're happy for you, Mitra joon."

Azar huffs from the back seat. "I still think you've been dating longer. Maybe you both just didn't admit it to yourselves."

I slam my door shut. This was supposed to be my moment of revelation and they're both annoying the crap out of me.

I head into the bakery and veer straight to the back wall, where thin sheets of crisp flatbread hang draped over a rack. The toasty, sourdough smell wafts over to me, beckoning me to the sangak adorned with black and white sesame seeds. Dad peruses the sweets in the glass display case, but Azar zooms over to me, ramming her elbow into my side.

"I've been waiting for this day," she says. "Are you going to tell Mom?"

I keep my eyes on the rows of fresh-baked flatbread. "I don't know."

"I'm sure she'll be cool with it."

"Maybe," I say. "Maybe not."

"Don't worry. She doesn't make a big deal about this kind of thing."

It's meant to be reassuring, but her certainty feels like a reminder: Azar is getting to know our mother, and I'm not.

"Just don't say anything to her yet."

"I won't." Azar chooses a sheet of sangak from the counter, folding it in its plastic sleeve. She smirks at me. "You picked a good one, Mitra."

The New Bennifer

Azar: Beatra

Azar: Meatra

Azar: or what about TraBea

Bea: what's happening?

              Mitra: I told Aziz we're dating

Azar: or we could go for the dark horse and use your last names . . .

Azar: Esfatega?

Azar: Ortesfahani?

Azar: too wordy?

              Mitra: I don't know how she went from "we're dating" to making up the word "Ortesfahani" though

              Mitra: Aziz, did you accidentally grab dad's hard cider instead of the ginger ale again?

              Mitra: you know there's alcohol in that?

Bea: WHAT

Azar: that was ONE time Mitra

              Mitra: but your words did sound remarkably similar to this gibberish

Azar: I'm not drunk!! I'm brainstorming your portmanteau!

Bea: wait, what's a portmanteau?

> **Mitra:** it's like the Lesbian Urge to Merge, but in name form

Azar: all the celebrity power couples have them!

Azar: TomKat, Brangelina, Kimye . . .

> **Mitra:** are any of these people still together?

Azar: OMG what about BEAM

> **Mitra:** I'm sorry you're being subjected to this Bea

> **Mitra:** she can't be helped

Bea: I'm not complaining!

Azar: you'll thank me later 😉

Little Gay Rebellions

REALITY HITS WHILE I put on my suit. I joked with Bea about how the Holy Trinity teachers would explode over the gay rebellion sewn into my fashion choices, but now that I'm faced with heading into the Palm of God's Hand, my knees shake. Bea and I have been keeping our *somethingness* undercover at school because Holy Trinity isn't exactly a welcoming environment. There's no Gay Straight Alliance, no *Everyone Welcome Here* sign in the receptionist's office. Our classroom windows have decals of Christian fishes and Celtic crosses, not rainbow flags.

We've managed to fly mostly under the radar out of self-preservation. Tonight, though, we'll be on display for the whole mass of sweaty, dancing students to see. There will be teachers and nuns and our conservative classmates and . . . Cara. I've thought about what this dance will mean for Bea and me—this big step toward a new thing we're becoming. But I didn't think about what it would mean for our lives at school. To be *out* there. Bea and Cara didn't hide their relationship last year, but they didn't broadcast it at school dances, either.

After I get dressed for the dance, my dad helps me with my tie in the hallway mirror. Our upstairs is small, the walls slanted in Azar's and my bedrooms by the roof, so my dad has to stoop whenever he passes under the low part of the ceiling. "I remember the last time I helped you get ready for an event like this. It was your sixth-grade dance."

"Wait, are there pictures of that?" Azar shouts from down the hall.

"None that you will ever find," I yell back.

"You were so little then," my dad says. "What happened?"

He looks at me in the mirror: black slacks and suit coat, teal button-up, and a thin black tie with spatters of purple spots. I gave myself a blowout for the first time since the New Year, so my coal-colored hair is smooth and wavy as it brushes my shoulders. I even let Azar do my makeup, so my lips are stained a deep plum and my eyes are edged with dark liner that makes me look a little bit like Jaleh.

My dad gets this look in his eye, and it's one I've seen dozens of times before: a look that says, *I remember when you were small enough to hold in just my two hands.*

"You're going to have a fun night." He pats my shoulders. "But . . . not too much fun, okay?"

"Dad." I can hear Azar and Gigi laughing over the synth-pop song pulsing in Azar's room.

"You listen too, Aziz," he calls. My sister and her best friend emerge from her bedroom on a cloud of vanilla and rose perfume. "No drugs, no drinking. No funny business."

"Got it," Azar shouts as she and Gigi thunder down the stairs.

"It's Holy Trinity," I tell Dad. "You don't have to worry. There are actual nuns chaperoning this thing."

"It's not just the dance I'm talking about," he says. "But after. You are staying over at Bea's tonight?" He hesitates. "Do Bea's parents know?"

He already knows the answer to his question. Bea's parents never know what's going on.

"I think so," I say.

"I trust you to be smart," he says before leaving me in the hallway. I can hear the layers under my dad's tone, the word *smart*. A sleepover with Bea means something more now that we're dating. I don't know what will happen tonight. Electricity zigs up my spine just thinking about it.

Azar's squeal resounds up the staircase. "Your *girlfriend* is here," my sister sings. She hasn't taunted me in musical form in a long time, but I guess she's full of inspiration now that she knows about me and Bea.

"Mitra!" Bea's voice booms. "Don't make me walk up the stairs in these shoes."

I meet her at the staircase, me at the top and her waiting at the bottom, already stepping out of one of her silver heels.

And, Jesus. I was not prepared for the sight of her. Bea's dress steals all the stars and swirls them up in cobalt blue, shimmering from her puff sleeves to the fan of fabric at her knees. A snowflake comb tucks into the soft coils of her hair. Somehow, she took a piece of shapeless fabric and transformed it into *this*.

I make my way to her, and her mouth swings open with her smile. "We're getting expelled tonight," she says. "There's no way they're letting you into the gym looking that good!"

I grip the railing to keep myself from toppling over with her words. We hesitate a few steps from each other on the staircase, just looking at each other, my heartbeat trilling loud in my throat.

I bring one hand to her waist, my head swimming on her floral perfume. I don't even know what to say to her. So I say the obvious thing, my voice small as a mouse: "You look beautiful."

Azar screeches from the dining room. "Stop being cute and come take photos with us!"

"One quick thing first?" Bea slips back into her heels and fetches a small white box at her feet. "I couldn't decide on a corsage or boutonniere for you." She pops the lid on a bundle of white bellflowers framed by tiny fern sprigs. "The florist said a boutonniere would be classiest with your suit." I hold my breath when she fastens the bundle to my lapel.

I find her corsage on the dining room table and present it to her: ranunculus, little fists overflowing with curvy white petals, abundant with beauty just like her. She grins as I loop the beaded bracelet around her wrist.

My dad lines us up by the window to take pictures in every possible group combination he can mathematically manage.

Bea and I used to smoosh into each other's personal space for photos, but now that we're living in a post-kiss world and wearing our fancy dance attire, a weird formality settles between us. I drape my arm loosely around her shoulders, the skin of her collarbone touching my thumb. "Closer," my dad says to me and Bea. But my muscles stiffen, aware of every point of contact between our bodies.

"Relax, Mitra!" Azar instructs. "You look like a robot." She and Gigi do their best robot impressions behind my dad.

I take a deep breath to try to ground myself, but it fills my lungs with Bea's warm flowery smell.

Bea slips out from under my arm. "Okay. I think we're good." The skin at her collarbone flushes red. "How about a family one?" She steals my dad's camera.

When we finally escape the house, Dad waves us out the door. "Make it the best day of your life!" he calls as Azar and Gigi cackle from the doorway. "Well, maybe not the *best* day. Have fun . . . be responsible."

I slide into the front seat of Gary, my face still flaming. "Kill me now." I flop my head back against the headrest.

"Forget your dad," Bea says, taking me by the shoulder. "We *are* making this the best night of our lives, okay?"

I swallow. "Even better than the Anti-Formal Friday where you got the high score on Super Cars at the arcade?"

She scrunches her nose at me, then turns the key in the ignition. "Way better than that."

I don't know what that means. I'm afraid to even let myself imagine.

Social Experiment

AT HOLY TRINITY, Bea and I take our time walking under the archway into campus. Everything inside me is at odds tonight. I've never felt more right with Bea, or more myself in my clothes and in my skin, and I'm stepping right into the bear trap of Holy Trinity. I admire Bea's optimism about *the best night of our lives,* but I'm petrified. We could be walking headfirst into disaster. We could get scolded, or sneered at, or worse. And even if people are chill, I might be too nervous to enjoy the moment. Will I be brave enough to take Bea's hand, or pull her in close to me for a slow song?

"You ready to do this?" Bea asks me as we follow the thump of a bass beat toward the gym.

I squeeze her hand, then drop it before we reach the chaperones at the entryway. "Only one way to find out."

We push in the double doors to the gym, which is decorated like an icy wonderland: Plush fake snow lines the walkway, and a forest of white cutout trees rings the perimeter. Geometric snowflakes dangle from the ceiling amidst zigzags of twinkle lights. Swaths of glittery white cloth drape over everything in sight. I expected it to feel like we were stuck in an endless PE period, but the gym is unrecognizable, and the spectacle of it all is actually dazzling.

"So this is where those big tuition bucks go." Bea laughs.

A few sets of eyes follow my suit, and the attention makes my heartbeat throb in my throat. Bea maneuvers us past the onlookers. "They're staring because you're hot," she whispers.

Bea leads us to a giant snowflake display in the corner where Max and Ellie are taking selfies with a life-sized abominable snowman. He's a muscly beast tufted in white fur, with a lumpy yeti face and fangs.

"Hey!" Max waves when they spot us. We take a moment to eyebrow-communicate how surprising it is that both of us have chosen to attend a school social event.

"You look really nice." I poke the fuchsia bow tie nested into Max's black button-up shirt. There's a hint of glitter dusting their cheekbones, probably from Ellie's epic collection of stage makeup. Not enough sparkle to catch negative attention from any assholes in attendance, but enough for me to notice. It's a delicate balance to be yourself at Holy Trinity.

"You two look amazing," they say.

Ellie pulls us each into a hug. She's wearing a black slip dress, and her pale pink cheeks glimmer with glitter to match Max's. I'm not surprised to find Ellie at Formal. Even though she's about as social and popular as the rest of our HolyHorror crew, she treats everything like it's a science experiment. *What would happen if I put dry ice in my Coke? What if I use this theater prop butter churn as a light saber?* I'm sure she's taking mental notes on her social research tonight.

"We miss you," Bea sighs.

"At least Max gets to see you during that Gay Studies class you're all in," Ellie says.

"That's what I call poetry seminar." Max smiles. "Because we almost outnumber the straights in our class."

Cara appears on the snowy walkway in a cherry-red dress, her dark hair straightened to frame her jaw. The muscles in my shoulders contract, but I draw in a deep breath and wave at her. This suit is classy and I aspire to act that way. Even though inside, my gut trembles.

It's hard not to compare myself to Cara. Max always says Cara has *striking* features: the heart-shaped tan face, the inky black eyes and hair, lips like a spring tulip. She's polished. Shiny. Like me, if I'd been run through a tunnel car wash. It's no wonder she steals everyone's attention onstage.

Cara clocks Bea, and I know what she's seeing: the gorgeous blue dress, the shiny curls, the glow of her cheeks. Bea is radiant. Cara hasn't seen her out of our stop-sign-red uniform in a while, and it shows.

Cara hands waters to Max and Ellie and waves at me and Bea. "Hey."

"I like your dress," I tell her. It's confident, just like her.

"Killer outfits," she tells us. "Did you see Ms. Acosta's chaperoning? The Weeknd came on and she asked me what song was playing. She called it a 'lively tune.'"

"Ms. Acosta likes R&B," Bea marvels.

"Checks out." It's eerie to be joking with Cara, like we would have pre-Halloween heartbreak.

An old Nicki Minaj song breaks through the speakers, and Bea takes my hand. "We're going to go dance, but we'll find you later."

Cara watches our hands interlock, a click of recognition in her eyes. "Oh." Something passes over her face, and she steps back. "Okay."

Beside her, Max's and Ellie's eyes widen in the twinkle of icicle lights. *You two?* Max mouths, gesturing between me and Bea. Ellie's mouth hangs open.

If they hadn't picked up on the infrared queer energy shift between Bea and me in poetry class the last week and a half, they definitely know now.

Bea guides me to the dance floor. "Oh god," I say.

"It's for the best!" Bea squeezes my hand. "Now it's all out in the open. Swift and painless, right? Like a Band-Aid."

Spencer stops his awkward back-and-forth sway to gawk at us. It's like I can see the gears turning in his head. My suit, our matching corsages, our clasped hands. Next to him, Jason and Leah catch our eyes and whisper something to each other, drawing a huffed laugh out of Leah.

"Painless," I echo.

"Forget about everyone else for a minute," Bea says. "Let's dance it out."

We wade deeper into the crowd, and Bea closes her eyes. I focus all my attention on Bea, trying to block out any stares around us. My panic can't last long. Bea dances like she's funneling pure joy. Something resets in my brain and it's like I'm seeing her through someone else's eyes: this curvy, curly-haired girl with more personality bubbling out of her than any one person should have the capacity to contain. And she's here with *me*.

Azar, in her ice-blue tea dress, finds us on the dance floor. "So," Bea says, "did Ethan show?"

"Who's Ethan?" I shout.

Azar beams an annoyed glare at me. "Nobody."

"That junior guy she's been DMing," Bea says. "The one who came to her volleyball tournament."

"Why haven't I heard about this?"

"Bea, that was in our *private* text thread," Azar grumbles.

"Sorry!" Bea raises her hands in surrender.

"He's not even here anyway," Azar huffs. "Can you go back to focusing on your *own* romantic situation and stop keeping tabs on mine?"

"Okay. Come on." Bea takes Azar's hands in hers, wiggling them back and forth until she's persuaded Azar into a grumpy dance. "So he didn't come. You can still have fun with us!"

Some classic '80s ballad drops, and Bea starts belting out the lyrics, daring Azar to join her. Azar gives up on her grouchiness and begins an off-key duet with Bea. Midway through the chorus, they both lock eyes on me. "Think we can get your sister to sing with us?" Bea asks Azar.

"No. There are too many witnesses!" When it comes to this type of fun, I prefer to observe rather than participate.

"But it's our first dance together."

"She's not going to do it," Azar says. "She's too freaked out. She looks like she's about to turtle all her limbs back inside that suit."

Bea laughs with her eyes shut, squeezing my shoulder. "You don't have to sing."

"I'm going to turtle my way over to the concession stand," I say. "I'll bring you back some water."

I take a breath as I step up to the drink station. "Mitra," Ms. Acosta calls to me from behind the table. She's wearing the usual head-to-toe black wardrobe, with a cardigan sweater and trousers and her red Keds, this time with a sequined snowflake brooch clipped to her chest. "It looks like you and Bea were enjoying yourselves."

I scramble to make out the words under her words—did she see

Bea and me holding hands? Can she tell we're more than just *super close friends*? Are things going to be weird in class now? But when she hands me the water bottles, she pats my hand and the corner of her mouth lifts up. "I think your outfit is lovely," she says.

I straighten my tie. "Thanks, Ms. A."

The music shifts to a slow song, and I wade through the crowd until I catch Bea near the corner of the gym, giving Azar a twirl. I wave to them both and set our waters on a side table covered in sequins and snowy cotton fluff. When Aziz spots me, she bows out and strolls back to her friends.

Bea circles her arms around my waist instantly and holds tight. "You found me," she says. "Didn't think you were going to get back in time for the song."

Her hair tickles my cheek when she tucks her face into my neck. "And miss dancing with you?" I say.

"You're not a turtle," she whispers into my ear. "You came here with me tonight. I told you, Esfahani girls are brave."

I sway with her folded into me, forgetting everyone else for a golden minute. Her body and the soft puffs of her dress fit perfectly against me. I've never let myself relax into her arms like this before, allowing every bit of space between us to dissolve into warm touch. Allowing her scent—bright perfume and earthy coconut and a little bit of salt from her sweat—to wash over me. Her heartbeat greets mine through the fabric of our clothes.

"Speaking of being brave." She pulls back just enough for me to make out her freckles, the grin playing on her lips. "I was wondering if—if I could call you my girlfriend?"

I've never been someone's girlfriend before. The word twinkles in the air around me, like it's embellished by its own string of icicle lights. "I'd like that," I say.

I touch my nose to Bea's, the both of us holding our breath. Maybe there are more eyes swarming now. This is the most out I've ever been—I should be scared. But that fear bursts open into some kind of glitter-bomb. I feel *free,* in this place where I never thought I would.

Her fingers find the back of my neck as I bring my lips to meet hers. I kiss her once, then twice, slowly and unafraid.

"School dances." Bea holds my tie in her fist as the song ebbs. "Not terrible."

Every Girl I've Ever Been

"**YOU SURE IT'S** okay for me to stay over?" I ask as we pull up to Bea's empty house an hour later. My heart hasn't stopped slingshotting through my body since I heard the word *girlfriend*. Thousands of sparklers burn under my skin.

"Okay with me," she says. "Probably not okay with my parents. They're at some real estate convention in Yakima."

"Will your mom get mad if she finds out?"

Bea drove barefoot, so I wait for her to pull the parking brake and put her heels back on.

"What is she going to do?" Bea turns to me. "Threaten to send me to Catholic school? I've already endured twelve years of preemptive punishment. This is, like, my reward," she laughs. She's still fizzing over with glee, and even my nerves can't spoil that.

The fabric of Bea's night-blue dress pours over the seat, and I nestle my hand in it. All these little moments I longed for with her—now they're falling into my lap like gold coins. I find her wrist and trace a swirl on her soft skin.

The touch makes Bea close her eyes. I want to savor the moment, but I can't escape my own questions. "What about when she finds out we're dating, though?" I ask.

Bea cracks an eye open at me.

"She still thinks I'm a bad influence on you. Ever since my dad took us to see *Rent* in eighth grade, remember? She kept calling it *unsavory* and *not a wholesome choice for children*."

Bea snorts.

"What would she say now?"

For a second, Bea looks exasperated, but then her expression softens. "What about *your* mom?" she asks gently. "Have you come out to her?"

"My dad might have told her." I thumb the buttons on my suit coat. "I don't know what she'd say. I don't know how moms are supposed to act in this kind of situation."

"I wouldn't use my mom as a shining example," Bea says. "But . . . hopefully Jaleh will be accepting. She should love you for who you are."

Bea falls quiet for a second, that nebulous word swinging in the air between us. Two weeks ago, Bea would've said *She should love you for who you are, like I do.* We can both feel her swallowing the words left unsaid.

And I know what it means that she can't say it anymore. I stopped telling Bea I loved her exactly because *love* changed its shape. A word I'd said a thousand times saturated itself in new meaning now that we're dating. I reached all these amazing new layers with Bea after we kissed, but we lost that.

The silence inside Bea's giant empty house presses on me. At the dance, the music and lights and crowd made me feel powerful and brave. But now it's just Bea and me alone in her living room, where we've watched horror movies and done our homework. How do I get romantic with Bea in the place where we once reenacted all the best songs from Moana in our pajamas?

I watch Bea do what she always does when her parents aren't around: take up space. She puts on a Rosalía album loud enough for the Spanish-guitar magic to ricochet off the pristine walls. Then she heads into the kitchen and pulls out a few bottles of liquor and every type of juice and sparkling water she can find in the fridge.

"We need cocktails," she says.

Bea presides over the drink-mixing process like it's a witchy incantation. Maybe focusing on the drinks is her way of channeling all the intense energy kicking around inside of her from the dance. When she spills some tequila, she curses under her breath. I wonder if she's spooled as tightly inside as I am. I wonder if her brain is flashing neon glow lights behind her eyes, internally screaming *We kissed AGAIN!!* I won't ask her, though. I want her to think I'm completely chill with what just happened.

Too bad she already knows me well enough to know that I'm not.

We end up with a drink concoction that's a hodgepodge of our cultures: orange and pomegranate juices, tequila, and orange blossom water. It's strangely delicious. I grip the drink like it's my life raft, keeping my eyes on the contents of my glass.

"Salud," she says, clinking her glass with mine. Our eyes lock as the glasses touch, then break away. The music switches to a song with a claptrack, and I feel each clap resound under my skin, insistent. Bea taps her fingers on the countertop. "Do you . . ." She hesitates. "Should we go upstairs?"

Yes. The right answer is *yes.* Upstairs is where we go when we're at Bea's house. Upstairs is where I want to be, because we kissed tonight and we're dating now, and we're home alone, and she's my best friend, and I've wanted this moment for forever. But my tongue has gone limp from panic, so I just nod.

We make our way upstairs, careful with our drinks on her parents' white carpeted steps. When we reach her room, Bea dresses down, sliding out of her heels and snowflake clip and earrings. She tosses her hair to shake it out of the partial updo from earlier.

I follow Bea's lead, taking off my suit coat. She reaches toward me to help me loosen my tie, and all my muscles melt when her hands touch my neck.

"How did it feel tonight?" she asks. "Going full-on Janelle Monáe at Holy Trinity."

I try to breathe as she slips the tie over my head. "Wearing a suit wasn't actually the biggest moment of my night."

"Oh, really?" That makes Bea grin. "What else happened?"

"I saw a yeti."

She grabs me by the collar. "Jerk." Bea stretches up on her toes to reach my lips. I thread my hands behind her waist to the cutout in the back of her dress, tucking my fingers in with the warmth of her skin there.

"I can't believe we get to do this," she whispers.

I know what she means. We're both moving slowly, like we're underwater or in a dream. Neither of us can believe this is happening.

I've spent thousands of hours with Bea in her room, reading and snacking and bursting out laughing together, and not one of those hours was spent like this: our lips and our breath falling into rhythm together.

Bea guides me toward her bed, the bed I've sprawled across a million times before, but this time my heart roars in my veins. I stretch out on the tangle of violet sheets and pillows and a handful of sweaters she must've rejected when she was getting ready for tonight.

She fits herself in beside me, resting her knees on mine, and for a few heartbeats we're silent. Her mouth hangs open in a smile.

"What?" My finger lands on her lower lip.

"Just looking at you," she says.

I squirm a little in her sheets. "We've known each other for, like, five years. You know what I look like."

"It's different this time!" she insists. "Just, let me look at you."

I turn toward her, resting on pillows that smell like her shampoo. She runs her fingertips from my forehead to eyelashes, cheeks to lips, studying me.

I let go of all my questions this time, not wanting to trample the moment with a flurry of thoughts and worries.

I brush the hair from her eyes and then rest my lips on Bea's. When I kiss her, it's like every girl I've been in these past few years steps forward. I'm thirteen and my heart's trilling the first time I ever see her smile. I'm fifteen and I want to curl up with her brilliant poems. I'm seventeen and terrified by the rush of sparks when she holds my hand.

My fingers cling to the ends of her curls, and she runs her hand along my waist as we nestle deeper into each other. When we've completely fogged up her glasses, Bea laughs and moves to set them on the bedside table. Then she hovers her hands over the closure of her dress.

"Is this okay?" Her fingers twitch at the zipper, nervous.

In answer, my hands take her place, unfastening the closure and zipping down to her hip. When she sheds her dress, she's left in her bra and underwear, covered in indigo lace. She's all soft brown skin and faint freckles now.

She catches me looking and tugs on her bra strap. "Too girly? Not military-approved?" She's teasing me, but there's a nervous edge to her questions. I wonder if she can feel the air buzzing between us like I can.

"Keep living your best femme life," I say. I begin with the buttons on my shirt just to give myself a breather, but Bea moves my hands aside and takes over. She fumbles on a few of the buttons and we both vent nervous giggles. Our laughter gives voice to the implausibility of this moment. *Bea is undressing me.*

She sets my shirt aside and reaches for the button of my pants. My belly button has never felt more exposed in my life. When I'm down to my black bralette and boy shorts, Bea shocks her cold legs against mine, making me yelp.

"It's February," she defends herself, nuzzling her nose into my neck. "Warm me up. Use that Sacramento magic you got in there somewhere."

We kiss until Bea falls asleep with her face pressed to my collarbone, her lips moving against me with her breath, until I can't tell where I end and she begins anymore.

Still Dreaming

I don't want to wake you, but
you should know that your exhale
just filled the sails of a thousand
invisible ships.

I don't want to wake you when
your sleeping heartbeat sounds
a drum that keeps the world turning.

I shouldn't wake you when your
cheek and my chest meet each other
like sunrise clouds spread over
a waiting ocean.

I don't want to wake you, but
when you closed your eyes gravity
melted away, and now blankets and
jewelry and lost socks dance around
your room.

I don't want to wake you, but
a whole universe just sprouted
in the space between your eyelashes.

I don't want to wake you. There are
stars for you to name and moonscapes
to skip through. And I'll be here
when you rise, still dreaming.

Queer Wizardry

BEA TAKES MY hand in hers as the elevator drops in Baldie on Wednesday. It's been five days since I held her in my arms in front of everyone at Formal, and I'm still in a trance. I feel like I got flung through the barrier between our universe and the next. Now I'm in a world where Bea and I get to kiss in the car after school, and slip each other flirty notes at passing period, and I'm also still expected to be Normal Mitra—eating breakfast and turning in French homework and remembering to sleep.

The elevator is blissfully slow and cranky, so we get a rare few moments alone at school. Bea leans into my side and rests her head on my shoulder.

"I can't believe I get to hold your hand," I say.

"At least while we're in our private metal box," she laughs.

The elevator bounces to a stop at L2, and she slides her arms under my blazer and around my waist, stealing one last hug. "This is why we're going to UW," she says. "Only a few more months. Praise Jesus."

When the metal doors part open, we drop our embrace. Cara appears on the other side of the doors, along with some junior boy with floppy brown hair.

Cara's lips lift into a brief smile. "Hey." She steps in beside us, straightening the collar on her red blazer.

She's had almost a week to process the news of Bea and me, but I keep reliving her expression when she first noticed Bea at the dance, and then her *Oh* when she clocked us holding hands.

I scan her face for some sign of emotion. She hasn't brought up Formal once in poetry seminar, and she's spent most of our class periods diligently working on her seminar journal. I'm desperate for *some* indication of what she's thinking. Has she been picturing Bea in that blue dress as often as I have? Does she regret breaking up with her? Is she jealous, or just surprised? But her expression is inscrutable.

The doors close and the junior boy beside us grins as the elevator drops again, all of his teeth showing. "Isn't this the start of a joke?" he says. "Three lesbians in an elevator?"

"I'm actually bi," I start.

"Don't even try, Mitra," Bea says. "Something tells me all nuance is lost on him."

"Right, it wasn't the start of a *joke*." He's still grinning. "It was the beginning of a tastefully made little video."

Great. Bea and I may have once been invisible nerds to most of the student body, but it seems we've suddenly become A Thing.

Holy Trinity tries to quash all relationship drama with its PDA rules: *This is an institution of faith, engagement, and education. Public displays of affection are in poor taste. PDA is banned if it makes others uncomfortable or becomes a distraction. Consider your impact on innocent onlookers.* But queer girls *existing* here is enough to cause a distraction. And we're constantly making the innocents uncomfortable just by living our evil gay lives.

"All right, Curtis." Cara jams her thumb into one of the elevator buttons, and we lurch to a stop at the next floor. She elbows him toward the exit. "Don't make me call your mother. Out you go." The doors close behind him.

Sometimes I forget. In the grand scheme of Holy Trinity, Cara and I are on the same team.

Bea glances at Cara. "Thanks."

Cara tucks her black hair behind her ear as the elevator touches down on our floor. "Don't mention it."

We take our seats in poetry seminar, with Max and me between Bea and Cara.

"How's the committee shaping up?" I ask Max. They were selected, along with a few other students, to choose Holy Trinity's spring musical.

"It's all right," they say. "But Grace keeps trying to convince everyone to vote for *Seven Brides for Seven Brothers*. I just can't. If they make me do sound design for that hetero hellscape, I'll quit." They sigh. "There's only so many times a queer person can hear 'Goin' Courtin'" without a part of them dying inside."

The bell sounds, and Ms. Acosta passes out a packet of readings for the day. "There are all kinds of ways to celebrate God," she tells the class.

"Like making out with your new girlfriend under the life-sized cross in the gym at Formal?" Max whispers to me.

"You trying to get me suspended?" I whisper back. Max pulls out a sheet of paper and jots something down.

Suspended? Never. But would it kill you to share some details? You totally blindsided us!

"We have many ways to give thanks, to appreciate the wonders we've been given," Ms. Acosta continues.

I pull out my own scrap of paper and set it on the armrest where Max can see.

I know. Sorry. How is Cara taking it? Max quirks their eyebrow at me and I keep writing.

Things have felt kinda awkward with her.

She'll be fine. She's just processing. Max pauses, tapping their pen. *I know she wants Bea to be happy. She wants everyone to be friends again. We all do.*

I glance at Cara as Max and I slip our notes away. She has her hands folded in her lap, her gaze out the window as she listens to the lecture.

She wants us to be friends again. And—maybe we could be. It's some type of queer wizardry to remain friends with your exes, but I've heard it's possible. We're a ride-or-die community.

Ms. Acosta holds up a thin blue book. "I believe Mary Oliver gave thanks through her expressions of awe and delight in the natural world God created. Today we'll explore some of her reflections on nature."

She turns to a page and begins reciting one of Mary Oliver's poems about hummingbirds in a garden. I try to turn my mind to the poem, but I get caught in my own thoughts.

Ms. Acosta finishes the poem, one of the last lines digging under my skin: *I visited all/the shimmering, heart-stabbing questions without answers.*

I thought all my unanswerable questions vanished the moment Bea and I kissed in the chapel. But the universe has other plans.

Majoon

AFTER SCHOOL ON Wednesday, Azar goes over to Jaleh's apartment for dinner. She's been spending her Saturdays there since our doomed brunch reunion, but this is her first weeknight dinner with Mom. Bea and I spend the evening video chatting our way through an American Government essay. It turns out she's way faster at finishing her homework when I'm watching, like she's waiting for me to give her a gold star.

Dad and I eat leftover lubia polo mostly in silence—Azar has always been the talkative one, and it turns out my dad and I don't have much to say without her constant prompting.

"You didn't want to join your sister tonight?" Dad asks.

I spear my green beans. "No."

"You know," he says, "if sometimes you want to go with her, I won't mind."

It's weird to think that our family is split in half, only a few blocks apart, eating our separate dinners.

As I'm taking our plates to the kitchen, our phones chime in unison.

Azar: hey can I stay over?

Azar: I finished my homework already

Dad: you have your toothbrush?

Azar: yeah Mom got me one

Dad: okay. We can pick you up on the way to school tomorrow.

He's concerned about her dental hygiene, but he's not worried that Azar is staying overnight with the person who used to be too high to remember to wake us up for school.

I bite my tongue.

Jaleh's apartment complex is on a dead-end street in the woodsy part of Highlands, near a northern loop of Kelsey Creek. We pull up Thursday morning at 7:45, way too early to pick up Azar for school, but I think my dad is as eager as I am to make sure her first overnight went okay. Instead of going to the door, I text Azar from the car:

Mitra: We're outside.

Our waiting energy is so tense that it feels like we're manning the getaway car for a bank heist. Part of me wants to scream *go, go, go!* and let Dad rip down the street in a screech of rubber. He glances at his watch about a hundred times until the front door swings open.

Azar appears dressed in her uniform skirt and blazer, her black curls held back with a red ribbon tie. She's carrying a mason jar of thick liquid in her hand.

My dad lets a sigh puff out from his lips. "Guess she survived," I say. "You can take your hand off the panic button."

"Morning!" Azar swings her backpack into the back seat and slides in after it.

"What's in the jar?"

"Oh. One of Mom's smoothies." She points the glass at me. "Want some?"

I forgot about Mom's smoothies. The taste of banana, coconut, and dates ricochets me back to before-addiction times in Sacramento. She'd be in the kitchen early in the morning, singing folk tunes over the whizzing of the blender. I'd ask her what was in the concoctions and she'd say *Majoon*. Literally: a combination of various items. Not a very reassuring answer to a kid with a suspicious palate. But her smoothies turned out delicious every time, and she was always making wild claims about their health benefits. *This one will keep your energy perky all day. This will help with that cold of yours. This will help you focus for your math test.*

When we moved to Bellevue, Azar started experimenting with her own smoothies. Hers were unorthodox: peanut butter and frozen strawberries and rosewater, coconut milk with dates, orange slices, and whole pistachios. I think she was approximating her own version of the perfect majoon, complete with grand proclamations: *This one will cure your bad attitude. Hopefully this one fixes your weird hair today.*

I hand the mason jar back to Azar after just one sip.

"How was your night?" my dad asks, turning to the back seat to give Azar her forehead kiss.

"Good. We made spaghetti and I taught her how to do a TikTok dance."

I picture them dancing and tripping over each other, laughing so hard they have to pause the music. All our history neatly erased. Dad nods along.

"I got a bunch of work done on the new series I'm doing for my Digital Arts class," Azar says. "I'm using photos of my friends as references, and editing them with some illustration and design elements to turn them into animals. I'm calling it *Wild Sides*."

"Can I see?" I ask.

"Not until it's done." Her words come out like an autoreply; she doesn't even pause to consider my request.

Aziz used to ask my opinion about everything. Back in Sacramento, I was part big sister, part babysitter, part mom. But since we moved to Bellevue, she acts like she doesn't need me anymore. And I almost get it—why turn to me when she has a glossier big sister in Bea, someone who shares her affinity for true crime podcasts and cold brew coffee and flamboyant fashion accessories? Still, it rankles that I don't matter enough to her to warrant any input into her art.

"Why do you always say that?" I turn back to face Azar. "You let Bea look at everything."

She raises her eyebrows at me. "Bea is interested in what I'm making. You just want to tell me what I should be doing differently."

"What?" All I've ever done is try to help, giving her suggestions on color and text placement and stuff.

"Girls," Dad sighs.

Azar glances down at her empty jar. "I'm just a kid to you. I'm not, like, a person."

Her words knock the wind out of me. "That's not true." I wait for her to meet my eyes again, but she won't look up. "Hey. I know you're not a kid anymore."

"Then ask me what *I* think about things. And let me make my own decisions," she says. I know she's not talking about art anymore.

She's talking about our mother.

Ready

Jaleh: Mitra joon, I would love to see you again if you're ready.

Jaleh: Azar said there are lots of beautiful nature areas in town. She showed me Weowna Park Trails recently. Would you like to visit a park together?

Jaleh: maybe we could see the Bellevue Botanical Garden?

Jaleh: I am open to whatever you'd like to do. Miss you, Mom

Clementine Fluffington, PhD

ON THURSDAY AFTER school, I sit twirled in a fleece blanket on my bed, late February sun reaching me through the window. I've been staring at Jaleh's texts since they barged onto my screen this afternoon. All I want to do is lie around reading Bea's favorite poetry and bask in our new girlfriend status, remember kissing her behind the statues and dormant rosebushes at lunch. Instead I'm huddled over my phone with a bead of panic-sweat on my forehead, rereading Jaleh's words for the hundredth time.

I try to picture meeting my mom at the Botanical Garden. I imagine her wandering through the rain garden and marveling at the hummingbirds taking sips of sweet nectar inside the bells of fuchsias. At the garden, you can't step off the walkway paths without destroying something. Everything is delicate and carefully cultivated. It's too gentle a place for my mother.

In Sacramento, my mom grew a sabzi garden behind the house: mint and basil and dill, cilantro and spring onions, little purple radishes that bit back with spiciness. The whole thing was wild and delicious, and we loved it. We folded her herbs into rice and fish dishes, and peppered them beside Dad's stews.

I wonder if she started a patio garden in her new apartment. And I wonder why she would she want to see me again, after I shut her down at brunch. What does she want from me now? Where does she think we can even go from here?

I set down my phone and pick up Hafez's *Divān*. It's a slim book, but the pages are dog-eared all over the place, with Post-its sticking out of different passages. It's been a while since I've turned to Hafez for guidance. He's like an oracle in Iranian culture, someone who helps you divine answers to your unanswerable questions. That's how he earned the name *the tongue of the unseen*. But he doesn't give you any easy resolution. His poems keep you wondering and they make you work. They hold up a mirror, and you have to look inside to understand what he's trying to tell you.

Sometimes Hafez's answers are profound and spiritual. Like the universe wound itself back in time to connect you with this centuries-old oracle, to grant you ancient wisdom. Other times, it's clear he's drunk. He has a lot to say about the tavern, and the cup, and the sweetness of wine.

Jaleh taught me how to consult Hafez for wisdom. At the holidays marking the turning of the seasons—especially Yalda and Nowruz—she'd pull out the *Divān* from our special shelf and flip through the pages while I thought up my secret question. *When will I get a best friend? Or What will happen with Mom and Dad arguing? Or Why don't I like the same things that other girls do?* Then I'd pick a page with my index finger and Jaleh would read the poem aloud to me, in English and in Farsi too. Her mouth would delight in all the sounds of his rhythmic ghazals. Then she'd help me make sense of the lesson.

Later, I had to make sense of his poems on my own.

Now I hold a question for Hafez in my mind, and even granting it that much space is hard to do. I know I probably shouldn't be asking a yes-or-no question. Hafez doesn't work like that; he's obnoxiously open-ended. But I'm desperate for guidance. I want Hafez to tell me what to do.

Should I see Jaleh again?

My finger flips to a page with the thirteenth poem and my eyes land on the first lines that call out to them:

My weary heart eternal silence keeps—

I know not who has slipped into my heart;

Though I am silent, one within me weeps.

I slam the book back on my nightstand. *Rude.* Hafez couldn't give me some gentle comfort in a time like this? I couldn't land on one of his poems about the coming of spring, or one of his wine-induced benders? He had to get right up in my face with his messy feelings, forcing me to look at the things I don't want to see.

I squeeze my eyes shut, the lines still looping behind my eyelids. When I was little, I didn't have to divine these answers on my own. I had a guide.

I pick up my phone and video call Bea's number. When she answers, she's lying on her back in the grass of her backyard, the flick of a cat's tail obscuring half the screen. Her smile releases the weight on my chest.

"Is that Clementine?" I ask. "Your neighbors are going to accuse you of catnapping if you keep this up."

"I'm not a catnapper!" She scratches the cat's tiny chin, and he rubs his whiskers against the buckle of her rust-colored overalls. "He comes to me willingly."

"You lure him with those artisanal smoked salmon treats," I say. "Catnapping."

Bea sits up abruptly, Clem coiling into her lap. "Something wrong?"

"How can you tell?"

"Your voice." She brings her face up close to the screen, like she's trying to put me under a microscope. "What's going on?"

I prop my phone up on the nightstand and tuck my knees into my chest. "My mom texted. She wants to meet for some sort of nature outing. If I'm *ready*." I drop my cheek to my knee. "I tried consulting Hafez. He was . . . annoying. I don't know what to make of what he was saying."

Bea sets her phone up against her water bottle in the grass and settles onto her stomach, propping herself up with her elbows. "You want me and Clem to help you interpret?"

A wave of warmth rushes over me. "You don't mind?"

Bea pushes her glasses up her nose. "I don't know if you know this, but Clementine's actually a scholar of Persian lyric poets."

The spotted cat sashays in front of Bea's phone.

"Clem's been holding out on me," I say.

I recite the three lines to Bea, and then read her the entire thirteenth poem for context. She listens with her eyes steady on me through the screen. At the end, Clem prances back onscreen and swipes his paw at me, knocking over the phone.

"Okay." Bea steals her phone back from the cat. "You know way more about what Hafez is thinking than I do. So what do you get from it?"

"He's being obnoxious!" I say. "Pushing the pain in my face. Like I didn't already know it was there. The whole poem is dripping with loss and desperation."

"But the poem is all about love, right?" Bea says. "Longing and sorrow too, but love is at the heart of it."

That makes me think of Bea and me. Even though our kiss started something magic between us, it signaled a loss too. We can't say *I love you* like we used to. We had to let go of our friendship-love to become something new.

It's not the first time I've let go of someone I loved.

"I mean, listen to these lines." Bea pulls up the poem on her phone and reads them aloud to me. "It's about a relationship with someone he loved. Someone who slipped into his heart."

My head sinks into my hand. "I'm not ready to let my mom back into my heart."

Bea watches me through the screen for a minute, petting Clem's spotted fur. When she finally speaks, her words are slow and measured. "But if you're hurting, doesn't that mean she's already there?"

I flop back against the bed. "You and Hafez are tag-teaming to destroy me today, aren't you?"

She chuckles. "I'm just saying. Maybe these lines are calling you out. Your heart has been silent. Seeing your mom again could be a chance to change that."

Hafez's message rings through Bea's words. I don't want to be silent. I'm in love with a brilliant girl who loves me back. My heart is the most whole and healed it's ever been. My feelings for Bea are stretching the edges of what I thought I could contain. Maybe I'm ready now to feel other big things.

I thumb through the *Divān* again, and then sit up. "Okay," I say. "Okay. I'll go see her."

"Is Azar going too?"

"No. She said if she comes, I'm going to use it as an excuse not to say anything to my mom. Which, true."

Bea swipes an errant raindrop from her glasses. "Need backup?" She smiles.

"Always."

Poetry Journal:
Unearthed

I buried you
when I was thirteen
in a back cavity of
my mind, layered over
with dirt and steel and
time—it was work.
Leaving you behind.

Now my sister draws
you vivid in splashing
paint with every story,
clawing at the careful
packed earth to pry
you free—you rise with
the silk of our history
draped over your arms,
open for an embrace.

Mom, you carried me
to bed and I pretended
to be asleep just to lay
rag-doll limp in your
arms. Mom: you left me

at school so late the
teacher fed me apples
meant for snack tomorrow.

I have questions for you.
What would you think
of me now if you really
knew me? Am I still that
rag-doll girl to you? And
did you bury me too?

I can feel this one viscerally. The effort the speaker puts into burying
the memory of her mother, and the pain of exhuming that memory.
It seems as though other unexpected memories and emotions could
surface in the process. I'd be curious to read more about what else
has been unearthed by this. Lastly as a mother: I don't believe it's
possible to really "bury" or forget your child. — Ms. Acosta

A Mother When It Mattered

RAIN SPLATS THE windshield for most of our drive to the botanical garden. Bea showed up bright and early at my house this morning so we could make a pit stop for peach Danishes at Mercurys. But now, in the parking lot outside of the gardens, the cream cheese pastry sits anchor-like in my stomach.

"Ready?" Bea zips up her mint-green rain shell. She bought an extra Danish for Jaleh, which is the definition of nice, but I still tried to talk her out of it.

I don't answer. The whooshing of blood is too loud in my ears to think. I texted Jaleh last night and told her I'd be coming with Bea, but I didn't tell her who Bea was. Maybe I should've just bit the bullet and come out to her over text. I open the car door and cling to Bea's hand all the way to the visitor center.

My mom is sitting on a bench beside the Zen-looking building, wearing a black jumpsuit and a jean jacket with a chunky turquoise necklace. Her curls branch out around her tawny brown face, shielded by an umbrella overhead. Umbrellas are a real rookie move in the Pacific Northwest because there's hardly ever enough downpour to warrant them. But I think about my mom going alone to REI and buying the first umbrella of her life, just so she can adapt to living in the city where her daughters live. And that twists my heart up.

I wave to Jaleh. Bea loosens her hand in mine, but I'm not ready to let it go. My mom will have to deal with any feelings she might have about me dating a girl; I'm not going to hide Bea for her sake.

Jaleh rises and smiles, shaking out her umbrella and pulling me in for a hug. When she hugged me at brunch, I was too angry and in shock to register anything else. This time I clock it: Her body feels different, because I'm different. Older and bigger in her arms.

"This is Bea," I say, gripping her hand again. "My girlfriend." The heartbeat in my ears reaches critical volume, and I'm embarrassed that my body reacts to this moment like it's a big deal.

Jaleh's eyes widen a little and she hesitates a second, then blinks away the surprise and gives Bea a kiss on each of her cheeks. "Nice to meet you," she says.

When she comes in to kiss my cheeks, her bunches of salt-and-pepper curls tickle my nose. *"Girlfriend?"* she whispers in my ear. The word comes out dipped in amazement.

"We brought you breakfast." Bea fishes the Danish from her purse and Jaleh's eyes light up.

"Thank you! I love these. I have a sweet tooth, just like Mitra's sister." She munches on the pastry as we stroll down the path.

"Oh my god, me too," Bea says. "Azar got me hooked on Persian candy. What's the thing that tastes like super sweet funnel cake?"

"Zoolbia," my mom groans. "My favorite. With saffron syrup."

"Yeah!" Bea says.

"But it's not as good in stores. I can teach you girls how to make it at home, easy." Jaleh watches my eyes when she extends the invitation. "If you like."

I shrug. I don't like zoolbia. It's too sweet and oily, and sticks in my teeth.

We amble down the trail, lined in maple trees and crawling ground cover. A stream trickles beside us, and then a forest of ferns and rhododendrons emerges.

"This would be a lovely place to write poems," Jaleh tells me, touching her palm to my shoulder. "Lots of natural inspiration."

My muscles freeze up around the touch.

"You like poetry?" Bea asks.

Jaleh pauses. "I do. I wrote a bit in college."

I didn't know that. Or maybe I did at one point, back in the time when we knew each other. I'm flustered to think about everything I don't know about my mother. The things I forgot when I shut away my memories of her, and the things I never got a chance to learn when her addiction took over.

"Cool!" Bea smiles at me. I know what she's thinking: *Your mom is a poet too.*

This thing I didn't even think to worry about knocks the wind out of me: Bea likes my mom.

Jaleh is charismatic and smart and interesting, so I shouldn't blame Bea for getting roped in. But I thought she'd be on my side. I thought she'd instinctively understand to hold back. Instead, she's acting just like Azar. Maybe next she'll tell me I've blown things way out of proportion, that I should forgive my mom like Azar has, because *isn't she wonderful?*

"It's been a long time since I wrote anything. But I have been trying to get more creative again." She touches the turquoise beads around her neck. "We had lots of art activities in my rehab program. I made this," she says.

She brings up rehab so casually, like it was a lifetime ago, like it's something we all dealt with and moved on from.

"That's beautiful," Bea says.

"Let's check out the Japanese garden," I say, walking ahead of them down the gravel trail. We reach an ancient gate leading to a manicured garden of Japanese maples. Dewy ground cover and budding azalea bushes ring around mossy lanterns.

"Peaceful," Jaleh says, breathing in the damp after-rain air.

Azar keeps telling me our mom is better now, and she does look tranquil here. My dad wants me to meet her where she's at today, to appreciate how far she's come in her recovery. And it's obvious that she's changed. But I can't release all the pain she caused. I can't gamble on the hope that I'll end up with a different mom this time: the one here in the gardens; the one who is calm and present and kind.

Because if she hurts me this time, it'll be my fault. I'm old enough to know better.

I take a seat on a basalt rock beside the stream, watching my mom and Bea as they both peek inside the doorway of a stone lantern.

"Maybe the home of a mischievous fairy," Jaleh says.

Bea laughs. "I used to have fairy tea parties with my tía when I was a kid. This would've been the best spot for one." Bea perches beside the stone lantern. "We'd put a few drops of tea in these thimble-sized cups she had, and spread them out on a maple leaf as our tablecloth."

"And did the fairies ever show up for teatime?" my mom asks.

"Sadly, no."

Jaleh reaches into a cluster of California poppies by the lantern, plucking the pointy green tip that covers the flower's petals before blooming. She rests it on her index finger like a slender cap for a garden gnome. "Maybe because you didn't give them hats for the rain," she says.

Bea grins and plucks her own cap from a poppy bud, placing it on the crown of a pine cone. She tucks it inside the lantern and nods at her creation. "There. Just in case any fairies happen to stop by."

When I was little, my mom read us stories about peris, Persian fairies. They were these beautiful spirits who flew around ancient Persia, causing trouble. Whenever she read us folktales about peris she put on this special voice, high-pitched and squeaky, kind of like how Azar sounded at the time. The peri voice never failed to make us laugh.

My head aches.

"Let's keep going," I say.

Bea follows behind me, waiting for Jaleh to catch up. I thought this was what I wanted—for her to buffer the rough places between Jaleh and me—but what I really want is for Bea to look at my mom and know the hurt she's caused. I want Bea to ice her out like I am, so Jaleh knows she can't fix everything with one field trip.

I want Bea to have my back.

We forge farther on down the trail toward the ravine. "We're reading Mary Oliver in our poetry seminar right now," Bea tells Jaleh. "She was a nature poet. She probably would've loved this place."

"Tell me about what you're studying!" Jaleh says. "Who is your favorite poet?"

"You're gonna make me pick one favorite?" Bea laughs. "That's impossible. But—can I give you a few? Classics, I love Lorca and

Neruda. Modern, there's too many. But Mitra got me into Anis Mojgani. His stuff is the kind of thing that just comes to life when you read it aloud." Bea glances at me as she wipes a drop of rain from her forehead. "If I had to pick a favorite, though, it would be Mitra."

My skin heats up under my raincoat. I steal a glance at Bea, her admission tugging up the corners of my lips.

"What a compliment," Jaleh says. "Have you read any Rumi?"

"Not yet."

"Mitra, you have to school her!" my mom scolds me. "He is one of our classics. Especially when it comes to love." She winks at us. "His words leave an imprint. Some of them, I'll never forget."

"Then *you* can school me," Bea tells Jaleh, like they're old friends. "What's your favorite?"

We reach the ravine garden, dense with Douglas firs and bare oak trees. Mist from the morning's rain sweeps down the canopy toward us. The suspension bridge stretches out before us, its rusty A-frame grounded in stone pillars.

"I have a few lines I kept on a note card that I stuck to the wall of my room when I was in treatment," Jaleh says. "They carried me a long way."

My mom and Bea stroll with me toward the bridge at the heart of the ravine. "I still have the Rumi lines memorized," Jaleh says. "They were: 'Love nourishes and mends. Love opens the clenched body, lets the soul breathe.'"

"I love that," Bea says.

My mom's henna-colored eyes land on mine. She's trying to tell me something. She reaches out for my shoulder again, but this time I pull away.

"I'm ready to go home," I tell Bea, crossing the bridge back toward the path. I can't handle another minute of watching the easy connection between Bea and my mom. Jaleh can show up now with her Rumi quotes and her fairy hats and her hand-beaded jewelry from rehab, saying that she's ready to be a mom again, but she wasn't my mother when I needed her. She wasn't my mom when it counted. And Bea should know that.

We walk the rest of the way back to the visitor center in silence. I want to sprint to Bea's car and lock myself inside, but I make myself turn back to Jaleh to say goodbye.

"Wait," she says, rifling through her purse. "I held on to this." She pulls out a small piece of paper and hands it to me. "Maybe Rumi's words will mean something to you."

I recognize the tattered note card, with its Rumi stanzas written in blue ink in my mother's handwriting. First in Farsi, which I can't really read, and then again in English. This little slip of paper was the one constant Jaleh kept, whether she was detoxing in the cramped white room of the hospital, or in the green dorm-style bedroom at rehab. For a flash I'm ten again, sitting on the armchair in her room on Family Day, eating cafeteria fries while my dad talked to Jaleh in the hallway.

"You've been gone for three months," my dad mumbled.

"I'm not ready to come home yet," Jaleh answered. "Things are easy here. Controlled. It's not like being at home."

"We can make it safe at home," Dad insisted. "What do we need to do? What's different there?"

"I have to be a mom when I'm at home," she whispered. "I can't be that right now. It's too much."

I stare at the note card with my mom's inspirational phrases on it. *Love nourishes and mends,* but love didn't keep her sober. It didn't fix her addiction. I wonder if these words did anything for her.

I wonder what makes her think she's ready to be our mom now.

You and Me

AS SOON AS we get in the car, I turn on Bea.

"You know she hurt me, right?" I say.

Bea's face blanches and she doesn't respond.

"I'm not shutting her out for no reason. She said and did terrible things to me and Azar and my dad. And you're acting like she's just this amazing, interesting new person you met. I thought you'd be in my corner."

My anger steams up the inside of the windshield and I cradle my head in my hands. I want to curl up into a ball in some high place, like a cat that doesn't want to be poked or messed with by anyone. Bea was supposed to be my rock today. Instead, she didn't even give a second thought to taking my mom's side.

Bea starts slowly. "I know. I understand that she hurt you. And I'm always going to be on your side. But—she's your mom." She takes off her fogged-up glasses, revealing her soft, earthy eyes. I look up at her with my head still in my palms. "Of course I'd want to get to know the person who made you. I'm interested in her because she matters to you. Even if you're not ready to let her into your life again."

I don't like the line Bea draws between my mother and me.

"I don't know what to do with this," I say. I'm partially referencing the note card in my lap, and partly talking about everything that just went down.

When I was little, I saw Jaleh the way Bea does now. She was *fun*.

Sometimes she would pull Azar and me out of elementary school early on a Friday for what she deemed "field trips." She'd bring us to Lake Natoma to feed the geese, or take us to the railroad museum. When we were *really* little, she'd take us to Fairytale Town to pet sheep and run around Arthur's Castle.

I loved our unauthorized field trips. They made it easy to forget the days she didn't show up. I kept forgiving her, kept letting her back in, because I was seven and I wanted to climb Owl's Tree house at Fairytale Town. I wanted to ride down the corkscrew slide, and I wanted her to catch me.

"I know it's a lot," Bea says. "You can go slow with her. And I'll be here, okay?"

When I've unwound from my cat pose, I reach my hand out for Bea's. "Sorry," I tell her. "Thank you for coming with me."

She holds my hand tight. "I have something to take your mind off of everything," she offers.

"You're really good at that," I say.

She reaches into her purse and pulls out a brochure. It's a little rained on and sugary from the Danishes, but it does the trick to turn my attention: a UW campus map.

"I signed us up for a visit," she says through her grin. "We get to stay in the dorms and eat cafeteria food, maybe sit in on a class or go to a poetry reading. Think of it as a preview of our college life to help us survive Holy Trinity until acceptance letters come in April. The best part is it's twenty-four hours together with no tartan skirts in sight!" She squeals. "It'll be just like we're already in college, living the life."

I take the brochure from her hand, unfolding images of sweeping cherry blossom fields and a brick complex overlooking Union Bay. Twenty-four hours with Bea in another city, away from the stranglehold of Holy Trinity, with the world's longest floating bridge between me and my family? Sign me up.

"We're getting out," I marvel.

"You and me," she promises.

Sometimes I forget that we're four months away from graduation. Four months from when Bea and I will be out of The Palm of God's Hand for good, away from Crossroads and Jaleh. Soon, it'll just be me and Bea, finally starting the rest of our lives.

I close the map in my hands. It's so thin for something holding our whole future.

"Did you ever think this is how it would be?" I ask. "All those times we talked about UW and pictured next year, did you ever think we'd be . . . ?"

I don't know how to finish the thought. *Together? In love?* How do I even give a name to what we are now? But Bea must know what I mean, because the corners of her mouth lift up.

"I imagined a lot of things." She smiles. "I had a lot of different versions of next year playing out in my head. But, no. I didn't see this coming."

"Clem didn't divine any answers about us from mystic poetry for you?"

"If he had any answers, he didn't tip his hand," she laughs.

Bea brushes a damp curl from her forehead, and I smile alongside her. She watches me for a long minute. When she opens her mouth, she's dropped her satisfied smile. "You were going to say *in love,* weren't you?" She blinks at me. "When you asked if I ever thought we'd be . . ." She motions between us with her hand.

Rain splotches on the window paint shadowy circles on her face. I watch the pattern of shadows slide over her skin as I try to breathe.

I could backtrack if I wanted. I could tell her *no,* and she might let me get away with the lie. But she's holding out an invitation for me, her words like a perfect apple in an outstretched hand.

"Yeah, I was," I tell her.

That grin resurfaces, this time spreading wide across her face. She leans closer to me and I sneak a kiss in the space between her eyebrows, then the tops of her cheeks, all the places I can never reach when she's got her glasses on.

When I pull back from her, Bea curls her hand around mine. Her lips part for a tiny exhaled laugh, and then she says it:

"I love you, Mitra."

And she breaks a spell, speaking the words we've left unsaid.

Heat rushes from my heart outward, filling my body, brightening all my insides.

Bea's ears and nose flash pink, but she continues. "Not how I love Max or Azar, or even how I loved you when we were thirteen. I *love* love you." She hooks her eyes on me when she says the word, daring me to believe her.

The moment vacuums the air out of her car, our little confessional booth. When I can breathe again, I lean toward her, pulling her tight to me. My lips meet her ear and the place below her jaw where her heartbeat races under her skin.

"I love you too," I tell her, my voice still washed out by her words.

Maybe our love is like the never-ending poem lived out loud: Together, we've created something bigger than either of us could dream up on our own.

While I hold her, and breathe her coconut smell, and try to catch up to my sprinting heart, my brain circles the moment again and again. *I am loved.*

Mitra

for ages before
those words, so many
things whispered *love*

love, love before we
could: I caught your
eyelash on my finger-

tip, saved it for you
to turn into a wish, you
drove us to school with

one hand on the wheel,
one looped around my
wrist: everything

whispered first, then
grew loud as drumbeats
pulsing under our kiss

Bea

kiss the dreams still sparkling in your sleep-
creased eyes and ignite them, there's oxygen
enough here to feed a fire as big as our

future crackling spitting sparks of all that
freed breath we bottled pent-up for years
sealed sacred, entombed in these pages alone:

watch our words and wishes realized, popping
fireworks in the chambers of our dark-cornered
hearts like fizzy champagne victory-cheers

in our blood, that's our love—and imagine
that explosion unleashed on a canvas like this,
just imagine the colors that'll rush out of us

Things That Don't Bother You
When You're in Love

- Endless days of red tartan skirts and blazers.
- Guys' eyes following you in the hallway, and having to wonder whether everyone knows about your dating life.
- Complicated exes who pop up at lunch and on break when you're just trying to have a moment alone with your girlfriend.
- Complicated mothers who text right when you're trying not to think about them.
- Rumi quotes that refuse to leave your brain.
- Reckless sisters who ignore your advice and forgive too easily.

The Only Thing That Matters
When You're in Love

- Each other.

Anti-Tartan

BEA AND I have become experts at finding covert ways to flirt on school days. She'll drive me and Azar to Holy Trinity in the mornings, but we'll stay behind in the parking garage, sneaking morning kisses behind the cover of trusty ol' Gary. When Max is feeling generous, they'll let us take our lunch to the sound and light ops booth in the theater for a private, closet-sized date. And Bea will slip folded-up notes in my backpack between classes. Sometimes they're haikus:

Did you cast magic
On my skin when you kissed me?
Everything shimmers.

Still, it's hard not to feel stifled here. We both can't wait for our UW weekend. We're so hyped about the college tour, you'd think we were counting down to Burning Man or Mardi Gras.

When the weekend finally arrives in the beginning of March, my dad takes us into Seattle, even though Bea insisted she could have driven us. Dad says it's no big deal to fight through twenty minutes of 520 traffic and circle the maze of campus streets and parking lots—he keeps claiming he wants to pick up jujeh kabob at Persepolis in the University District nearby, even though there are a bunch of Iranian restaurants where we live. When I heckle him about his flimsy excuse, he furrows his eyebrows at me.

"Let me have this, Mitra," he says. He keeps glancing from me to Bea and back again in the rearview mirror, and he's radiating Dad Energy.

"How old is the student you're staying with? And what's her major?" he asks.

"She's a sophomore," I say. "So, nineteen? And she's a Language and Lit major."

"Lit majors are the ones who smoke marijuana," Dad mumbles to himself.

"Wasn't your mom a Lit major?" Bea whispers to me.

"Look," he says to me. "I know you two have had many sleepovers. But you're dating now. Things are . . . different. You know what I'm saying?"

"Yes, Dad. Jesus." I roll down the window to distract from the tidal wave of embarrassment.

"I'm talking about safe sex, and Jesus cannot help you with that."

That's it. I have died. I have died, and now I'm just a ghost trapped in this vehicle. "Dad. Stop."

He hits the brakes for a kid on a longboard as we turn onto The Ave. "Mitra, your relationship is serious, so I have to be serious too."

"We got it," Bea squeaks. I grip her hand on the car seat between us until my knuckles turn white. *Sorry,* I mouth to her.

Dad gets us as close to Red Square as he can before we get stuck behind a food service truck. "We can just get out here and walk the rest of the way," Bea offers. She's as ready as I am to open the doors and tumble-roll out of the moving vehicle.

Dad's eyes shift between Bea's and mine again, a bead of sweat forming on his temple. "Okay, girls. Just be respectful of each other."

It's small comfort to know that my humiliation is probably dwarfed by his panic right now.

Bea sputters in laughter as soon as we grab our bags and hop out of the car.

"Glad you're amused." I take her elbow and tug her down the brick path, trying to put distance between us and the car as fast as possible.

"At least he cares," she says. "My parents probably don't even know queer sex is a thing. I bet they think it's like, us in a room with the door closed, invoking Satan via ritual sacrifice."

"Maybe they're better off thinking that."

I shake off the embarrassment, but there's a different feeling fizzing up underneath it, like Pop Rocks tingling in my stomach.

A night alone with Bea.

She's dressed as anti-tartan as possible today: shimmery eye shadow and matte peach lipstick, a Black Belt Eagle Scout band T-shirt, and purple jeans. And the Pegasus loafers. They're the one accessory that makes a seamless transition from uniform to civilian life. I'm wearing my "fancy" flannel, checkered blue and turquoise with utility pockets, and denim jeans cuffed above high-top sneakers.

"Soon we can dress like this every day," I say.

"Maybe I'll get a bunch of piercings. And my new uniform will be a rotation of different queer band T-shirts."

"What about me?" I ask.

"You'll never have to wear a tartan skirt again. Or any skirt, if you don't want to. Just androgynous shirts and . . . pants with lots of pockets."

"That sounds pretty dreamy." I squeeze her hand as we pass a crowd of students.

"Maybe we can get an apartment after freshman year. I'll make you pancakes," she says.

"When have you ever made pancakes?"

"I can learn."

We're a city away from our parents, on a college campus with forty-five thousand students, probably none of whom are nuns or priests. We're sharing a dorm room this weekend, and we have free rein to explore all of campus and the U District. We can do whatever we want.

What *does* Bea want?

The night of Winter Formal, Bea and I went further together than we ever have, and it left me completely dizzy. But I'm still getting used to even *that* level of intensity with her. Now that we've said *I love you,* I wonder if she'll want more. If she'll expect more.

That sets off a blitz of panic thoughts. Bea and I share a library of poetic accounts of the most embarrassing and vulnerable stuff we've ever experienced. But we've never really talked about sex. Maybe because we were scared, or because we didn't know how to talk about it. Maybe because this potential was brewing all along.

I haven't had sex. I haven't wanted to before now. But I figure Bea and Cara have. When they were together, Bea would tell me about their firsts—date, kiss, *I love you.* But at a certain point, she stopped sharing. I probably shut down any details with my awkwardness— sex has always been this mysterious, language-defying thing to me. Maybe she didn't want to tell me about it because she knows I'm inexperienced and thinks I wouldn't get it.

I want to go there with Bea. But I also like reveling in our slow simmer and teetering at the edge of where we are now. Once we have sex, I won't ever come back to this *before* feeling. I'll be flooded in the unknown *after.*

I've been there with her once already, when we morphed from *friend* love to *this*. It's deeper and scarier and infinitely more beautiful here, and I also know we can't go back to that other love. A swallowtail can't retract its wings and turn back into a caterpillar.

And now that we've transformed into something new, I don't know how to say these things to Bea.

Things like: I'd like to touch you.

I'm scared.

I don't really know what queer sex is, either.

I want to find out with you.

I don't know how to tell when I'm ready.

I'm trying to be Bea's girlfriend now, which in my head looks like being sexy and confident and also mysterious and *cool*. Not some self-conscious bundle of feelings screaming *I'm scared and I don't know what the hell I'm doing!*

"Hey." Bea grabs my hand, forcing me to look up from my sneakers on the brick path. Her eyes are giant and cast copper by the bright March sun. "We're free." She grins.

We stop in the center of Red Square, arms linked, and look around. The complex is dominated by old brick buildings, like Holy Trinity's campus magnified in scale by a million, except all the sculptural touches above the doors are different: evergreen trees, open books and scrolls, old-timey crests with birds on them. No old dead white priests here. The library looks like a cathedral with its spires and stained glass, but there are no saints' faces in the windows. I'm tickled by the fact that this holy-looking building houses books. It's like they worship *knowledge* here.

"We're supposed to meet her by the bells," Bea says, scouting out a congregation of golden bells atop the building beside us. We cross a throng of students toward the entrance to Kane Hall, where a short girl with fair skin in a purple W sweatshirt stands on top of a bench to rise above the crowd. She has straight jet-black hair and winged eyeliner game that would put Azar to shame.

"Beatrice? I'm Jae!" She gives us a hearty wave. At first I can't figure out how Jae spotted us, but then I remember our overnight bags and the fact that we're clutching each other like lost children at a carnival.

"I'm Bea, and this is Mitra," Bea says.

"Welcome to UW!" Jae hops down from her post on the bench. She's shorter than Bea, but she projects her voice like a true tour guide. "Ready to be a Husky for the weekend?"

We follow Jae in a daze northward through campus, weaving through the bustle of UW students. Modern buildings with walls of windows loom above us. There is so much green space here—grass lawns dotted with students playing Frisbee, gates of towering Douglas firs, buildings coated in ivy. Squawking ducks and geese punctuate our stroll, along with the shouts and chatter of students roaming all around us.

Bea keeps her fingers knotted with mine as Jae leads us to a ginormous 1970s-style residence hall. The gray stucco sides of the building accordion with hundreds of windows from each dorm room. Inside, we pass a front desk to a student lounge packed with couches and coffee tables. There's a wall-mounted flat screen and a pool table in the corner. Bea breaks away and jumps onto the couch, spreading herself across the faded cushions. "Think of the horror movie fests we could have here!"

I try to picture us on next Halloween, on this couch—hosting the college version of our HolyHorror night, with new friends and no parental supervision. This time, instead of sitting with several inches of buffer zone between us, I'm curled into her arms as she's singing *don't dream it, be it* in my ear.

I pull Bea up from the couch and sneak a kiss before Jae leads us onward. I feel a little bit like a mouse in a maze as we wind our way through the endless hallways to Jae's room, stopping to drop our bags off on her floor. She's decorated the dorm room with string lights and posters of classic book covers, but she wasn't given a lot to work with: The room is a narrow white pentagon with one window and a wooden desk and chair. Her desk is burdened by stacks of textbooks and a few framed photos. The space makes me feel even more like a mouse.

Then there's the bed: a twin bunk bed with one extra twin mattress laid out on the floor beside it. It reminds me of summer camp. I guess I didn't have to worry about whether Bea would expect more this weekend. We'll be sleeping a spitting distance away from our camp counselor the whole time.

"Lucky, right?" Jae pats the bottom bunk. "I have a double, but my roommate transferred out, so I have room to host prospective students."

"Mitra!" Bea's voice flashes with excitement. "Come look." I meet her at the window, which she's cranked the few inches open that the architecture will permit. "You can see the bay from here!"

I tuck my face over her shoulder to take in the view with her. I see trees, and hundreds of cars swirling around the student parking lot, and the tall stadium lights of a nearby athletic field, and beyond that—the bay. The narrow gray snake of the 520 bridge cuts through it. "We can see home," she says.

I thought we'd feel worlds away out here, a giant lake between us and everything we know. But it's not so far after all.

"Do you want to settle in, or are you ready for a tour?" Jae asks. Bea is already springing up and down.

I want it all at once. I want to curl up with Bea on the bunk bed and map out the next four years of our fantasies together, and I also want to race around campus like caffeinated children, pointing out every potential delight.

"Show us everything," I say, taking Bea's hand again.

Overheard at UW

Student with bite-marked arm: "Tell the RA to get the air horn. That goose snuck into the lobby again."

Long-haired bro: "Why is it that you have enough money for tickets to every music festival, but I have to spot you five dollars for your breakfast burritos?"

Girl in Husky pj's: "Get Taylor and meet me in Callie's room. That pre-med guy just ghosted her. Bring chocolate."

Eyeliner girl: "I'm not going out with him again, unless I can put it on my résumé as babysitting a man-child."

Coffee-stained-shirt kid: "Can't come tonight. Econ test on Monday. That's fine, just leave me here. Go on without me. Let me waste away with my ramen and my nine-hundred-page textbook. Have fun."

Bea: "Do you think they'd stop us from sharing a dorm because we're dating? Or are housing assignment rules so gendered and archaic that it wouldn't occur to them to ask? Maybe this is the one time it'll work out in our favor that people assume girl couples are just *really good friends*!"

How to Be a Queer Girl 101

BEA, JAE, AND I get Korean fried chicken at a pocket-sized restaurant on The Ave for dinner, and after sunset Jae invites us along with her to a party. I've learned today that Jae is an extreme extrovert, something I didn't know book nerds could be.

"I thought we were going to sit in on a class. Or, like, a poetry reading?" I say.

"Don't worry," she says. "This isn't a frat party on Greek Row or something. I'm more of a whiskey and art-party girl. My friend's band is doing a house show tonight."

I'd rather hole up in some obscure coffee shop or library corner and plot out our college life together than navigate a room full of drunk strangers, but I can still hear Azar's words in my head: I'm a *turtle*.

"Besides, you can go to all the classes and readings you'd like next year!" Jae says. "You're young, you're only here for the weekend. Let me show you a good time! We gotta do something more memorable than an open mic night."

Bea looks pretty stoked about the idea of a college party. I think she's drunk off the waves of social energy emanating from Jae. At Holy Trinity, her aversion to Catholic school pushes her deep inside her shell; I forget sometimes that I'm at an entirely different end of the introvert spectrum from Bea.

I want to keep Bea smiling this big. Always.

Jae takes us north of campus to a house with cars parked bumper to bumper out front. The windows are rimmed with rainbow flags and a Black Lives Matter sign. "Taryn!" Jae shouts through the open front door. A girl with bleached blonde hair, light skin, and an eyebrow piercing greets us. "I brought chips and salsa," Jae says. "And baby queers!"

My cheeks burn.

"You're the prospective freshmen?" Taryn waves us inside, where a dozen of her friends look over at us. "From that Catholic nunnery?"

For a second I feel like I'm back in tartan. Taryn lets out a laugh. "I'll get you drinks. Make yourselves at home."

The walls of Taryn's house are covered in screen-printed portraits of women, some of whom I recognize from history class, most of whom I don't. Light from her front windows filters through a collection of tropical plants. All the secondhand sofas and coffee tables have been cleared from the living room and pushed against the walls to make room for a makeshift stage and dance floor.

Some of her friends smile at us as we find an empty spot to sit on a couch. One of the girls has a full sleeve of ocean-themed tattoos under a pastel tie-waist top. The guy next to her has chin-length black hair and a button-up shirt covered in lemons, with bright green bracelets on his arm. *All* of them have made fashion choices that would guarantee them Service Work at Holy Trinity. I peek down the hallway at the silhouette of a person in tweed pants and printed tee that says *Reading Is Sexy*.

Bea and I exchange a look that says: *These are our people.*

At least, these are who I'd imagine our people to be. I don't know what I'd dress like or act like if I had the freedom these students have. It makes me wonder what Bea will be like when she's completely unleashed from Holy Trinity and her parents' house. She'll be like a star gone supernova. Most of me thrills at the thought of seeing her come fully into her own. And part of me worries if I can keep up with that radiance.

Taryn brings us red wine in mason jars. "I love your art prints," Bea tells her. "Is that Sylvia Rivera?"

"Yeah! I had a hard time with that print at first, but it turned out okay."

"You made these? All of these?" Bea gapes at all the portraits surrounding us.

"Yup. I'm a Visual Art major. I mostly work with textiles, but the screen-print portraits are a hobby of mine. Trying to get enough pieces together by senior year to do a gallery exhibit."

"That's awesome!" Bea grins at her. I wonder if she knows who all these figures are in the portraits.

"What are you into?" Taryn asks us. "When you're not praying and shit?"

"Um, writing," I start, taking a sip of the bitter wine. "Poetry."

"You're poets." Taryn smiles. "Rad. What are you working on?"

"We started writing a poem together when we were thirteen," Bea says. "And we're still going. Many, many volumes later."

My stomach flips a little around the wine.

When we first started The Book, we were ridiculously secretive about it. Bea would hide it under her mattress at her house, and I'd bury it in my underwear drawer to throw Azar off the trail. At school we passed it back and forth under our desks or in the empty girls' bathroom, like we were doing some covert ops. Eventually we realized nobody cared that much about what we were writing, so we got less cryptic about the whole thing. Still, there are only a handful of people who know about the never-ending poem.

I don't know why Bea would tell a stranger about it.

"Damn! That's a long poem!" Jae says as my cheeks prickle pink. I feel embarrassed, and I don't know why. Maybe because The Book is the most private and sacred thing in my world, and Bea is airing it out for these super smart college students.

"Can we hear some tonight?" Taryn points to the front of the living room, where a couple of people are assembling equipment. "Finn is setting up the mic and speakers and stuff for the music later. You could do a little slam poetry session if you want."

I almost choke on my drink. Bea drums her fingertips on my back. "That's okay," she says. "We don't have anything with us."

A group of people comes in through the back door, shouting Jae's name. "I'll be back," she says.

Our student guide strolls out the back door to join her friends in the yard. I shouldn't need Jae to hold my hand at the big-kid party, but still, nerves spark in my stomach.

One of Taryn's friends, with short black bangs, deep brown skin, and a vintage Hitchcock T-shirt, takes a seat on the floor beside us.

"Tar, did you do the art reading yet?"

"Mind-blowing," Taryn says.

"What are you learning about?" Bea asks.

"We're reading profiles on contemporary artists, and this week's was Yayoi Kusama."

"I've read about her!" Bea says. "The polka-dot lady."

"Who?" I look to Bea.

"She is a *trip*," Taryn says. "She creates neon sculptures of pumpkins and, like, psychedelic orbs covered in polka dots. Plus she made these things called Infinity Mirror Rooms, where you're basically in a room full of never-ending stars and dots. Ricki, let's take a field trip to the Smithsonian! I want to go see it."

Ricki shakes her head. "I feel like that exhibit's going to give you a visually induced high, and you don't want that," she says. "Need I remind you of the time you tried mushrooms?"

"But this is immersive art!" Taryn argues.

Bea pulls up images on her phone to show me an elderly Japanese woman with a fire-engine-red wig, surrounded by blobs of primary colors and giant polka-dot-flecked gourds.

I'm not sure I understand this kind of art. It's a lot for my eyes to handle, even through the small screen of Bea's phone. I can't imagine being surrounded by an entire room of these aggressive colors.

"I guess she was looking at a red flower tablecloth as a kid, and had this hallucination of the pattern repeating everywhere into the universe," Ricki says. "She said it represented infinity, the endlessness of space and time, and self-obliteration. She's been painting polka dots ever since. Can you imagine getting that existential as a *child*?"

"The same thing happened to me as a kid," Taryn says. "Except it was with my bowl of Froot Loops."

"Bullshit." Ricki swats Taryn's arm.

"The woman made a piece of art called *Macaroni Pants*," Taryn says. "Macaroni glued to pants, Ricki. We're obviously one of a kind."

Bea giggles. Taryn takes Bea's phone and pulls up an image of booty shorts plastered with pinwheel macaroni, spray-painted gold. "Behold," Taryn says. "The Macaroni Pants."

Bea scoots next to Taryn and scrolls through the images. "Wait, there's more!" she says. "It's part of a series. *Macaroni Shoes, Macaroni Dress, Macaroni Handbag* . . ."

"Shut up." Taryn leans her head on Bea's shoulder as they stare at the various forms of noodle-based art.

My stomach does its own pinwheel watching them laugh together. "I don't get it," I say.

"She's challenging our ideas of femininity," Taryn says.

"And it's a commentary on industrialist capitalism," Ricki says. "All that machine-made food sprayed gold."

Bea turns to Ricki. "I saw photos of her antiwar, anti-capitalist performance stuff," she says. "She gathered a group of naked people, splattered them in polka dots, and stood on the Brooklyn Bridge."

"A woman after my own heart," Ricki says.

Bea straightens her glasses, vibrating with enthusiasm, clearly having the time of her life, surrounded by queer nerds. I feel like I've missed out on How to Be a Queer Girl 101.

I wish I knew anything about Yayoi Kusama, or contemporary art, or even polka dots. I'm completely at a loss listening to Bea and Taryn and Ricki get philosophical about the themes and statements in Kusama's artwork. How did I not know that Bea likes visual art?

I thought getting out of Holy Trinity this weekend would give Bea and me a chance to bond over all the things we have in common. Instead, it's pointing out how different we are.

Maybe these aren't our people. Maybe these are *Bea's* people.

But then, who are my people? I try to imagine a house somewhere on The Ave tonight with a dimly lit living room full of comfy couches and free-flowing chai. Everyone's curled up reading their favorite books in silence. If there's music playing, nobody has to dance to it. That's my kind of party.

Taryn's friend Finn turns on the mic and more people flood into the living room. "What's up, Eighteenth Street! We've got some music for you tonight." Finn and the band dive into an energetic folk-pop song with a guitar, fiddle, and banjo.

Jae bounces her way back into the living room when the music picks up tempo. Taryn hops up and takes Bea's hand, tugging her toward the crowd of people gathering in front of the band. "Let's see your moves, poet!"

Bea, Taryn, and Jae move their way across the makeshift dance floor toward the band, stomping in time with the fiddle. Taryn twirls Bea and she kicks her Pegasus loafers up behind her. They're both grinning, Taryn mouthing along to Finn's lyrics.

Watching Bea dance is like watching a flower unfurl. She was designed for it. She spins and flies and twists her arms through the air like she's channeling power straight from the music. She's in her element here, in a hive of people we've never met before.

I've never been like that. I've never walked into a room and felt like it was mine. The only person who ever made me feel so at home is now carving her own space in a swarm of strangers.

Bea spots me glued to the couch and snatches my hand in hers. "You thought you could sit this one out?" Her voice rings with warmth and wine. "No way."

She pulls me onto the dance floor and wiggles my arms until she's uncorked my stiffness. I try to let the tambourine and banjo take over, washing the worry from my body. But it stays solid in my belly like a stone.

Bea pulls me close for a moment, her face tucked into the collar of my flannel as she sways us back and forth. Everything buzzes inside me. I try to reshape my mind into the way I felt the night of Formal—when dancing with Bea felt triumphant and beautiful. When everything was finally coming true with her, and all that potential joy spouted out of me.

We break apart and form a circle with Jae, Taryn, and Ricki. The banjo twangs a driving beat, sprightly and persistent, and Taryn takes Bea's hand again to spin her around to the sound. Bea dances with closed eyes and a spreading smile.

Enjoy this. Feel happy, I command myself. But the buzzing feeling inside me is louder now, and I know it's not just the alcohol. My muscles crank tight around my worry.

I feel like I'm losing something I only just found.

Out of the Nunnery and into the Party House

IN THE MORNING, Bea takes a shower in the communal bathrooms—brave—and puts on a floral dress and jean jacket. I hop in after her, then throw on jeans and a mustard button-up shirt, scrunching the waves of my hair with shea butter. After, I sit on the bunk bed in Jae's room and watch Bea do her thing: the curl balm, the eyeliner, the highlighter, the mascara, and all the other products I don't even know the name for. She shares the dorm mirror with Jae, chatting about Jae's boyfriend visiting from Western next weekend as she fixes her curls.

My girlfriend, my brain keeps chiming. I can't believe she's my girlfriend. This person who understands the existentialist symbolism of polka dots, who matches her dress to her Sunday morning mood, and writes me poems when she's bored in class. This girl. My girl. For now.

We hug Jae goodbye, and then we pick up bagel sandwiches at a corner shop, heading to the quad to eat breakfast.

Gray skies dominate overhead and beads of water still cling to the grass. It's early enough that the quad is mostly empty. We make our way down cement stairs to a grassy field zigzagged into triangles by brick walkways. The bricks ripple in waves over old tree roots of the Yoshino cherry trees flanking the field. They're cartoonish in their squat stature and gnarly branches, each one bursting with fists of rosy buds. A few pear trees already pop with soft white blooms and constellations of pink filaments, filling the breeze with their crisp, perfumy smell.

One of the buildings in the quad has a turquoise dome atop it, kind of like the dome on a mosque, which is comforting. I wonder how many Muslim students go to UW. And I wonder how many religiously confused students like me go here too. Maybe I'm not the only Muslim-Zoroastrian raised-in-Catholic-school weirdo.

"Look!" Bea pulls me to a tree and we inspect the branches up close, where tiny pink buds break out of their fuzzy green robes. In a few weeks the whole quad will be bursting with cherry blossoms.

Bea points us to a wooden bench next to a lamppost in the shade of cherry trees. The trees above us are mossed over from winter rain, with ribbons of amber bark gleaming through. Shoots of new branches spring out of the limbs.

I eat my sandwich to the sound of Bea's chatter. My eyes stay on a dancing wall of ivy on a building across the quad, like a million little hands waving back at me. When she's finished her bagel, Bea prods me with her elbow.

"You're being quiet this morning," she says. It's an observation, not a demand. But I can read the questions threading under her words.

"I think I have my first wine hangover," I say. I don't know what Hafez was going on about when he wrote all those odes to wine. He had plenty to say about *last night's wine still singing in my head,* but I don't remember him ever writing a poem about *this morning's nauseating headache.*

Bea brings her hand to the back of my neck. Her fingers dance around my hair, and I close my eyes for a second, remembering how lucky I am.

"What's up?"

I don't know how to tell her about the voice in my head chanting *not enough, not enough, not enough.* So I tell her an easier truth. "I think you'll be really happy here."

Bea plucks a tiny white pear blossom out of my hair. "We'll be happy here," she says. She cups the blossom in her hands and leans her head on my shoulder. "I'm glad we came. It's like I can see a way out now."

"Out of the nunnery and into the party house," I say. "That could be your memoir title. But you know we could never invite your mom over if we lived in a place like Taryn's. She'd call it a *den of sin.*"

"I don't care." Bea takes my hand. "I think I'm going to tell my parents we're dating."

I shift so I can face Bea on the bench. "Really?"

"I think I just needed to be able to picture next year. I'll be out of their house in like six months. When we're here, what they think won't matter anymore." She breathes in the quad's cherry air and smiles at me. "I'm going to do it."

I take her chin in my hand and kiss her. "And you think *I'm* brave."

The Ortega Family Rosary

Bea: guess what I did?

Bea: hint: the Ortega family rosary is getting lots of overtime action right now

                        Mitra: how did it go??

Bea: a transcript of our conversation:

Bea: "remember all those times you thought Mitra and I were dating?"

Bea: "well, it turns out that was a great idea"

Bea: "so glad you encouraged us to make that happen"

Bea: they both smiled and said "thank you for telling us"

Bea: but it was the same kind of "thank you for telling us" I got when I was six and I admitted I put Silly Putty down the garbage disposal on purpose because I wanted to find out what would happen

                        Mitra: uh-oh

Bea: then they went into their room to have a Private Discussion

                        Mitra: let them have their tantrum. You did a big thing!

                        Mitra: time to increase my attempts at getting on their good side?

Bea: that's a lost cause, honey

Bea: but I love you for trying

Ashes and Abstention

FRESH OFF THE tail of our weekend of freedom, we have another mandatory Mass: Ash Wednesday. The day when burned palm fronds are ground down to dust and smudged on our foreheads in the sign of the cross. I don't understand every ritual in Catholicism, but this feels like a very goth holiday to me. The chapel's silence presses down around me.

Since UW, I try not to spend too much time in silence. When things get quiet, my mind carves out space for its worries, digging and digging like a dog hunting a buried bone. Things have been so good—*too* good with Bea, and a part of me worries something this golden won't last. So instead of letting the fears flood in, I'm trying to stay in the moment. Bea's pinkie nudging mine on the pew between us. The scent of her coconut shampoo, clean and warm even as Father Mitchell smokes up the chapel with the sway of the thurible. The sound of her breaths in my ear.

Her foot kicking my shoe. Hard.

That's when I find her note scribbled on the back of the donation envelope.

Bored. Entertain me!

I grab one of the little golf pencils in the hymnal rack and write back.

Time for quiet reflection and prayer, Beatrice. Jesus is your entertainment.

I'm being cruel, I know. But sometimes her frustration and impatience in Mass is *my* entertainment.

Hungry, she writes. *Take the host wafers and run.*

Father Mitchell's tone is solemn and the service is punctuated by prolonged silence. When he does speak, it's all about death and the confession of sins.

"Today marks the beginning of Lent," he says. "We must purify our hearts, atone for our sins, abstain from that which we desire, and labor toward a more pious and holy path, so that we can greet Easter with a spirit of celebration."

"The cafeteria's probably empty." Bea's voice prickles my ear. I guess she's given up on the golf pencil. "We could go steal some quesadillas." She curls her fingers around mine, and her touch hums electric up my skin.

So much for abstention.

"You just wanna get me alone again," I whisper. We're still trying to keep things PG at school, but ever since we said *I love you,* we've been kind of permanently entangled like octopi.

"Where's the crime in that?" she says.

I can't buy into the doom and gloom of today's sermon when Bea's sitting next to me, smiling her mischievous smile, burrowing her fingers into the warm pleats of my skirt. I want to tell Father Mitchell that sometimes, desire is beautiful when it's realized. And maybe it's the thing that will purify my heart.

We rise and follow a line down the center of the church to receive our ashes. "What are you giving up for Lent?" Bea asks Max, up ahead of us. She has not bought into the practice, but she's still respectful of the fact that Max is earnestly Catholic.

"Doom-scrolling," they whisper. "I uninstalled all the social apps from my phone."

"May the Lord bless you and keep you." Bea pats their hand sympathetically.

"You can do it," I encourage them.

"What about you?" Max asks Bea. "What are you giving up?"

She looks back at me, pressing her lips together. "Giving a fuck?" That has Max chuckling under their breath. "Especially when it comes to my parents."

We reach the front, and Father Mitchell dips his thumb in a bowl of ash. He marks our foreheads with the sign of the cross, and a little bit of the ash flakes into Bea's eyelashes.

"From dust you came, and from dust you will return," he says.

I carry that sentence all the way back to the pew with me. There's a kind of poetry in it, like a nod to the grandness of the universe. We came from stardust, and we're made of the same elemental particles as Jupiter and diamonds and air. Maybe we will be a part of all those things one day: the same celestial dust.

It feels romantic to me. But that's probably because of the girl two inches to my left, tipping her head onto my shoulder with a yawn, exhausted from our marathon video chat last night. If I could kiss the top of her hair right now without incurring the wrath of the church ushers, I would.

Instead, I use my fingertip to draw out the specks of ash from Bea's eyelashes. "Giving a fuck?" I say. "Really?"

I don't get Bea's parents. They have no interest in showing up for her day-to-day life, but they still manage to make her feel like she's a bad daughter.

She knows this is what they do. She even jokes about it. But that doesn't soften the blow of their judgy comments.

"Well, I'm not giving up kissing you," she tells me.

"Never," I say. "Jesus wouldn't want that."

Father Mitchell calls us to pray, and a hundred kneelers flop to the floor, the sound thundering through the chapel.

"I'm not toning anything down for my parents anymore," Bea says. "I think when Cara and I broke up, they were relieved, like they thought I was going to live out the rest of my high school days in hermitude. Just, like, studying and crying and not making out with anybody. Well, surprise!" She chuckles. "And you're not even Catholic. So I've really dialed up the sacrilege. But they can feel the way they're gonna feel. I'm sick of keeping my queerness all tidy and palatable for them." She slides from the pew and onto the kneeler.

"That's big," I say. But inside I'm replaying the Halloween breakup reel: the late nights, the inconsolable tears, her face when Bea told me *they say you never forget your first love.*

She looks back at me over her shoulder, her hands clasped up on the pew in front of us. "I'm not hiding you."

The determination in her voice makes me grin.

Bea closes her eyes in prayer. "Kneel, you heathen," she whispers to me. I join her on the kneeler, and I try to reflect and I try to pray. But then Bea rests her ankle over mine, and I'm caught on that warm point of touch.

I've never observed Lent, but if I did, maybe it would be the kick in the butt I need to stop worrying about Bea and next year and Cara. Not that I can just pray my way out of my own disastrous thoughts. But it *is* the season for divine intervention.

A Thespian Moment

BEA AND I get to poetry seminar right before the bell on Friday, and the only armchairs left open for us are on opposite sides of the circle from each other. One of them is next to Cara. I spend a good thirty seconds staring at the two empty seats, panicking like I'm in a high-stakes game of musical chairs. Finally, I flop down beside Cara. I'll take one for the team. That's what a good girlfriend should do. Bea settles across the room, skimming the last few pages of our reading.

Cara gives me a nod. She's focused on a packet of papers in her lap, highlighting different sections of the text.

"What's that?"

"Script," she says. "Spring musical rehearsals started." In an unprecedented turn of events by Max's selection committee, Holy Trinity will be performing *Les Misérables* this spring. It's a bold choice for such a conservative school, what with the sex workers and all. But Max said the new drama teacher, Mr. Sherman, is cool and *up for a challenge*. Cara is starring as Cosette.

Seeing Cara's multicolored highlighting takes me back to last fall's production of *The Crucible*. The five of us used to hole up in our favorite booth at Pho Ever on Eighth Street, drinking bubble tea and slurping down salty, hot pho while we ran lines with Cara. She played Abigail, and I helped her rehearse so many times that Bea said I should've been the understudy to John Proctor. And, not gonna lie, I would've rocked his flowy pants and wide-brimmed hat.

We all got really into the script one day, belting the dialogue and gesturing at each other across the table. I shouted the line *God is dead!* right as the waiter brought us another piping bowl of soup, and he looked horrified as he splashed the soup on our table. "Sorry," Cara had said, wiping up the broth with her napkin. "We were having a thespian moment." We all burst out laughing.

As weird as things are with Cara now, I kind of miss those days. "Good luck with rehearsal," I say.

Ms. Acosta rises from her desk holding a small yellow book. Our homework for poetry seminar this week was to read Kahlil Gibran's *The Prophet.* Gibran was a Lebanese American poet, not Iranian, but my family claimed him as our own anyway. We kept *The Prophet* on a special shelf in our bookcase in Sacramento: the shelf with our Farsi and English editions of the *Divān,* a collection of Rumi, and the *Rubaiyat* of Omar Khayyam. I liked to think of it as the Ancestor's Shelf.

"Over the past few days, you've read excerpts on life, love, and loss from Kahlil Gibran," Ms. Acosta says. "This book starts with the story of a prophet about to leave a city where he has been stranded. As he watches a ship arrive on the shore to take him home at last, he realizes this is his final opportunity to impart his wisdom and teachings to the local townspeople. The poems that follow express his philosophy on life, his personal truths, everything he wanted to share before departing."

Cara shifts in her chair next to me, flipping through the photocopied pages of *The Prophet.* Her long, inky hair spills onto the armrest between us. She smells like fabric softener and citrus shampoo, and her poetry packet is all marked up with her brilliant thoughts, dotted with Post-it flags. I shrink into the opposite side of my armchair.

"Consider the task of the prophet," Ms. Acosta says. "You have a limited amount of time, limited words within you, and you're asked to share your truth before you leave. What would you say? Who would you say it to?"

Cara's eyes flit over to Bea. I drop my gaze to the blank page in front of me.

"We're going to do something different today. You've all gotten more comfortable with each other, and I want to stir things up a bit. I'll match you with a partner to discuss this prompt with," Ms. Acosta says. "After your brainstorming, you'll each write your own poems in the style of the prophet."

I wonder what Cara's prophet poems will be like. They'll probably radiate with wisdom and certainty, with titles like *Achieving Power Lesbian Status* and *How to Be Flawless at Life*.

"Now, for your partners," Ms. Acosta says. "Max, you'll be working with Tala. Lilith will be with Bea. Rashad, team up with Olivia. Cara, you'll pair up with Mitra."

Cara's eyes flash on Bea's, then mine, as everyone gets up to shuffle to a new seat. I wonder if she and Bea have some lesbian ex-girlfriend telepathy going on. My stomach twists as I turn toward Cara.

She sets down her photocopied packet and sighs. "This is kind of a tough prompt."

"Yeah?"

"I mean, the idea that I can have my own prophecy, without taking into account my parents' prophecy, and their parents', and their parents'. It's like, me and my brother growing up in the US and getting a good education, those were their biggest dreams. I'm living out their prophecy right now." Cara's black eyes fix on me. "I don't feel like I get to have my own."

"I get it," I say. Cara hasn't been this real with me in a while. But the two of us have always shared this territory. She understands what it's like to be a second-gen immigrant kid. We both carry our parents' stories on our shoulders.

Now that I think about it, it's all pretty Catholic. The guilt, the sacrifice. The idea that we're born tainted, whether through "original sin" or through our parents' traumas.

"You don't get to make your own prophecy when you're inheriting a story that someone else already started writing," I say.

My mom must have had a prophecy for Azar and me before her addiction clouded over everything. I wonder what she imagined when she was seventeen and her family left Iran. I wonder if she ever pictured raising girls who would grow up freer than she had been.

Cara tucks her hair behind her ear. "But then, the whole point of my parents' sacrifices was probably so that we could live out our best lives, you know? So then maybe I *should* be living my truth and all that. Or, I don't know. Is there a way to do both?"

"Maybe that's your prophecy," I say. "Figuring out how to do both."

"So what's yours?" Cara asks me, glancing over at Bea. "Is it about *love*?" I hear the edge in her voice, and maybe she's just trying to tease me, but it makes my skin prickle.

"Maybe."

"It should be about how to hold on to something good when you've got it." She laughs. "How to not screw things up, like I did." She pauses for a second and then swallows. "I'm happy for you, really."

My throat turns dry.

She's probably trying to be nice, to poke fun at our awkward situation, name the fact that I'm dating her ex. But all I hear in her words are these rivers of regret and jealousy. Cara wishes she'd never broken up with Bea.

Across the circle, Bea waves her hands in the air as she describes her prophecy to Lilith. My heart beats so loud in my ears that I feel like I've gone underwater.

I was wrong about Cara's prophet poem before. She's already got the title on lock: *How to Make Your Ex's New Girlfriend Dissolve into Insecure Puddle: Three Simple Steps.*

Poetry Journal:
The Prophet Prompt-Shore

I see the ship on the horizon,
black speck marring the smear
of uncomplicated blue, dragging

dread through my heart. It promises
everything: a world outside the
sealed tomb of Holy Trinity, ticket

off this island, maybe ecstasy and
maybe terror, boat barreling toward
change, falling off the map of waters

we know. Will you climb aboard
with me? Or are you watching the
waves for your own omen, another

freight without anchor? Time rinses
through me like wind, I have so much
to tell you still, or more, things I

dreamed we could be to each other.
But my mouth understands the
uselessness of its own language.

I have no prophecy for you. Just
this heart, this open hand, a wish
to stay here on the shore with you.

Well done, Mitra. You mention not having a prophecy for the reader,
but Gibran's prophet wasn't expected to foresee the future. Only to
reflect on life as he saw it. You have some meaningful reflections
here on the preciousness of time, change, and connection (between
the "I" and "you"). I'd like to see you deepen these, perhaps in a next
poem. How have these three themes presented themselves in your life
before? — Ms. Acosta

Love Triangle

AFTER SCHOOL ON Friday, we give Azar a ride to her friend's house by the country club. Neither Bea nor I feel like going home yet, so we pull up alongside Kelsey Creek in Gary and park by the stream. It's rushing with water from the months of rain, bulldozing bits of dirt and grass from the banks of the creek as it runs. Everything is some variation of green now: grass, moss, trees draped in their lichen coats.

Bea flexes her hands out on the steering wheel. "Did you hear that Emily T. got mono? She had to drop out of the musical."

"Yikes."

Emily T. was supposed to play Éponine, which is sort of a major role to recast this late in the game. Cara is probably freaking out right now. I feel bad that Cara's in such a tough spot, and then I feel proud of myself for not delighting in her misfortune. Maybe I'm growing. Maybe I'm finally shaking off the unease that settled in after Cara's weird comments in poetry seminar.

"What are they gonna do?" I ask. "God, I hope Mrs. Hastings doesn't volunteer to fill the role like last time." *Little Women* isn't the same when one of the Little Women is sixty-three.

Bea bites her thumbnail when she looks at me. "They're kind of desperate right now. Cara asked me to step in."

"Wow." That little seed of growth shrivels up. "I get that she's freaked out, but what was she thinking? I mean, has she read the script? Éponine and Cosette are, like, locked in an angsty love triangle the whole play." I laugh. "Not something you want to sign up for with your ex. What did she say when you turned her down?"

Bea's eyes shift across my face. "I didn't turn her down. I want to do it."

My stomach elevator-drops out of me. "What? Why?"

"It's my last chance to do a musical before we graduate," Bea says. "I think it'll be fun."

I unbuckle my seat belt and turn toward Bea. "But she shattered your heart."

"And I'm not heartbroken anymore, obviously." Bea gestures between the two of us. "Does it really bother you?"

I drag my hand down my face, trying to pin down something, any logical argument that'll make Bea see the disaster this could become. But my heart tramps loud, and my mind is a slew of panicked thoughts I can't own up to.

Cara said it: She had a good thing with Bea, and she screwed that up. Maybe this is Cara's way of roping Bea back in.

Bea must see that, right? And she's choosing to say yes to Cara anyway.

I try so hard to stamp out the voice that takes my worst fear and turns it into a taunt: Bea said yes because some part of her still wants to be with Cara.

Bea might love me, but Cara was her first love. Cara changed her in a fundamental way. Bea won't ever forget what that feels like.

My mom's voice floats through me, carrying Rumi's words. *Love nourishes and mends.* Maybe our relationship really has mended Bea's broken heart. But I can't gamble on that.

I drown out Rumi's words with my own truth: *I can't lose Bea.*

"I just . . . don't think you should do it," I say. It's the only argument I can land on in my flood of worry. "Please. Think about it."

Bea turns to face the windshield and leans back in her seat, watching the creek flow by. "You have to trust me," she says. "After everything we've been through, you have to know I'm in this with you."

I don't know how to respond. I love Bea more than anything. But all I can see is her tear-streaked face on Halloween, and so many nights after. She cried until her stomach hurt, until she felt like she couldn't breathe. She was devastated and drained empty.

She must know that doing the musical can't be healthy. And all those nights rehearsing scenes saturated in longing and envy and love—she has to understand that those emotions could bleed into real life.

"You don't see it like I do," I say. "I know you love me. I do. But— this won't lead anywhere good, okay? It sucks that Cara's in a tight spot with the musical, but you can't be the one to come running anytime she needs help. She can figure this out without you."

Bea shakes her head at me and cranks her keys in the ignition. "All right, Mitra." She pulls onto the boulevard and heads east.

"Where are we going?"

"I'm dropping you off at home." Her voice is tight and small. "You can't even say that you trust me, can you?"

Bea's eyes harden on the road ahead. "Is this because of everything with Harper?"

If there's a bruise I never want to push with Bea, it's that one. All throughout her relationship with Cara she was insecure, thinking she wouldn't be taken seriously, wouldn't be trusted because she had cheated on her last girlfriend. Freshman year, Bea had been dating this girl Natalie, but then she met Harper from Our Lady of Mercy. Bea was fourteen, and they were at Snowflake Lane drinking cocoa like straight out of a Hallmark Christmas rom-com, and they kissed. I told Bea a million times that she should forgive herself, but she was sure she'd have to bear the shame of her mistake through all her future relationships for the rest of time. When Cara broke up with her, it only reinforced that belief.

"I'm—it has nothing to do with that!" I tell her. "I'm just saying the play is a bad idea."

Bea won't look at me when we idle at a red light. "You always said you didn't judge me for what happened. That it was okay, and that people make mistakes. I thought you, of anyone in my life, would see past what I did. But I guess everything you said only held up when we were friends, huh?" Her fingernails dig into the steering wheel. "Now that we're dating, you don't trust me. You think I'd cheat on you."

The Harper thing hadn't even crossed my mind. It's not about the fact that Bea cheated before. It's that I don't know if I can trust her to love me—*really* love me—the way she loved Cara.

"Hey." I brush her shoulder. "Come on. That's not what I'm saying."

Bea pulls up to my house and shifts the car into park. "I'm doing the play." She stares ahead. "It's on you whether you want to trust me or not."

She punches the unlock button and waves me off with her hand. I'm left in the driveway with my backpack, my head spinning. Rumi made false promises. Love doesn't mend, it ruptures.

Important Women

RIGHT AFTER I started at Holy Trinity, the school hosted a mother-daughter day. Or *Important Women's Day,* as they labeled it last-minute, to be inclusive for girls without moms. The receptionist handling sign-up assured my dad that Azar and I could attend as a pair, and we wouldn't be the odd ones out. I didn't want to go, but Azar was totally enticed by the agenda: dressing up in fancy, non-uniform clothes, having a special brunch at school on a Sunday, and then taking an afternoon boat cruise around Lake Washington. She picked out a lime-green dress and put clips in her hair, while I tried to fade into the architecture in my navy sweater.

As soon as we got to school, my sister and her new best friend glommed onto each other like magnets. And she wasn't the only one—most of the girls ditched their Important Women for friends, leaving the moms to gather at their own tables in the auditorium with mimosas and cinnamon buns.

So the receptionist was right: We weren't the odd ones out for coming without a mom. *I* was the weirdo for not having any friends.

I took a seat at a vacant table decorated with blue hydrangea blossoms and a pink tablecloth, eating from my paper plate of scrambled eggs and hash browns. The eggs weren't anything like the turmeric ones my dad made at home. The speaker system rotated through a short inventory of emotional women vocalists, like Adele and Taylor Swift.

When a Celine Dion song came on the stereo, a voice burst out from right behind me. *"For all those times you stood by me . . . for all the truth that you made me see . . ."*

I turned to find Bea dragging a folding chair beside me.

"How do you know all the words?" I asked, already smiling.

Her eyes pinched closed as she barreled on. *"You were my strength when I was weak . . . you were my voice when I couldn't speak . . ."* She grabbed the straps of her faded overalls as she sang.

It had only been a week and a half since the fateful paper scrap introduced us. We'd started sitting beside each other in first period, but I'd never seen her outside of school hours. Today she wore a bright orange shirt under her denim, with glitter swept beneath her eyes and a fake daisy pinned in her curls.

"The song's played three times already," she said, halting her ballad to take a bite of her cinnamon roll. "If it plays a fourth time, I'm hacking into their music system."

"Or you could just give in to it," I said, thumping my fist against my chest like Celine Dion.

Her eyebrows popped above her glasses. "All right. Your turn." The song transitioned to another Adele track, and Bea tugged at my arm. "Don't act like you don't know the words!"

"Hello," I whispered back at her. *"It's me."* My voice gained courage as I sang my way through the opening lyrics to Adele's ballad.

By the end of the song, we were racing each other around the auditorium hallways, screaming *"Hello from the outsiiiiiiiiiide"* so loud that a staff member asked us to please use inside voices.

When we caught our breath, Bea took my hand and bounced it between us. "Let's be friends," she said.

Maybe it was that easy for her to make a new friend. To choose me. But I had never had a best friend before. I'd had kids that I talked to in class and sat with at lunch by default, and a few birthday party invites, but never this. I'd never had a Bea.

That's why I had been so resistant to owning my feelings for Bea. That's why I had the rule about never letting my love for her show. There was a reason I kept silent for years. I knew what I could lose.

Poetry Journal:
The Prophet Prompt #2: Broken Shells

Kahlil wrote *Pain is the breaking*
of the shell that encloses your
understanding. I was reckless

with my words, let them rip
through my world like an animal
unleashed, I splintered shell homes

to mineral blades beneath
my soft feet. She used to laugh
like unfiltered joy booming free

until my words spoiled the peace
between us. So if I'm standing in
the prophet's place, people waiting

for some wisdom, I say: hold your
tongue, bolster the cavern of your
heart's home, calcium builds

eggshells but also bones, be un-
breakable: make yourself the
hardest thing you know.

Poignant and painful musings on change, Mitra. A few reflections for this prophet. Does hardening the shell truly protect the speaker? Or does it limit their potential for a greater capacity of understanding and connection? I'd be curious to see what happens if the speaker were to break open the shell! — Ms. Acosta

Fight

BEA DOESN'T TEXT me back over the weekend, and she won't talk to me at school today. She sits across the crescent of seats from me in poetry seminar, sinking into the deepest of the old armchairs. I only let myself look over at her when she's writing, when I know she won't be looking back at me.

The silence pressure-cooks anger inside me. I'm mad at myself and Bea and Cara, and I don't even have a place to put my anger, because of the new never-ending poem rule: No writing angry. No fighting with each other through The Book. So I focus my energy on poetry seminar instead. I reread the pages of *The Prophet* during our free-write time, hoping they'll somehow make things different.

But Kahlil Gibran can prophesize all he wants; it won't change the fact that I screwed up, just like Cara warned me not to.

Nowruz

ON SATURDAY WE'RE two weeks away from the Persian New Year, Nowruz. Since moving to Bellevue, it's been a low-key holiday in our house: Azar makes sticky, almondy love-cake, my dad makes fish and herb-flecked sabzi polo, and I try to grow my own wheatgrass and hyacinth for the Haft Seen altar. We listen to Iranian music, and sometimes Bea comes over to read Hafez with us, and we fall asleep on the couch with our bellies full of rice. It's a pretty tame way to ring in spring, but I like it.

This year is different. Jaleh confers with Dad on the phone, and then he tells Azar and me that Jaleh is having the two of us over to her apartment on Sunday for an early Nowruz dinner.

It's not a question. And I don't have any good excuse to get out of it; Bea and I have barely talked all week, so I can't say I have plans with her.

He drives us over to her apartment in Highlands on Sunday evening, even though it's walkable from our house. "It's not even Nowruz yet," I tell him. "I don't see why we have to do this."

Azar has spent most of her Saturdays at Jaleh's since she cycloned into our lives a little more than a month ago, but I haven't even seen her apartment yet.

"Nowruz is a time for fresh starts," Dad says. "Why don't you give her a chance?"

He doesn't need to remind me. I'm only in the car because the guilt and weight of the holiday have been crushing me. Nowruz is all about renewal and cleansing out old energy to make way for the promise of a bright new year. My spirit is all wrong for the holiday: I'm clogged by tension with Bea, hung up on old history with Jaleh. Nowruz is supposed to be a time of visiting and honoring your elders too—a chance to pay your respects to the adults in your life who matter to you. With Jaleh only a few blocks away this Nowruz, I'm confronted by the glaring reality that she's been alone and unvisited for the past four years.

I keep envisioning the Nowruzes she spent apart from us: She stands alone at the kitchen counter of some amorphous apartment in Sacramento that I never visited, eating takeout kabobs and rice from an Iranian restaurant. The worst part is when I imagine her setting the Haft Seen by herself. It's supposed to be an altar of seven items starting with the letter *S,* each one representing intentions for growth and new life in the new year. Seven symbols to represent her wishes, to welcome in love, health, wisdom, renewal. And patience.

I wonder what her intentions are this year.

Dad idles on the street outside the apartment while Azar leads me up to the front door. Jaleh has a silver hamsa on the doorframe with a blue cheshm nazar in its center. The sight of the hamsa and its evil eye tugs me back in time like a bungee. I passed this hamsa every day on my way in and out of the Sacramento house as a kid. It used to mean *home* to me. And now it's here.

Azar slips off her Toms at the door and waits for me to follow suit. I don't like that she knows all the rules to our mother's house, and I know none. I kick off my high-tops. "Be nice," she says. She opens the door without knocking.

Inside, Jaleh is playing classical Persian music with violins and sitar, the *dum dum dum* of a tombak drum welcoming us in. The apartment air is perfumed with parsley and cardamom and frying rice.

"Hi, girls!" She's at the kitchen counter, which is brimming with bunches of green herbs. She wipes her hands on her apron and opens her arms to us. "Nowruz Mobarak!"

"Mmm, smells good, Mom." Azar accepts her hug.

"We brought you this," I say, holding out a plastic pot with a hyacinth bulb with three thick stems sprouting from it. Two of the stems erupt in purple blossoms.

"Beautiful." She smiles at me. "Thank you, Mitra." She places the hyacinth on the little Haft Seen she's set up on a coffee table in her living-dining area. The apartment is tiny and new and also jarringly familiar. Art prints of calla lilies that she used to keep in her bedroom in the Sacramento house now hang behind her couch. A lime-green armchair from our old living room nestles into a corner by the window.

When we were little, Azar and I would make forts with the armchair, draping bedsheets over it and piling the tented area inside with pillows. Mom would pop her head under the sheet to hand us snacks. When it was time to tear down the fort, Dad would stomp around like a giant and bellow at us while he whipped away the sheet, with us screaming and laughing inside.

Everything in this new apartment is colorful and loud, just like my mother, though it's more orderly than I remember.

Jaleh sees me taking everything in. "Azar, show her around?" she suggests.

Azar directs me around the rest of the small apartment, and I register all the other familiar touches: the Persian rug in the hallway, the green glass lamp. There's a framed photo of Azar and Mom and me from at least ten years ago on the back patio of the Sacramento house, our faces smiling and stained from eating watermelon. In the bathroom, a wire jewelry hanger dangles with all of Mom's necklaces and earrings. I run my hand over the familiar pieces: abalone, gold, turquoise, jade. Each one of them strikes a different memory in me.

"This is my room." Azar points me toward a small bedroom with twin beds. "*Our* room," she corrects herself. She's stuck a few photos of friends on the walls, and the desk is covered with rough sketches for future art project ideas. One of the dresser drawers is jammed shut on a leg of her pajama pants.

My stomach wobbles as I take stock of Azar's side of the room. I knew she'd been spending more time here, but I didn't expect this.

While I've been distracted with my own stuff, Azar has been building a life here with our mom.

Azar catches me eyeing her favorite hoodie draped over the desk chair.

"You left that here?" I try not to sound accusatory, but worry rises up the back of my neck.

"Whoops." She balls it up in her hands and tosses it toward her overnight backpack. "Forgot it last time."

"Girls, do you want to help with the kuku?" Mom calls from the kitchen. I swallow the dread rising in my throat and join her at the counter. I assign myself the task of soaking barberries and chopping walnuts for the herby egg frittata, while Azar and Mom rinse handful after handful of herbs.

"You watching the tahdig this time?" Azar asks Mom, sniffing the pot of frying rice suspiciously.

"I am. I promise." Jaleh rolls her eyes. "I burned it *one* time. Azar won't let me forget."

"Um, it's the most important part of the meal," Azar says. "And you keep forgetting to check on it."

"I'm not forgetting," Jaleh insists. "You can't disrupt the tahdig. It needs to rest undisturbed if you want it to taste good."

"You make it sound like a cranky baby," Azar says. "It's rice, Mom. Just look at it and see if it's browned enough."

"I don't need to see it to know when it's done," Jaleh says, tapping her prominent nose. "I can smell it."

"She can smell it when it's smoking," Azar mumbles to me, and the two of them laugh, Jaleh swatting Azar with the tie of her apron.

They're so comfortable with each other. They weave in and out of conversation like a practiced dance.

It used to be easy like that with my mom and me. She'd get out the step stool in the kitchen of our Sacramento house and I'd sit there while she cooked, keeping her entertained with stories. I'd grind saffron with the mortar and pestle while she diced onions and sauteed them in olive oil and turmeric until they sizzled. She'd let me swipe drops of pomegranate syrup from the jar before swirling it into the stew. We worked together in synchrony, stirring and singing as we cooked, when she was healthy.

When she wasn't healthy, the onions scorched. She'd wander off to her bedroom with the stove still burning until smoke plumed from the kitchen. Whatever happened to the khoresht and rice, she'd blame it on me.

Now we crowd all our food on the bar top and pull stools up to the counter for dinner. The spread smells like my childhood. There's ash-e reshteh, the thick and herby noodle soup, and rice with crispy tahdig, and dilly white fish, and a plate of barberry-studded kuku.

I try to remember the last time Azar and I had dinner with our mom. And that makes me think of our recent sermon about the Last Supper. When Jesus had his last meal with the apostles, he knew one of them would betray him. He predicted one of them would deny knowing him too.

At our last family dinner together, I wonder if my mom knew we would leave her. If she knew that my dad was about to make her move out for good.

"You went all out!" Azar says as she helps herself to a scoop of sabzi polo.

Jaleh takes a deep breath before speaking. "It's all the dishes I missed making for you two while we were apart."

Azar squeezes Mom's hand and then passes me the serving spoon. But I just stare at her.

Is that what Jaleh wants from this dinner? Overfeeding us tahdig won't wipe away the past few years, no matter how delicious her fried rice tastes. She acts like she can make up for all the time she wasn't around—to rebuild her relationship with us, like she can assemble bricks out of the dust of things long ago demolished.

I hold the empty serving spoon in my fist as anger mounts inside me. "Are you ever going to apologize? For everything you did?"

Azar sets down her fork full of fish with a sigh. But Mom looks up at me and holds my gaze.

"I thought my words would mean nothing," Jaleh says. "I went back on my promises so many times before. How could an apology mean anything this time? I wanted to show you both that I am different through my actions."

She rests her hand over mine on the countertop, covered in a tablecloth still stained from the punch at my fifth birthday party. "I *am* sorry."

I don't know what I expected those words to feel like. I thought they'd mean *something* to me, but instead they land flat. "Okay," I say, finally dipping the serving spoon into the bowl of ash-e reshteh. I'll eat her apology meal, because it would be self-inflicted torture to refuse a Persian mom's cooking, but I don't want her to think she's forgiven.

The kuku tastes earthy-green and salty and nutty. Each tart barberry explodes a new sense memory of Mom's cooking inside me.

When we're finishing our plates, Jaleh turns back to me. "How are things going with you and Bea? She's lovely."

I focus my effort on gathering the last grains of rice on my plate while Mom lingers in my silence.

"She and Bea had a fight," Azar blurts out.

"Aziz!" I shoot her a warning look. She might be comfortable with telling Mom all about her personal life, but I'm not.

"What?" Azar says. "Bea wants to do a part in the school musical with her ex-girlfriend. Mitra's insecure because Cara is really talented and pretty, and Mitra's scared Cara's going to try to steal Bea back. And Bea is pissed because Mitra doesn't trust her even though they told each other they *love* each other."

I glare at Azar across the table, and she just shrugs, packing her mouth with a cardamom cookie. "You've been a dark cloud all week. And you've given me limited details to work with," she says. "So I had to ask Bea for more info. You didn't even tell me you two said *I love you!*"

The nan-e nokhodchi flour puffs out around Azar's words, and she ends her monologue coughing on the dry chickpea powder. *Serves her right.* Mom pours her some chai in a clear tea glass.

My hands clamp down on the tablecloth. I've fought hard to keep my life private from my mom since we left her. The more I let her in, the more power she has to hurt me.

"That's hard, Mitra," Jaleh says. "But to be in a relationship, you must trust the other person. My therapist says it takes time to build trust, like laying bricks one by one. But love and trust must go hand in hand."

Her tone is instructive, like she's guiding a child through a difficult math problem.

"That's rich, coming from you. I didn't ask for your advice." My words are directed down at my empty plate. "You don't know the situation. You've only met Bea once. And you don't know me." I work up the courage to look at her. "And you don't know anything about trust."

"Mitra," Azar says, but I ignore her.

I want Jaleh to understand: I'm drawing a line between us. She will not slip into my heart like Hafez said. I don't need her.

"I can figure this out on my own. That's what I've been doing for the past five years, and I've been doing just fine."

"I understand." Jaleh takes a breath and a slow sip of chai. "I don't like unwanted advice, either. In fact, on Friday my boss told me it was a *bold choice* that I wear a nose ring at the office."

"What?" Azar balks. "Do they have Holy Trinity dress code at your work or something?"

"Sometimes it feels that way," Jaleh says. "I've been there for barely a month, and already he has an opinion about everything I do. Even when I'm successful in obtaining a grant for us, if it's not in the way *he* would do it, he'll have something to say about it."

Jaleh and Azar dish about Jaleh's boss and her new job while we finish dessert. I focus on drinking my chai and eat a nan-e berenji and a couple of khorma, letting the sweets serve as my excuse to refrain from talking. The rice flour cookie melts like a cardamom cloud on my tongue.

When she finishes her last cookie, Azar heads to the couch and stretches her legs out across the cushions. "Think I want to spend the night tonight, Mom. If you can drop me at Dad's on your way to work in the morning?"

"Sure." Jaleh glances at me. "Mitra, would you like to stay over too?"

I try not to register the hopefulness in her voice. I keep looking over at her Haft Seen, the hyacinth and apple and vinegar and all the other items laid out carefully on her altar of intentions for the new year, and I wonder what she wants from me. Maybe she wants me to snap back into being the daughter I was before, grinding saffron side by side with her in the kitchen, laughing and turmeric-stained. Maybe she genuinely wants to get to know me as I am now. But maybe it doesn't matter what she wants.

"I should head home," I say.

She can read it in my voice. *Home.* We both know where home is to me, and where it isn't.

Jaleh nods. "Give me a minute to clean up and I can give you a ride."

"No." Energy mounts in my legs as I scoot back from the counter and take my plate to the sink. "I can walk."

"It's dark out," Jaleh says. "It could rain."

"It's Bellevue," I tell her. "It could always rain."

"Don't be stubborn," Azar shouts at me from the couch, where she's curled herself into a big fleece blanket.

"I'll be fine." I head for the exit without hugging either of them goodbye. "Thanks for dinner." When I close the front door behind me, the hamsa on the doorway stares back at me with its evil eye.

Amends

IT DOES RAIN. I walk home along the tree-lined streets of my mom's new neighborhood to the titter of water high up in the evergreen branches, and the flow of Kelsey Creek somewhere beside me. I feel like the creek too, all churned up and carrying long-lost things that swirl and bump together. If everything could just settle inside me, maybe I could see clearly again.

The only way I know how to settle is to talk to Bea. I want her to tell me everything will be okay, and that maybe someday things with my mom will look different. Bea is so good at magnifying hope. I miss her with everything I have. But she wants to insert herself back into the world of the person who hurt her, pretending she'll be immune to Cara's charm this time, as though we won't all end up regretting it.

Just when I'm cursing the dark, spooky streets of Highlands, my dad rounds the corner and calls out my name.

"What are you doing here?" I ask, even though I'm glad to see him.

"Azar texted," he says, falling into stride beside me. "She said you left angry. I wanted to walk with you." He puts his hand on my back, then lets it swing beside him.

"Thanks." I go back to listening to the water, all the raindrops murmuring *Bea, Bea, Bea* when they chime against the pine needles.

"I know you're upset with your mother," my dad says. I guess he's the only person Azar didn't blab to about my fight with Bea. "But I think you should give yourself the opportunity to get to know her again."

My dad and I have always shared the same internal, quiet sense of order. We set rules and we follow them and they keep us safe. I don't know why he decided to violate that order by bringing Jaleh back into our lives.

"You're one to talk," I say. "It's not like *you* came to Nowruz with us. You're not the one being asked to make amends with her."

"It's different for you and your sister. She's your mother." Dad sighs. "When she called last summer, I tried to think about what it would be like to not see you and Azar for years. I couldn't imagine it," he says. "It's too painful."

"Just because it's hard to think about doesn't mean it was the wrong choice," I say. "That doesn't mean you get to push me into seeing her."

Dad slows his step and looks at me. "You think it's easy for me to give up time with you two? To see Azar spending her weekends there?" He runs a hand through his dark hair. "Your mom has a disease, Mitra. She did not ask for this. The addiction hurt us in many ways, I know. But it hurt her just as much. She has worked very hard to stay sober. She deserves for us to recognize that."

Our footsteps on wet cement carry the conversation for the rest of the journey home.

Jaleh doesn't know me, Azar doesn't listen, and Dad keeps betraying his own better judgment. I know the one person who would understand. And I've pushed her away.

Bea, what would you say now?

I try to summon her voice in my head, picture the answers she'd have for me. But my imagined version of Bea pales in comparison.

I want her to wrap me in her arms. Work her magic and make all my troubles feel dwarfed by her love. I want that warm-skin smell of hers, and the vibration of her laugh through my body.

More than anything, I want to trust her. Trust her the way I did when she was only my best friend—when *love* meant something simpler and different than it does now.

What Would Kyla Do?

DAD LETS ME borrow the car to take to school on Monday morning while he carpools to work. I pick up Azar at Mom's apartment early, and then chomp my thumbnail at every red light on our way toward Medina. Azar eats leftover baklava with a glass jar of majoon in the passenger seat and she puts a plastic-wrapped square of kuku in the car's cup holder for me. She watches me out of the corner of her eye.

"If you want to make things right, make them right," she says through a mouthful of flaky phyllo dough.

"You're assuming the fight was my fault," I say.

"Knowing you, it probably was," she laughs.

Azar makes it sound so easy to fix things with Bea. I don't know what *right* would even look like at this point.

I shouldn't be allowed to have real, grown-up relationships. I need childproofing, like safety scissors or outlet covers, but to protect me from my own dating self-sabotage. If Bea forgives me, I swear I'll be careful and thoughtful and smart from here on out.

When we pull into the underground parking garage, I shift into park and turn to Azar, my lip caught between my teeth. "How?"

"Okay." She claps her hands together, gearing up like she's my phone-a-friend lifeline during some critical moment of a game show. "Tell her you were wrong. Apologize. Be supportive. When in doubt, gifts don't hurt."

"But how do I actually . . . feel different about her and Cara?" I sigh into the steering wheel. "They were *in love*. Like, fight-a-war-for-you, name-a-boat-after-you kind of love. That doesn't just disappear when one person says they're done. And then Bea's going to sign up to be onstage with her every night? The two of them up there singing love songs with Spencer, who—no offense—might as well be playing one of the prop suitcases. He has no stage presence." I catch my breath. "It's a recipe for disaster. At least *one* of them will catch feelings again."

Azar turns to me, folding her arms in front of her. It feels so formal, like we're about to hold a press conference or something. *Breaking News: Big Sister Bungles First Attempt at Real Love.*

"My friend Kyla was in the same situation once. She was super insecure because her boyfriend Cooper was in Yearbook with his ex, and they were always staying after school late together to work on the spread, and then there was an end-of-the-year house party for Yearbook staff and there was a hot tub . . . it was a whole thing."

"What did Kyla do?" I can't believe I'm asking about the relationship drama of some sophomore I've never met. I've hit a new low.

"Well, she didn't want to be controlling and push Cooper into his ex's arms, so she faked it 'til she made it. She told him she was glad he had extracurricular hobbies and that she wasn't worried about him and the ex."

Azar munches the last of her baklava. "Plus, she took up Ultimate Frisbee, and they had their own games and parties and stuff, so she got invested in that and stopped obsessing over what Cooper might be doing."

"That's actually helpful," I say.

Azar grins. "Don't sound so shocked." She flicks the crumbs from her lap. "I should mention that they broke up. But it had nothing to do with the Yearbook thing. Kyla fell for one of the handlers on her Ultimate team. That's a story for another time."

We head into campus, and I hustle through the hallways toward Bea's locker. She isn't here yet, of course. I sit with my back against the lockers and hug my backpack to my chest. *Tell her you were wrong. Apologize. Be supportive.* I rehash Azar's pep talk in my head until I see Bea's scuffed-up loafers in front of me.

It's been over a week since she smiled at me.

I reach my hand up for Bea, unsure if she'll accept it, but she takes my palm in hers and hoists me up from the floor. She's got waiting eyes and her lips are poised in silence.

"I trust you," I say, the words kicking every rib on the way out of my chest. "Of course I trust you. I'm sorry I freaked out." I plumb my hands into my blazer pockets. "And it had nothing to do with the Harper thing. I promise. I would never hold that against you, okay? I know who you are, and I know I can count on you. You deserve to do whatever you want. Do the play."

Bea brings her fingers under my chin and tilts my face up to look at her. "Thank you," she says, the first glow of a smile rising over her face. "I get that it's awkward and uncomfortable for you. But you have nothing to worry about."

I tuck a lock of hair behind my ear and grab something from my backpack. "I brought you The Book," I tell her. "Nothing angry. Just . . . me trying to figure out how I can be better."

She takes The Book from me and bolts her arms around me. "I don't like not talking to you. Let's not do that again."

If we were somewhere private, I'd dot kisses on her cheeks and draw my lips to hers until she felt my resolve. But I'll settle for squeezing her tight instead.

When we break apart, Bea's face brightens and her eyes flash behind her glasses. "Jesus Christ, Mitra. I have a *week's* worth of stories I've been dying to tell you."

I try to relish the sweetness of being back in Bea's good graces. But this is the first lie I've told her since we started dating. *I trust you.*

I want to mean it. But I don't.

Mitra

us is a word generous
as your resounding faith
in me, a word I'll labor

to earn, reach for the one
real truth: love that presses
my ear to the heart-

beat of everything, as
certain as four years of
poem-gifts you've etched

in me, even as my feet
fix in the mud of
my own limitations

you nourish me, inject
oxygen in this starving
place—so I'll scramble

for your love, fight for
fingertips brave enough to
find the pulse of us again

Bea

again my mom's eyes swirl a cartwheel of
rosary beads harboring holy Marys and
Our Fathers under her tongue in my honor

like I'm a problem her incantations can fix
only she's too polite to name that to my face
so she and my dad plaster platitudes over their

disappointment: that's nice about you and Mitra
but you can't tell your abuela you know she has
a fragile heart, and why do you have to be so

loud about who you are in your clothes and your
poems and your music, can't you restrain yourself
like all the boxed-in queers before me, forced

to call lovers friends—I won't do that to us, Mitra
I'll make every kiss a protest, every hand-holding
second a silent riot, a revolution brews in our love

Something Just for Me

IT'S SUCH A relief to be back in Bea's good graces. Couples therapist Azar really pulled through this time—I keep reminding myself to fake it until I make it, just like she said. Maybe I don't fully trust Bea yet, but I can show up and be a good girlfriend, and trust will follow.

I'm leaving poetry seminar on Friday when Ms. Acosta calls after me. "Mitra, can you stay behind a moment, please? I'd like to speak with you privately."

Bea drops my hand in the doorway and both of our cheeks rush with redness. *Sorry,* Bea mouths at me as she steps out of the classroom. We had already converted into weekend mode, so we both got sloppy about cloaking our gayness at school. Poetry seminar is small enough that it can feel like the one place we don't have to hide at Holy Trinity. And with Max and Cara in seminar, our class roster is like 40 percent rainbow flags already. But I have to remember that this is still a conservative Catholic school, and as cool as Ms. Acosta is, she's still an ex-nun.

I take a deep breath as I shut the door between Bea and me. Through the little window in the door, I can see Bea pacing out in the hallway.

"Um, hi," I say to Ms. Acosta. I've been baring my soul to her in our poetry journals all term, but it's still hard for me to open up to people in person.

She steps behind her wooden desk and opens the top drawer. "Peep?"

"What?"

Ms. Acosta pulls a paper tray of yellow marshmallow bunnies from her drawer and shows it to me. "I stocked up early for Easter." I watch her pull out one of the bright bunnies and bite off its head. "I know the Easter bunny bears no relation to Jesus's resurrection, but I must admit these are a sentimental favorite of mine. They've been around since I was a kid. Don't tell Father Mitchell." She winks at me.

I take a bunny from the tray and squish its mallow fluff between my fingers. Ms. Acosta takes a seat on a khaki-colored armchair and I settle in the chair beside her, nibbling on my bunny's ears. They send a sharp crunch of sugar through my mouth. "I thought we could talk about your college decision making," she says.

"Oh." My face slackens. I try to recalibrate from the worry I felt a moment ago, when I expected her to reprimand me for holding hands with a girl in class.

Ms. Acosta tilts her head at me, the little chain on her glasses swinging. "What were you expecting?"

"I don't know." My mouth flaps open and closed like a sock puppet. And then I just blurt it out: "I'm bisexual."

Ms. Acosta nods slowly. "All right."

"In case knowing that will affect whatever else you were going to say," I scramble.

She adjusts her glasses and watches me patiently. "How would your sexuality affect our discussion about college decision making?"

"You're a *nun*," I tell her, too loudly. "I thought you wouldn't want to help me out with college stuff if you knew that."

Ms. Acosta gets quiet for a minute and clasps her hands in her lap. "I have a daughter," she says. "She's forty-five now. She lives in Vermont, with her wife."

My eyes magnify times a million. I didn't know anybody at Holy Trinity had a queer kid. Or that anybody would acknowledge it, if they did.

"I used to have an idea in my head about what it meant to be gay, to have a gay child," Ms. Acosta tells me. "And it turned out that idea prevented me from really seeing, from really getting to know my daughter for several years. I missed out on what was."

She raises her index finger in the air. "Remember what Pope Francis said?"

"Realities are more important than ideas," I echo.

Ms. Acosta nods at me. "I'm interested in your reality, Mitra," she says. "Now. About your college choices. I talked to the guidance counselor, and she mentioned that you've applied to Reed College."

"Yeah." I'm still in shock about Ms. Acosta's queer daughter, and now I'm trying to process the fact that she talked to the guidance counselor about me.

"That's my alma mater, and I taught there for eleven years. I'm still in touch with Professor Gutierrez, an associate professor of poetry in the creative writing department. At one point in time, he was a mentee of mine. If you're up for it, I'd like to work with you on developing a portfolio of poems to submit to the department head."

She fishes out another Peep. "It's not typical for incoming freshmen to be accepted into the creative writing major, but it is possible."

My brain does a full system reboot. "Why?" I say. "Why would you help me?"

Ms. Acosta smiles. "I think you have talent. And incredible prom-ise. The writing in your poetry journal has really blossomed over the course of our class. I hope it's okay, I shared one of your poems with Professor Gutierrez already, and he was interested in seeing more."

"Really?" I don't know how to respond to her praise. I stare out at the shimmering edge of Meydenbauer Bay through the window.

"I don't know. Reed is supposed to be a tough school. And it's really expensive. Bea and I already decided we're going to UW together if we get in."

"You don't have to commit to attending," Ms. Acosta says. "This is a time to explore your options. It's a great opportunity to see what's possible for you next year."

Nobody has ever sat me down and talked about my future like this. My dad always encouraged us to go to college, but that's because he sees it as a survival strategy, a way for Azar and me to stay afloat as kids of immigrants without much of a safety net. At Holy Trinity, most teachers have treated me like a non-Catholic oddity at best, and at worst, a soul beyond saving. Ms. Acosta speaks of my future like it's a thing worth believing in. Like *I'm* worth believing in.

It's an intimidating offer, but I don't want to miss this gift Ms. Acosta is handing me. And Aziz's words come back to me. For the first time in a long time, I'll have a project all on my own. Bea has the play, and I can have this.

"Thank you," I say. "Okay. Yeah. I want to work on the portfolio with you."

"Lovely," she says, standing. "Why don't you work on a few new pieces, and we can gather some of your best work from your poetry journal, as well."

I feel lighter when I stand up. "I'll start putting stuff together," I tell Ms. Acosta.

She pulls another Peep from the paper tray as I head for the door. "One for your girlfriend," she says.

Things You Don't Worry About
When You're Writing Poetry

- The fact that play rehearsal runs until after nine p.m. some nights.
- What happens at said rehearsals between Éponine and Cosette.
- Why it takes your girlfriend so long to respond to your texts.
- Your girlfriend asking you what happened on Nowruz, and *When are you going to see your mom again?*
- The fact that your mom and dad went out to tea alone together "to talk and catch up."
- Why Azar leaves more of her stuff at your mom's house every time she visits.
- The fact that Azar wants to spend more and more weeknights there.
- What your future will look like.

It's Not Lying, It's Being Kind

I READ ONCE about an oil painter who said that everything he saw in the world around him was filtered through his oil-painter eyes. When he looked at the million shades of green in a sun-dappled tree, the gears in his brain started whirring. He saw exactly which yellows and greens and blues and browns he'd mix on his palette to re-create the colors. Painting was the way he made sense of everything he saw.

After two weeks of working on my poetry portfolio for Reed, I feel the same way about poetry. It gives me a place to filter everything— the questions I can't ask my mom, the perfect tingle of Bea's lips on mine, the weird discomfort while I wait out the *Les Mis* rehearsals.

When I run my hand through Bea's hair, my brain offers up a slurry of words, trying to tack down the soft comfort of her curls. Early spring sun on the bay stirs up all the colors sleeping under the winter-gray, and I want to name them all. Poem stanzas flit behind my eyelids at night, and I scribble them on the scratch paper on my bedside table. Sometimes it's just a word I wanted to wrap up and keep for later, like *translucent* or *cumbersome*. These word-gifts greet me in the morning, waking me like strong coffee.

Ms. Acosta says she can see the change. She hands my portfolio pieces back with smiley faces and underlines and a few suggestions or questions. The notes are things like *deepen this* or *keep going here*. I never thought someone besides Bea would understand or care about what I have to say. And I kind of can't believe that the person who *does* understand is an almost-eighty-year-old devout Catholic lady.

This morning after class, she told me she set up a visit at Reed for me this weekend, complete with an invite to sit in on one of Professor Gutierrez's classes, Poetics of Resistance and Resilience. I almost broke down and bear-hugged her right there, but the news came with a blow of guilt to my gut. Reed is way too expensive for my dad to afford, and if I told him I wanted to go, he'd try to make it work, even if it meant making major sacrifices. I don't want to put him through that. And I'm already set on going to UW with Bea. We're counting down the days until UW acceptance emails go out next Monday. It feels selfish imagining a future outside the one we've dreamed up—something just for me.

I haven't told Bea about the visit, or Ms. Acosta's plan to help me put together a portfolio for their writing program. I don't want her to feel like I'm making plans without her. I feel weird about the whole thing, almost like I'm cheating on her *academically*. But I've decided it's not lying, it's being kind—why worry her with the possibility that we'd take separate paths next year when there's no way I'll end up going to Reed? Bea and I have finally found a way to transform our friendship into something more. I'm not going to complicate that with a far-fetched wish.

Still, something inside me keeps chanting *go, go, go*. Just for the weekend. Just to see what it's like. Ms. Acosta believes in me and my writing, and she put all this work into arranging a visit. It would be rude to waste her kindness.

I just have to get my dad to agree to let me go. I don't know why I'm so nervous to ask him. It's not like I would lose anything if he says no. But my fingers fidget when I think about putting words to this wish.

I work up the courage to broach the topic over dinner on Tuesday, when Azar is at Jaleh's for the night. "Dad." I grip the bowl of lentils as I spoon some for him. When Azar is away, we've taken to eating all the foods we love that she hates, and watching the space documentaries she'd get bored of if she were here. It's actually pretty fun.

"I have to ask you something."

I bite the inside of my cheek. Saying this out loud will make it real.

"My poetry teacher arranged a tour of Reed College in Portland this weekend. It's a good school, and she wants me to consider it. She used to work there." I try to measure my voice so he can't tell that I've gotten my hopes up.

"Anyway, she's been helping me put together a portfolio of writing samples for them. I want to go check it out, but it's far away, and I'd need a car." I steady myself with a breath. "Would you maybe go with me?"

My dad sets down his spoon and smiles at me. "That's my Mitra joon!" Pride beams out of him. It's probably because I just told him I've been doing extra homework by choice. Every parent's fantasy. "It's a smart decision to look at all your options. I'd love to take you."

Excitement chases the guilt around my stomach until they weave together. I want to relish my dad's pride in me, but it's singed at the edges by my selfishness. He may love that I'm working toward something and exploring my options, but the price tag at Reed remains.

"Thanks." I scoop him the last of the lentils. The gesture does double duty: gratitude and penance. Food is love in our house.

"It will be fun," he says. "I loved my university days." Dad gets a wistful look in his eye, probably recalling his glory days of yore at

Berkeley. I don't know much about that time in his life, but I know he was a member of the computer science and aerospace clubs. I'll never know how he had the time and skill to hit on my mom while he was busy building all those remote-controlled airplanes.

"And, a chance for us to have a father-daughter road trip." He claps his hands together.

I try to smile and be grateful. But as the guilt about my dad drains away, it's replaced by nerves. I'm still not ready to tell Bea.

HolyHorror Group Chat

Ellie: y'all we need a BREAK

Ellie: rehearsals have been running us ragged and I want some down time with my HolyHorror crew!!

Max: agreed. it's been too long.

Max: also I've heard *I Dreamed A Dream* approximately thirty-seven times this month

Max: the despair is starting to seep into my soul

                        Mitra: don't give in, Max!!

Bea: well I know Mitra needs a break because she's been working on a Secret Writing Project that she won't tell anyone about 💀

                        Mitra: no I haven't!

                        Mitra: it's just stuff for poetry class

Bea: you do remember I'm in the same class, right?

Cara: can you take your relationship squabbles outside, ladies

Cara: we're trying to problem-solve here

Bea: what's our cure?

Bea: karaoke night, Netflix marathon, drown our sorrows in pho?

Cara: I think the whole cast needs help honestly

Cara: Spencer and Jack are supposed to be acting out a bromance for the ages, but they keep bickering like an old married couple between scenes

Cara: and, no offense Bea, but your chemistry with Spencer is nonexistent

Cara: not that I blame you

Bea: is he a wet noodle onstage, or am I just gay?

Ellie: both!

Cara: we need some serious cast bonding if this show is ever going to make it off the ground.

Ellie: cast plus Mitra 😊

Max: our honorary stagehand!

Cara: leave it to me.

Leveling Up

IT'S BEEN MORE than a month now since Formal, since Bea held the word *girlfriend* between us like a string of twinkle lights. We thought it would be silly to make a huge celebration out of a one-month anniversary when she's been my person since we were thirteen, and I've loved her for years. Our relationship wasn't scraped clean that night we defined our *something*: We just added a new layer. But we still wanted to mark the moment.

On Wednesday after school, Bea parks us downtown and we pick up coffee. We walk down to the waterfront at Meydenbauer Bay Park, strolling the paths that cut through the grass. The air smells salty and green and gusts of wind push sailboats along the bay.

When we get to the end of the semicircle pier, Bea sits down on a bench and tucks her legs into the warmth of her skirt. I settle in beside her.

"When did you know?" She curls her hand around mine, warmed by her coffee cup.

"Know what?" We've been talking about the last month, and Formal, and our first kiss, and everything leading up to that; I know what she's asking, but my heart rumbles around my chest as I stall. Wind whips my hair over my face from off the choppy bay, an outline of Mount Rainier visible in the distance.

A smile grows across Bea's face, and she loops her arm through mine. "That you loved me. In a different way."

I swallow the foamy end of my coffee, and I tell her about that night the summer after our sophomore year. I tell her about reading the never-ending poem together on my rooftop in the dark, and seeing a part of her that maybe only I got to see. She grins through my story, just listening.

"You know when I knew?"

I don't know. I've wondered, but never asked.

She squeezes my arm for a beat. "That day you took me to the pool."

"Really?"

"I mean." She clears her throat, looking at the red speck of a kayak out on the bay. "I'd thought about it before then."

"Yeah?"

"Of course!" She straightens her glasses to look at me. "Like, how could I not? It was on my mind when you came out sophomore year, and . . . last spring too. But it never felt like something that could really happen until that day we went swimming." She kisses my ear.

"It was my belly button, wasn't it?" I say, and she laughs, startling a nearby duck into flight.

"It was the belly button," she concedes.

I think of all the moments between us—in poetry class, at her house, trying on the suit for Formal—between that day at the pool and the day we kissed in the chapel. A world of moments when she loved me, and I didn't know it yet. Each of them a gift.

"We haven't gotten to talk like this in a while," Bea says, pulling a curl away from the edge of her mouth. "I've been caught up in the play. And you've been so busy writing."

"Sorry." I hate that I'm not telling her about the portfolio and Reed. I just don't want to rock the boat when things are so good between us. "We only have a little while left in poetry seminar, and I want to make the most out of it."

"But we only have a little bit left of senior year," she says.

"I know." I lean my head on her shoulder as we watch ducks and boats bob on the water. I want to have a gift for her too. "You're right. I'm going to take you on a date," I say.

Bea wiggles beside me on the bench. "Is this, like, the next stage in your efforts to *romance* me?" She laughs. "Like, Awkward Flirty Texts, Volume Two?"

"We're leveling up," I say.

Kowabunga

TODAY IS THE day. Buried in the bottom of my backpack are my civilian clothes: black jeans, white shirt with rolled-up sleeves, and my forest-green zipper hoodie with some of Ellie's home-drawn queer pride pins fastened to it. Just knowing they're sleeping under my religion textbook, waiting for 2:45 to roll around, makes the day brighter.

We're going to the Bellevue Art Museum's Monsters, Villains, and Superheroes exhibit at 3:10. As soon as school gets out, we'll perform a Houdini-like transformation out of our uniforms in her car. Then we'll speed over to BAM to have our socks knocked off by all the freaky toys and posters and relics of old comic book characters. Bea loves this kind of stuff, so I thought it would be perfect for our first-ever museum date.

When the last bell rings, I speed walk through the hallways of Holy Trinity to escape as fast as I can without getting written up for running. I'm supposed to meet Bea at Gary in the parking garage, but a hand catches my wrist just as I'm about to exit Hot Guy with Crucifix.

"Wait." Bea pulls me toward the windows at the front of the building.

"What?" I try to catch my breath from the speed walking.

"Um. I have to talk to you about something."

"Can you talk while we're in the car?" I glance out the window at a handful of crows on the plaza. "If you keep me much longer, I'm gonna have to start stripping down in the middle of school."

Bea's nose scrunches in a smile. "Wouldn't be the first time. But. Okay. How would you feel about a change of plans this afternoon?"

My heart sinks. "What do you mean?"

"I guess our cast-bonding thing is going to be today? Like, right now. Cara just sent out details in the group chat."

My hand loosens its grip on the strap of my backpack. "But today is supposed to be your day off from rehearsals. We had a date."

"I know." Her eyebrows furrow behind her glasses. "I'm sorry. But I really need this."

She flops back against the windowpane, her eyes staying on me. "I've been panicking. Dress rehearsals are just around the corner, and we're supposed to be off book by next week, and I still can't even remember everybody's names! I know I'm joining the play late, and nobody expects me to be as up to speed as Emily T. would've been by this point. But I don't know the cast and crew that well, and it's making things really hard. I'm not ready."

Bea is breathing fast and talking faster. "What was Emily thinking, getting mono in the middle of spring musical season? She just *had* to share a Gatorade bottle with her whole pickleball team? Who does that?"

"Easy," I say. "It's going to be okay."

"I know you really wanted to go see the exhibit," Bea says. "If you want, you can still go. But you're invited to the cast thing, if you want to come with us instead." She reaches for my hand. "You know they all miss hanging out with you."

The little conspiracy theorist inside me says *Maybe Cara knew you two had a date planned today, and she orchestrated this whole cast-bonding event to try to sabotage your relationship.* But Cara would have to be a Bond-villain evil mastermind to pull off that kind of scheming. I drop my inner tinfoil hat and push down the thought.

"I don't want to go to BAM without you." I feel like a toddler who didn't get their way, but I can't hold back my disappointment. "I'll come."

We give a ride to Max, Ellie, and one of the stagehands, Jessica, and meet the rest of the cast and crew on Third Street in downtown Renton. There are maybe thirteen of us, mostly main cast and a few members of the chorus and tech crew, most of us matching in our red uniforms like we're preschoolers on a field trip.

We stroll up to 8-Bit Arcade right at four o'clock, Cara checking the time on her phone. "Perfect," she says. "They just opened. We have five hours before they kick out minors." She pulls a giant plastic bag of change from her backpack. "I brought enough quarters for everyone. And Mr. Sherman said pizza's on him." She whips out a debit gift card and Spencer whoops. "Courtesy of Holy Trinity's theater department budget."

I forgot how serious Cara can get about organizing fun. Back in our HolyHorror party days, she'd arrange every detail: the dry ice, the multi-flavored popcorn options, the perfect acoustics for our Rocky Horror singalongs. It's been a while since I've been on the receiving end of one of her thoroughly planned parties. I just wish it weren't today.

We line up at the red-and-white entrance to 8-Bit, next to the cartoon window dressing with Homer Simpson and Donkey Kong and Super Mario, and Cara doles out a handful of quarters to each of us.

Inside, the arcade is dim, lit by the rainbow glow of dozens of retro pinball machines and arcade games. Stools line up beside a bar counter where milkshakes and soda, and later beer, are served. The back door is propped open, leading to a wooden patio with a few picnic tables and patio umbrellas.

Spencer and Jack, who play Marius and Enjolras, start chanting *PIZZA! PIZZA!* and pumping their fists in the air, striding up to the bar counter. Jessica and Ellie flop into matching plastic orange seats to race side by side in a '90s-style Super Cars game.

Cara sets her backpack down by the wall and points at Bea. "You and me," she says. "TMNT rematch."

Bea cackles. "Is this why you planned our cast party here? Just so we get a second chance at defeating the Foot Clan? It's never gonna happen. I swear, that game is just a quarter-eating machine."

"Check your attitude!" Cara says. "Come on. I'll let you be Michelangelo." She gives Bea a toothy grin. "If anyone's gonna take down Shredder and Krang, it's us."

Bea rolls her eyes. "They're your quarters." She shrugs, squeezing my palm goodbye as they make their way to the Teenage Mutant Ninja Turtles multiplayer game.

Bea and I came to 8-Bit a couple times on our Anti-Formal Fridays, but I didn't know she had ever come here with Cara. Did they come on a date? Did they share a milkshake, and flirt-brag about who was the best at Ms. Pac-Man, and kiss in the dark corners of the arcade?

My stomach roils. I slide up to the bar and take a seat on a pleather stool, and I order a slice of black olive pizza from the bearded guy behind the counter. The cheese puddles with oil and the crust is crunchy and hot, and does nothing to help my nervous stomach. I take my slice over to a row of pinball machines and find Max playing a retro Star Wars game.

I watch them flick the pinball a few times before I work up the nerve to ask, "Do you go to all the play rehearsals?"

"No." Max sighs as the pinball game resets, pulling another fifty cents out of their pocket. "But I'm at more of them now that we're almost to dress rehearsal time. Why?"

"No reason."

I glance over my shoulder at the TMNT game, where Cara and Bea are laughing with their hands punching the game's buttons and twirling the joysticks. Cara bumps her shoulder into Bea's, casting her eyes down at Bea for a second between moves. "Nice kick," she says.

"How many times do you think they've been here?" I ask. "They have all these weird inside jokes about Teenage Mutant Ninja Turtles."

Max follows my eyes over to Cara and Bea at the TMNT game, Cara reaching over to Bea's control panel to push a button. Bea smacks her hand away.

"Okay," Max says. "Stop thinking whatever it is you're thinking."

"What am I thinking?" I set my half-eaten slice of pizza on the edge of an abandoned game.

"I know what you're thinking, because it's the same type of stuff *I* think." They point their index finger at their chest. "With Jessica. Things have been going great, we've been talking every day, we're like *thisclose* to dating. And still my anxiety takes some little speck of worry, like, why did she take an hour to message me back tonight? And it takes me on a whole roller coaster of panic over nothing."

The TMNT game beeps out a cheerful tone, and Cara and Bea high-five. "Mikey for the win!" Cara cheers. "Have you been practicing without me?"

I can't watch. I take my uneaten pizza out to the patio, Max following me, and we take seats at a chipped picnic table. "What if it's not nothing?" I ask.

They shake their head, pulling the hair from their eyes. "Bea would never do something like that to you. And remember how terrible things were for all of us after they broke up? We stopped hanging out, and we couldn't even eat lunch together anymore. It's *good* they're chill around each other again. There's only a couple months until graduation. We don't have that much time left together. Now we can all be normal."

I can make out Bea's laughter through the crowd of voices inside. "Okay."

Ellie skips out of the arcade toward us. "I just demolished Jessica," she says proudly. "Super Cars *and* Donkey Kong." She flexes her hands out in front of her. "Told her not to take it personally. I've been working the switchboard for theater for two years. These hands are *nimble*!"

Behind her, Bea wanders onto the patio, taking a seat beside me on the bench. "There you are!" She grins at me. "Oh my god. We killed! I mean, we took out three of the bosses. It's not like we got to Shredder or anything. But still!"

"I pity any villain who tries to take you on," I say.

"Want to go a few rounds with me?" She jingles a stack of quarters in her palm. "You pick the game."

I look over at Max, who pats me on the back. "Sure," I say. We all follow Bea into the darkness of the arcade, the edges of her clothes lit red and orange and green from the glowing pinball machines.

I walk up to the TMNT arcade game and drum my fingers on the buttons. "Teach me your ways," I tell Bea. "How many people can play this?"

"Four."

I motion to Max and Ellie behind me, but Ellie waves me off. "Next round! I'm going for the Stranger Things pinball."

I spot Cara at the bar counter on a swivel stool, finishing a bite of pepperoni pizza. I swallow the lump in my throat and wave at her. "You in?" She smiles and raises her bag of quarters.

The quarters drop *plunk plunk plunk* into the machine, kicking the '90s rock theme song into action. Bea bounces her shoulder into mine as the four of us take position at the game. "How do we play?" I ask.

"Just, punch stuff," Cara says. "I call Leonardo!"

I take Raphael and Max picks Donatello, leaving Bea as Michelangelo again. The game starts with the turtles erupting from a manhole in a burst of neon colors, twirling through the air with their swords and nunchucks.

"They're pretty beefy and muscular for reptiles," I say.

"You just have to buy into the premise." Cara laughs. "They're turtles and they're ninjas and they're trained street fighters. We don't ask questions."

"Shh! It's starting!" Max says as the voice-over shouts *Kowabunga!* The turtles leap down from the top of a steep skyscraper, and then we roll into a fire-ravaged building facing down the Foot Clan.

"Attack him, Raf!" Cara shouts beside me as a purple-clad warrior kicks down a door to lunge at me. I jab at the buttons and joystick like my life depends on it. Raphael waves his swords around, kicking and punching the warrior until he twirls through the air and hits the ground with an electronic *BOOM*.

"That's my girl!" Bea ruffles my hair before grabbing her joystick again. We play valiantly with Ellie leaving her pinball machine to cheer us on, all of us squealing and jumping and probably spraining our fingers, until we get defeated by some warriors on hoverboards.

When the game chirps out its final song, Max pulls us into a four-way hug. "We did it," they breathe.

"And did you see how Mitra deflected that manhole cover to take out the Foot Clan warrior?" Bea wraps her hand around the back of my neck and brings me in for a kiss.

"We made a good team," Cara says.

I catch my breath and pull Bea over with me to the bar counter for a milkshake, still riding the high of our kiss.

Maybe Max was right. Maybe this is the start of the five of us being normal again. Who knew a few rounds of '90s arcade games could work like family therapy on us.

Half-Truth

Bea: what are you up to this weekend?

> **Mitra:** road trip with my dad

> **Mitra:** going to Powell's to say hi to all the books

> **Mitra:** I think we're gonna visit Reed College while we're there

Bea: oh cool, why?

> **Mitra:** just to check out the campus

> **Mitra:** my dad wants me to

> **Mitra:** no way it'll top our UW weekend though 😊

Bea: I mean, that would be impossible!

Bea: unless another girl professes her love to you while you're in Portland

> **Mitra:** unlikely

> **Mitra:** I'll miss you

Bea: have fun, love

Bea: but not TOO much fun 😉

Bea: smell all the used books at Powells for me!!

Sour Cherries

THE FRIDAY MORNING of the trip, jitters wake me up early and I head to the kitchen to make breakfast for Dad and Azar. Dad bought sangak from the market on his way home from work yesterday, so I fit a long sheet of it into the toaster oven. It's baked on a bed of pebbles, so the bread's flat, crispy surface ripples with the fingerprints of all those little rocks. I find walnuts and feta and bright red radishes in the fridge to go with it.

On the top shelf of the fridge, there's an unopened jar of sour cherry jam with my name on it, written in Jaleh's handwriting. Azar brought it back from her visit with Mom on Tuesday. The jam is hard to find in the States because of trade embargos with Iran, so most people have to haul it across the border when they visit Canada, or track down the right variety of cherries and make it themselves. It's a big deal when someone blesses you with the gift of their coveted sour cherry jam.

I haven't been ready to crack the seal on the jar yet. It feels like I'd be accepting my mom's apology. I heard her words on Nowruz and I believe she's sorry. And I think she genuinely believes things will be different from here on out. But I don't know if I can believe she has changed deep down. The mom who can't stay sober is still inside her somewhere, lurking, waiting to come out and wreak havoc again. An apology can't change that.

Azar arrives at the dining room table in her pajamas as soon as the toasty smell of sangak reaches her room. We make rolled-up sandwiches and wait for Dad, who is nowhere to be found.

"Can't believe you get to skip school today," Azar says as she munches. "You're missing Good Friday Mass."

I totally forgot today is Good Friday.

"It's not technically Mass," I tell Azar. "It's a liturgy. No Eucharist."

"How do you remember this crap?" She chucks a walnut at me. "We're not even Catholic."

"They only let me skip today because they knew I was going on a college tour."

"Right." She chuckles. "Only you would sign up to spend your weekends doing *more school*."

"No such thing as too much learning," I tell her. "Where's Dad?"

When he finally runs into the dining room, Dad's wearing his work slacks and polo shirt with his ID badge slung crooked around his neck. Judging by his wild eyes, he's in Peak Stress Mode.

"What's going on?" I drop the sangak sandwich on my plate.

Dad ruffles his hand through his sleep-styled hair. "I'm so sorry, Mitra joon. There was a data breach at work, some ransomware attack. They're flooded with customer calls. My supervisor just phoned, and I have to be there. They're calling everyone in."

"But we're going to Portland today. I'm scheduled for a tour in, like, four hours."

"I know." He kisses the top of my head, then Azar's. "I'm sorry. I can't take you. But I spoke with your mother, and she's offered to drive you. She can take my place. Okay?"

"No, Dad—I can drive myself," I bargain. "It's only a few hours from here to Portland. I'll be fine."

"Mitra, it's too far," he says. "I don't want you driving there and back alone. And you'd need a car for the whole weekend. I need our car for work." He rips a hunk of sangak in his hand and gobbles it on the way to the door. "This was a nice offer from your mother, to drop everything at the last minute and help us out. Be gracious, okay?"

I don't even have a chance to rebut. Dad hops into his shoes by the front entrance.

"Aziz, your mother will drop you off at school before she and Mitra leave for Portland. Mitra—make it a great trip," he shouts on his way out. "Make it the best weekend of your life!"

Azar and I stare at each other for a minute in the wake of Dad's whirlwind. An entire weekend alone with my mom.

Fuck.

SOS

Mitra: help!

Mitra: unplanned road trip detour

Mitra: my dad has a work emergency so my mom has to take me

Mitra: SOS

Bea: oh no! I'm sorry beautiful ☹

Bea: why don't you and your dad just reschedule?

Bea: if it was gonna be a father-daughter weekend thing anyway?

Bea: Powells will still be there for you another day!

Mitra: we were supposed to visit Reed this weekend

Bea: thought that was your dad's idea to go though?

Reed

I DON'T KNOW how to respond to Bea's text. I leave her question hanging in the air between us like a spider dangling from its silk.

After we drop off Azar at Holy Trinity, Jaleh and I ride south in near-silence. "Do you want to play your music?" she asks me when we pass through Tacoma, as if music will make this less awkward.

"What do you want me to play?" I pull out my phone.

"I don't know what you listen to these days," she says. "Show me what you like."

A weight settles over her words. It's like everything has to be a bonding activity with her. Everything is a way for her to make up for lost time.

I scroll through my music to a playlist Bea made for my birthday in December. Jaleh drums her fingers on the steering wheel and hums along to all the songs she doesn't know.

We cross the Columbia River, the water border between Washington and Oregon. I've only been to Portland once, and that was when Dad and Azar and I road-tripped north from Sacramento on our way to Washington. The Columbia River sprawled wider than any river I could imagine that day, the green struts of the bridge spanning on and on.

That was the day we left Mom behind.

"Thanks for taking me," I tell Jaleh when we pass the Portland sign with a white stag leaping above it. "Did you have to miss work?"

"It's no problem." She waves me off with her hand. She has three gold rings on her right hand, two of which I remember from our life before, and one of which is new. "A lot of my grant writing can be done remotely. I'm glad to be with you."

We stop to drop off our bags at the apartment Dad rented in the neighborhood north of Reed. Because my dad wanted to make a whole father-daughter road trip out of this weekend, he opted for us to stay off campus together in an Airbnb instead of signing me up to bunk with a student guide. When we unload our stuff, I sit on the edge of the bed and make myself write back to Bea.

Mitra: He scheduled something on campus for me and I didn't want to back out. Just got to PDX. It'll be okay. It's just one weekend.

I'm mad at myself for telling her these half-truths. She might understand if I told her about the tugging of *go, go, go* in my brain, about Ms. Acosta's belief in me. But I don't want to taint that image she has of our escape to UW next year. She's finally able to envision a way out, and feels confident enough in that future that she even told her parents about us dating.

After ditching our bags at the apartment in the Hawthorne neighborhood, Jaleh and I drive right onto campus. She takes a small wooded lane up to a brick and stone castle flanked by cherry trees bursting with pink blossoms.

"I don't think this is it," I tell her. "We're supposed to meet the student guide at the arts and sciences building. Eliot Hall."

Jaleh points to the engraved letters above the double front doors. "It says Eliot Hall," she tells me.

The building looks like some kind of Tudor fortress, with

stone-framed bay windows and gables peaking up from the roof. Whereas UW housed towering modern architecture and a cathedralic library, this place feels like a wooded haven straight out of the English countryside.

I want to pour a cup of tea and curl up with a Mary Oliver book in one of the seats beside the vaulted windows. This place is a fairy tale, not a backdrop for everyday language and science and lit classes. I can't believe people go to *school* here.

My student guide, Amalia, is waiting on a stone bench by the front entrance. "Welcome, Mitra!" She smiles. Amalia keeps her red hair braided in a simple line down her back, and she wears cargo pants and a green thermal shirt. Her keys jingle from a carabiner clipped to a hoop in her pants.

Very practical and utilitarian. I think I like Amalia.

My mom and I introduce ourselves and tell our guide about the apartment we rented for the weekend. "Normally I'd start you off with a tour," Amalia says. "But it's almost time for my poetry class, and I know you're scheduled to sit in, Mitra. Why don't we head to class and then do a tour after?"

My body thrums with the same critical levels of excitement that Bea probably felt when Jae invited us to the off-campus party at UW.

A *college literature* class at a nonreligious school. My brain does a little tango around my skull.

I look to Jaleh, and she gestures for me to follow Amalia. "I'll find a place to get some work done," she tells me. "Text me when you're out of class. Enjoy yourself."

When we step into the classroom, I do a double take. I expected an amphitheater-style lecture hall, with four hundred undergrads crammed in for a PowerPoint lecture from a professor hooked up to a headset mic. That's what Jae said some of the 101 classes at UW look like. Instead, the classroom is as small as the poetry seminar room at Holy Trinity, but with a rectangular table in the center, ringed by chairs.

"What is this?" I ask Amalia. "Where does the professor lecture from?"

"There aren't a lot of lectures here. Classes are pretty small, so a lot of our courses look more like this, discussion-style. We only have about fourteen hundred students." She smiles at me. "It's not so overwhelming when you end up with, like, the same eight classmates day after day."

The class size is small enough that even my extreme degree of introversion doesn't ring any alarm bells.

Another nine people join Amalia and me at the table, followed by Professor Gutierrez. Except nobody calls him that: They all greet him with *Hi, Davíd!* I almost choke on my own saliva when I hear it. If we called our teachers by their first names at Holy Trinity, we'd be handed a toilet brush and sent straight into Service Work.

The class starts by reading Maya Angelou's poem "Still I Rise," and then they jump into passionate discussion. I watch the students ping back and forth with their analysis.

"The images are incredible," a guy with straight dark hair says. He reads out a few of his favorite lines so we can savor the imagery.

A girl with a nose ring and dyed blue hair speaks up. "The tone of defiance is so great. Like, she talks about being sassy, haughty, sexy!

She's celebrating all these riches she has, that her oppressors are furious they haven't been able to strip from her."

"She describes all this abundance throughout the poem," a girl with a yellow hijab says. "Certainty, hope, laughter. Then at the end of the poem, she names them as gifts from her ancestors."

"What can we learn from Angelou and this poem? What does she have to say about resistance and resilience?" Professor Gutierrez asks. I can't even call him *Davíd* in my head.

"It seems at first like it's a statement just about the one speaker, but it ends up being a rallying cry for this wider movement," Amalia says. "Rising up from hatred and struggle and celebrating and loving yourself."

"The speaker keeps echoing that refrain, *still I rise*," a girl with box braids and glasses says. "But she's not just talking about herself rising out of the discrimination she's faced as an individual. She's speaking to a larger uprising, of all Black folks rising out of the oppression of slavery and structural racism."

I listen as they shift into talking about broader themes in writing from poets like Langston Hughes, Adrienne Rich, James Baldwin, and Nikki Giovanni. They talk about poetic tradition and aesthetic and the intersection of politics, and how poetry can be a catalyst for resilience in the face of struggle.

Half of what they talk about soars over my head, and that delights me.

"What do you think, Mitra?" Professor Gutierrez turns to me. He's been guiding and moderating the conversation today, but it feels like he's more of a collaborator than some all-knowing, untouchable professor.

My skin turns sizzling hot. "I'm not up to speed on the readings," I say. I'm very aware that these undergrads are at least two years older than me, and super intellectual, and I don't want to be caught making a fool of myself in front of them. "I don't know if I have anything good to say."

"Forget about *good*," the professor tells me. "And forget about the readings. What do you think? How do you think writing can be used as a tool for resistance?"

"Well, writing is helping me survive Catholic school," I joke.

Professor Gutierrez grins, and a few of the students laugh. But my humor doesn't deflect the question. They all sit quietly, looking at me, waiting for me to say more.

Maybe it's the freedom of total anonymity here that motivates me to speak up. After this weekend, I don't have to interact with a single person in this room again. Or maybe it's that I want to live up to Ms. Acosta's belief in me. Either way, I find myself wanting to be real with the class.

"It's the only place I can talk about what I'm going through, and it doesn't make me feel boxed in," I say. "And I feel like it connects me to the people who came before me, who struggled way more than me. Kind of like how Maya Angelou talked about her ancestors."

"How so?" he asks.

I've already spoken more than I ever planned to when I stepped into the classroom, and a part of me wants to shake my head and let the focus shift to someone else. But I'm also bolstered by Ms. Acosta's encouragement, and even Hafez, who reminded me that I was not built to be silent.

"Poetry is really important in Iran. It's how we tell stories, and how we remember our history, and even how we understand our future.

"My mom told me that my great-great-grandfather wrote poetry back in Iran. The British were occupying at the time, and mining oil that they took back to Europe for themselves. My great-great-grandfather wrote poetry in protest of imperialism and distributed it on pamphlets across town. And that was enough to get him exiled from the country for years.

"He had to leave his home to escape death threats. So I think poetry is a powerful tool. His life was at risk just because of the words on those pamphlets—they were perceived as a powerful threat. Because his poetry was a force for resistance. It's a force for change."

"Well said," Professor Gutierrez says.

At the end of class, the professor stops me to chat. "Mitra, I'm glad you could join us today. I heard about you from Carlotta."

"Who?"

"Your teacher at Holy Trinity," he says. I feel like he just dropped some secret knowledge on me by whipping out Ms. Acosta's first name. "She was a mentor of mine while she taught here. She had wonderful things to say about you."

"Thank you." My cheeks flush pink.

"She sent me your portfolio, and I'd love to have you as a student next year. I think you'd fit right in as a Reedie. You'll find our students are just as passionate and thoughtful about their education as you are." He hands me an envelope of information on Reed's English department.

"Besides," he says, "from that story you shared today, it sounds like poetry is a family legacy."

"Thanks, Professor. It was a great class." I wave goodbye and duck out of the room before I can embarrass myself by the neon glow of pride beaming out of me right now.

I think about how he said poetry is a family legacy for me. I haven't thought of it like that. It reminds me of what Cara said when we were paired up in seminar—that her prophecy doesn't exist in a vacuum; it's tangled up in the prophecies of her parents, and their parents, back throughout their history.

Maybe that's what Bea and I are creating when we write the never-ending poem: We're living out our legacies, bringing our prophecies to life. There's a reason The Book has no terminal punctuation, no end and no beginning. We're only adding the latest verses to something that our ancestors began. Just another epic love poem in the story that started long before we ever picked up our pens.

Rescue Mission

Bea: how's Portland?

Bea: more importantly: How are you??

> **Mitra:** Portland is kinda perfect
>
> **Mitra:** so many trees!!
>
> **Mitra:** so many nerds!!

Bea: you liking Reed?

> **Mitra:** I'll never get in, and we def can't afford it
>
> **Mitra:** but it's been fun to try on for the weekend
>
> **Mitra:** though no professions of love so far 😏

Bea: good to know!

Bea: you surviving the unanticipated mother-daughter road trip?

> **Mitra:** six hours with Mom so far and still holding it together

Bea: need me and Gary to get in gear for a rescue mission?

> **Mitra:** things are actually feeling okay with my mom
>
> **Mitra:** I don't know what it is, something's different here
>
> **Mitra:** or maybe we're different?

Bea: I'm glad, beautiful

Bea: I'll tell Gary to abort rescue mission

Bea: and just think: When you come back, it'll be UW acceptance day!!

Bea: we can start burning our tartan and buying all things purple!!

Bedtime Story

"THIS IS THE Canyon," Amalia says as she guides me and Jaleh on a tour of campus. "It's a natural preserve. To the east, you'll find Reed Lake and the Centennial Orchard, and to the west, the Fish Ladder."

Inside the Canyon, we spot weeping willows and Crystal Springs Creek and a little cluster of American goldfinches. And on the Great Lawn, I spot more queer-presenting nerds than I ever have in my life. Students playing banjos, wearing flannel and nose rings, with undercuts and home-dyed hair, reading *Stone Butch Blues* and *Fun Home* in the grass. Maybe *everyone* is queer here.

We eat dinner at Commons with Amalia's friends, and then she takes us to the Paradox for a poetry slam. The performances knock the wind out of me, each line spinning the seeds of new poems in my mind. One of the poets spouts sassy and rhythmic verse, peppering her performance with more than enough curse words to make Jaleh go wide-eyed. My mom still gives a hearty round of applause when she finishes.

"Any last-minute sign-ups out there?" The host, in their rumpled blazer and bun of dark coiled hair, scans the room for any takers. "Someone want to give an off-the-cuff performance tonight?" Their gaze lands on me. "I'm looking at you, Junior Mint. You look like you've got something to say! And we're a forgiving crowd, aren't we?" The audience claps and hoots in response.

I wave back and forth like I'm trying to divert a landing airplane.

To her credit, Jaleh doesn't say a word, and the host moves on to another member of the audience.

Still, I picture myself standing up there at the mic next year. Maybe I'll be panicking inside with my hands stuffed in my pockets, but I could be brave in front of a small and supportive audience like this.

After the poetry slam, Mom and I return to the Airbnb, which is a mother-in-law-style apartment attached to a home. Big windows fill the studio with green from the Douglas firs outside. There are two full beds with a bedside table in between them, a mini fridge and a bathroom and a TV, and not much else.

It's a cozy room, and I'm exhausted from the day. My mind has been on hyperdrive here, imagining a future immersed in fellow nerds who teach me about the Canyon wildlife and read in silence with me on the Great Lawn. Maybe they'll teach me banjo, and I'll write nature poems under a willow tree by the creek.

I can see myself becoming braver here. I'd learn to be a better writer, and I'd learn exactly how much I *don't* know, which thrills me. But it's more than that. This place would give me the space and peace and motivation to become the fullest version of me.

But that's not the future I mapped out with Bea. And UW has so much to offer too—it's buzzing with constant motion, boisterous and active and big. It's beautiful in all the ways Bea is beautiful. I want to be with her, and she'd be happy there. She'd suffocate in a place this small and quiet. Bea didn't even apply to Reed—when we first looked at colleges together online, she immediately skipped past it when she saw the student enrollment. "It's almost as small as Holy Trinity," she'd said. "I can't do another stifling little school where everybody's in each other's business."

I don't know why I keep downplaying Reed to Bea. Reed is something I can't have, and that should be enough to turn off my runaway thoughts. Still, that little part of me that chanted *go, go, go* pokes at the edges of my consciousness as I try to sleep.

My mom slips under the white sheets of her bed and pulls out a book and reading glasses. I didn't know she wore glasses now. The dim lamplight from the bedside table draws shadows in the wrinkled corners of her eyes, igniting all the silver strands in her curls. She looks older. And she also looks just the same as she did when she tucked me into bed as a kid.

She points the cover of her book toward me: *Americanized* by Sara Saedi. "Want me to read some to you?"

My mom used to read to me before bed all the time. It was almost never kids' books—we read biographies and novels, essays and scientific nonfiction. *It will expand your mind,* she used to tell me.

The memories tumble over me in an avalanche. The low whisper of her voice as Azar and I tunneled into our blankets. Her cup of chai steaming warm on the table beside my bed. The dance of her fingertips over my eyebrows and down my nose, trying to coax me to close my eyes. She wouldn't leave my side until I fell asleep.

It was my favorite part of the day because it was a time she dedicated only to us. No work, no chores, no Dad. Only Mom's steady voice as she painted worlds for us in the shadows of our bedroom. When she read *The Lacuna* out loud, the vivid colors of a Mexico City kitchen burst to life around me. I felt my hands sink into cold plaster at Frida Kahlo's home. We baked sweet breads and slipped into warm water lagoons together. She invited us, night after night, into these enchanted lands with her.

I swallow down the surge of images and burrow deeper into bed, turning my head away from my mom.

She's inviting me back. I can step into those worlds again with her if I want to. And step back into her life.

"Just a couple pages?" I say.

I pull the sheets over my eyes. In the dark, her voice sounds the same as it did when I was little. And just like before, I fall asleep to the lull of her words.

Wanting

Wanting is trouble. It pries open
my ribs, peeks inside, sees what
I'm lacking. Then it dazzles me
with movie reels: a perfect sparkly
image of what could be. Wanting
is a hungry beggar. It craves too
many things: a mother, a forever
love, a future. I learned long ago
that wanting was the problem. But
maybe wanting is the compass
propelling me forward, the map
and the muscle and motor, toward
a future as wide as my desires.

Imagine

IN THE MORNING, we visit the Canyon again with coffees and breakfast burritos from the dining hall. I watch salmon fling themselves up the Fish Ladder, working against the current of the creek to return to their birthplace and lay their eggs. We walk all the way along the creek to Reed Lake, finding a spot to sit near a pedestrian bridge by the water. Canada geese squawk and peck and fluff their feathers in the lake. A trickle of students passes by on the trails while we eat our breakfast.

My mom watches as I eye all the passing students. "You know," she says, "I had a wonderful time at UC Berkeley. But I would have enjoyed something as intimate and green as this."

"What was it like?" I ask her. "College."

She sips from her to-go cup. "It was a hundred new experiences every day. It's a once-in-a-lifetime feeling. I tried every new opportunity I could."

"Like what?"

"I joined the foreign student association. I took a pottery class. I even tried aerial acrobatics."

"Seriously?"

"Not for long." She laughs. "I fell a lot." We watch a goose dive in for an awkward landing on the water, its wings wagging every which way. "It's not the same as what you do, I know," she says, "but I also dabbled in poetry."

"What kind of stuff did you write?"

"Wild things," she chuckles. "I was all over the place. Some political writing about home. I made a chapbook, even. Tin House published it. It was a very small distribution, but I was proud. I held a reading on campus when it released."

I can't believe my mom is a published poet. Last time she brought up her writing at the Botanical Gardens, I was too angry with her to really listen. This time, I'm curious about the life she lived before she was my mother.

"Do you still have a copy of the chapbook?"

"I'm sure I do," she says.

"Can I read it sometime?"

Jaleh's cheeks lift with her smile. "Of course."

I pick at the last scrap of tortilla from my breakfast burrito and toss specks of it toward the geese. "I bet Reed would be a great place to host a poetry reading." I curb the thought. That's as far as I can go in allowing myself to picture a future here. A life away from Bea is a life I don't want to imagine, even if it would make me happy.

Mom watches the birds waddle closer for their tortilla treats. "I know you prefer not to hear advice from me . . . but I can tell that you see yourself here," she says. "It's okay to want this, Mitra. I want you to follow your imagination, your passion." Her voice is generous with permission. "Do what feels right to you."

Water glazes my eyes before I can even register an emotion. The muscles in my throat bolt tight.

They're simple words. But those words make Jaleh sound just like the mom I remember from before her addiction, when she wanted everything good in the world for me.

At our Nowruz dinner, Mom had said she wanted to show me she was sorry through her actions. And here she is, showing me again and again.

I dig my hands into my sweatshirt sleeves while she looks out at the lake. "Thanks, but we can't afford it," I say. "And even if it wasn't too expensive, I'm probably not going to get in. They only accept like a third of applicants."

I focus on breathing, watching a turtle on the water. It stretches its scaly limbs outward from its shell, soaking in the sun on a fallen log. When its head extends from the safety of its shell, it blinks back at me, looking surprised. Its tiny turtle mouth stretches wide.

"Good things can happen, you know," Mom says, resting her hand over mine. "Maybe this good thing will even happen to you."

Good Things That Can Become True

We can drive the long way home from Reed—take 101 up the coast.
Stop at Seaside for saltwater taffy, detour to Tillamook lighthouse.
We'll listen to the gulls chattering loud and joyful.
We'll listen to each other's stories again.
We'll come back on a trip someday—
Just the two of us.
I promise.

Dear Heavenly Angels

"HOW DARE YOU." Bea smirks at me when I step through the chapel doors on Monday at lunch, distracted by the email app on my phone. "No phones in church." She snatches it out of my hand.

"Mature," I laugh at her.

"You know what Father Mitchell would say." She slips my phone in her pocket. "You don't need iMessage to talk to God."

I sink straight into Bea's arms, wrapping myself up in her. It was a long, exciting, confusing weekend, and the aftershocks of all that change still rumble through me. And being gone the whole weekend made me wonder what happened at the *Les Mis* rehearsals, and whether Cara coaxed Bea into any more "cast bonding" parties.

"Missed you," I tell her.

"Excuse me?" she mumbles into my ear. "While you were off gallivanting in Portland, I was coerced into making Easter Sunday dinner with my parents. I think they've finally detected that I'm pissed at them for how they've been acting since I told them we're dating. My mom and I made empanadas in complete silence. It took *hours*. God, I missed you."

"I'm sorry, Bea."

"On the plus side, I think they're realizing that their whole hands-off school of parenting has epically backfired. The empanadas were just a first installment of them trying to 'get involved.' They said they're getting tickets to see me in *Les Mis*."

"That's something," I say.

"I know. Their first appearance at a Holy Trinity function, outside of those *your child is a problem* parent-teacher conferences. It's, like, a marquee event."

"See?" I say. "Easter miracles do happen." I'm teasing her, but I know how much it means to Bea that her parents are taking an interest in her life, even if she won't say it out loud.

I pull away from her arms, sneaking my phone out of her pocket in the process.

"Hey!"

"I have to know," I tell her. "Don't you want to be put out of our misery?"

Today is UW acceptance day. I've been refreshing my email since six a.m. to hunt for my admission letter. I won't find out about Reed until they send me a snail-mail letter, because they're as old-school as Ms. Acosta.

"I'm not ready." Bea blinks at me. "I want one more normal chapel lunch with you before everything changes. Just . . . tell me about your weekend first, and then we can check our emails together?"

I hand over the phone and pull her up toward the first pew. "Okay."

Bea stretches out down the pew, molding her sweater into a pillow in the center of the row. I join her, stealing part of her makeshift pillow and sprawling out across the other half of the bench.

"A whole weekend. Alone. With your mom." She hands me a plastic-wrapped leftover empanada and I trade her a bag of Red Hot Blues chips.

"It was kind of . . . nice," I say. "And also awkward and scary and weird. But things felt more like old times with her. It reminded me of how she was before."

The crown of Bea's head nuzzles into mine. "What about Reed?"

I bite into the empanada to stall. "It was small," I say. "The nature preserve was cool. And we went to a poetry slam on campus."

"Yeah?" she says through crunches of chips.

"This empanada is amazing," I say, deflecting. "I can hardly taste the hostility."

"Trust, me, it's there," she sighs. "Subtle flavoring."

I scoot up the bench just enough so that I can kiss her forehead. It's such a simple gesture. But after so long spent suppressing my feelings for Bea, I don't take even one forehead kiss for granted. Each touch lights wonder in me.

"How was play practice?"

"Kind of bittersweet. It was our last weekend rehearsal. Ellie baked us all dinner rolls in honor of Jean Valjean's stolen loaf of bread." Bea wiggles closer so that we're face-to-face, upside down. "Dress rehearsal is on Friday. We're allowed to invite people to attend."

"Does that mean me?"

"Absolutely."

"Can I throw roses at you from the audience? And puffy-paint a shirt that says *My girlfriend is a star*?" It's a joke, but she knows other questions simmer right beneath the surface. *Can I be your girlfriend in public? Can we be open in a place like this?*

A smile hints at her lips. "We have less than sixty days left in this convent. And our admission letters land today. What can anyone do to us now?" She kisses my nose. "Go for it."

I want to stay in this moment forever, in the space between her lips and my skin. In the second before our future hits, when everything feels wild and possible.

A solitary bell clangs from somewhere high above us, vibrating the benches. Twelve thirty. "All right." Bea licks the red chip dust from her fingers and fishes our phones out of her blazer pocket. "Let's do this."

We sit up and knot our fingers together on the pew, our free hands refreshing our emails. I swept through my inbox last night so that for the first time in the history of my account, I have zero unread messages.

Nothing yet.

Some tiny part of me wishes the admissions officers would play God and make this decision for me. I'd get into UW, but not Reed, and then I could be certain of the plans Bea and I laid out. Or the opposite—and then I'd be forced to follow that voice in Portland that kept goading me, saying *This is a place you could be yourself.* The admissions gods could release me from the push and pull between choosing myself or my future with Bea. Since returning from Portland, my stomach has been churning around the impossibility of the decision. I have no idea what I want. Except this: "I want to spend next year with you," I say. And the next, and the next.

"God owes us," Bea says. "She'll make it happen."

"Should we pray or something?"

Bea stares at me, and she looks ready to punch me in the arm, but instead she drops my hand and flops down the kneeler. She clasps her palms in front of her and shuts her eyes.

"Dear heavenly angels," she booms. "Please take pity on us. We're queer. We don't belong here. Please, do us a solid and send us to college. If you do, we promise to never haunt your chapel again."

"Heavenly angels?" I ask.

She flashes an eye open at me. "It's kind of rude to pray to God only when you need something."

Bea slumps back from the kneeler and reloads her email app for the zillionth time. "Mitra!" Her shriek rips through the empty church. She leaps up onto my lap and points the screen toward me. She hasn't even opened the email yet, but the subject line reads *Congratulations!*

I curl my arms around her waist and press my nose to her temple. "You did it!"

"Those angels pulled through!" She yelps.

"This was all you," I tell her. "You worked *so* hard in school. This is your dream. You deserve this."

She leans back to look for my phone. "Anything?"

I reload again. "Not yet." I swallow. Adrenaline rushes through me. Maybe the admissions gods overheard my thoughts, and now they're toying with me. Holding these two futures out of reach, waiting to see which one I fight for the hardest. My heartbeat vibrates in my ears.

"When was your email sent?" I ask.

"Two minutes ago. Must've been mid-prayer." We sit there staring at the screen of my phone, tapping the reload icon again and again like lab monkeys waiting for a reward. A pebble of doubt tumbles down into my stomach. It rattles louder and louder with my worry.

What if she got in and I didn't? What if I wanted a life with Bea too much, and the universe decided to yank it out from under me? Do people get punished for hoping too loudly?

I click off the screen and slip the phone back into Bea's blazer pocket. Heat floods my face.

"No," she says, always sure. "Give it some more time." She hands the phone to me to unlock and then takes over the task of refreshing my email while still perched on my lap. I watch her stubborn fingers on the screen from over her shoulder.

Inside, I add my own part to Bea's prayer. To anyone who's listening: I've changed my mind. I want to make this decision myself. Please, please let me get into UW. Please don't take away the future we've promised each other. Let me choose Bea.

Prayer Works

Inbox (0)

[refresh]

Inbox (0)

[refresh]

Inbox (0)

[refresh]

Inbox (1 unread message)

From: UW Admissions

Subject: Congratulations!

Dear Mitra,

CONGRATULATIONS! I am pleased to invite you to join the University of Washington's Class of 2028.

This acceptance is in recognition of your hard work, academic excellence, and other achievements. As a future Husky, you will be able to share your talents with a diverse group of outstanding students from all around Washington State, the country, and the globe. Your UW community eagerly anticipates welcoming you onto our Seattle campus for your first quarter of undergraduate studies in Autumn, 2024.

This emailed offer of admission is just a first step. Soon, you will receive a mailed envelope of important messages and directions to enroll in your first quarter at UW. To secure your spot as part of the Freshman Class at UW, you must accept this offer of admission by May 1, 2024.

Now is your moment to celebrate! Share the good news of your acceptance to UW with those who have supported you—family, teachers, and friends alike.

With heartfelt congratulations from all of us at the University of Washington,

Adina Williams
Director of Admissions

Mitra

love to see you beaming
dimple-happy in the
fullness of our future:

you've been certain
while I've spiraled in
unknowns, my worry

a renegade kite while
you've been the stone,
steady me with brilliant

conviction hardened in
your bones—maybe you
dreamed these words

before I ever wrote them:
that's belief, Bea, and
you stir a courage as tough

and elemental inside me
like carbon, like oxygen,
this gift of your love

Bea

Love like ours lassos the gleaming moon
so we can dip our fingers in its liquid glow
coat our skin 'til everything we touch laughs

speckled by moon-print swirls: it's in our DNA
to fling dreams in the dark no hope for soft
landings, we mark our stories on the world

recklessly but sometimes they snag a divine
ear, sometimes our bold visions strike music
compelling even static stained glass angels

to dance, we remember those saints as miracle-
makers but the real miracle is the faith we
ignite in each other, devotion to a story

still unfolding—let's litter the pages in our
moon-glitter fingerprints, a future we bless
with reckless love and belief in one another

Pre-Show

Bea: text when you get here!

                                Mitra: just walking in. You're gonna do AMAZING!!

Bea: YOU TRYING TO INFECT ME WITH ALL CAPS WHEN IM ALREADY HYPED FOR THE PLAY

                                Mitra: I KNOW!! THAT'S HOW MUCH I BELIEVE IN YOU. YOU'RE GONNA KILL IT TONIGHT

Bea: THANKS LOVE!

                                Mitra: IT'S THE TRUTH!!

Bea: GLAD YOU CAME!

                                Mitra: WOULDN'T MISS IT FOR THE WORLD

Bea: OK I COULD GO ON ALL NIGHT LIKE THIS BUT DIRECTOR'S CALLING HUDDLE!

                                Mitra: GO BE AMAZING

A Heart Full of Love

THE REST OF the week floated by on a cloud of Bea's excitement. All of the *what-ifs* we'd been harboring for the past four and a half years got scraped of hesitation. Now everything is *will be*.

Walking back onto Holy Trinity's campus on a Friday night feels counterintuitive, especially out of uniform. It transplants me back to the night of Winter Formal when Bea and I wore our best queer formal getups, ready to demolish expectations. But this time I'm alone, so I go low profile with a navy button-up shirt and gray jeans, a bundle of sorbet-colored dahlias in my fist.

Turnout tonight is solid for a dress rehearsal: Kids from every grade linger outside the auditorium, along with a handful of teachers and staff. A few die-hard parent volunteers have set up tables to sell tickets for opening night, including Cara's mom, but most parents won't attend until the finished production starts. Bea's parents, still riding a wave of wanting to look like they're trying at parenthood, already bought their tickets for the official performance. She wouldn't say it aloud, but I could tell how much it meant to Bea that they committed to showing up.

I shoulder my way through the crowd and take the crew entrance stairs up toward where Max is seated. They texted earlier telling me to meet them and Ellie in the sound and light ops booth before the show. Aside from the thin silver cross at their neck, they're decked head-to-toe in black: crisp jeans, collared shirt, and lace-up boots. The monochrome is required for stage crew, but they also just look like they're wearing one of their favorite weekend looks. I join Max in the booth and smoosh my face sideways into theirs, like a cheekbone hug. Up close, I can appreciate Max's flawless mascara job.

"You look dashing," I say.

They sweep the dirty blond hair from their eyes and grin. "Thanks. Stage crew attire usually goes unappreciated, but, you know. We run the show. I like to look the part."

"Plus, Jessica's here," I say.

Max gets flushed. "We're going out for dessert after."

"I want all the details later tonight. So how's the show shaping up?"

"Fine?" They hesitate. "Young Cosette has a cold, and Jack tried to punch Spencer yesterday. But I'm sure it'll all come together."

I pat their shoulder. "Godspeed."

Ellie busts into the ops booth with wild eyes. "That track lighting can burn in hell!" she hollers.

"Hi, Ellie."

Her hands curl into fists and she plops down at the light switchboard. "Hi, Mitra." Max guides her in a deep breath. When she's done fuming, she turns to me. "Bea reserved you a seat up front. Look for her yellow jacket. It's five minutes 'til curtain."

"I should let you two get to it, huh?" I back away toward the door. Tech crew is surprisingly hardcore about booth boundaries, and I don't want to jinx my welcome. The first time Max invited me up here, I felt like I'd been indoctrinated into some blood-binding cult.

As I leave, Ellie drums her hands on the light switchboard. She brings the houselights all the way up, and then flickers them on and off like lightning. Fifth graders in the audience squeal at the effect and everyone murmurs, rushing to their places. Through the bustling auditorium, I spot Ms. Acosta's unmistakable cloud of white hair in the back row.

Bea's vintage varsity jacket jumps out at me as I step down the aisle. She's saved me a seat right up at the front, so I'll have a fantastic view of all the crying and dying and misery. The lights dim and I slouch into my seat, letting my eyes adjust to the shipyard backdrop onstage. The orchestra's string section plays the opening notes of the overture and I drape Bea's jacket over my knees. We found it at a thrift store junior year, and it has the name Royal monogrammed on the back in fat cursive letters. She insists it imbues her with queenly energy.

Sitting here holding my breath as the stage lights rise, I'm a ball of pure excitement for my girlfriend. All my nerves about Bea and Cara's stage time finally start to soften. Azar was right: Bea got to have her hobby, and I found mine, and now I can revel in Bea's performance without getting jealous. I feel very grown up and proud of myself, like I'm finally reaching the queer utopia where everyone is friends with their exes and there's zero weirdness or envy.

And if I do get a little jealous, the play ends in a week, and all that extra time with Cara will be over, anyway.

In the beginning of the play, Young Cosette and Young Éponine are played by two fifth-grade girls. Mini Éponine looks a lot like Bea did when we first met: round tan face spattered with freckles, with costume glasses and a puff of short brown hair. It's hard not to hear little Bea's voice when the girl speaks.

Midway through the play, Bea takes the stage as grown-up Éponine in a tattered corset dress and dirt-smudged makeup. Stage lights ignite her eyes and shimmer over her skin. She joins Spencer at the edge of a painted river backdrop.

"So I have met you at last!" When she speaks her opening lines, her voice cuts clear through the whole auditorium.

Her devotion to Marius rings in every word. It's like she's been practicing for this her entire life. Bea *is* a queen.

Cara and Ben, who plays Jean Valjean, join her onstage. I know Cara's a brilliant actor—and she shines as Cosette the way she shines in everything. But it's hard for me to train my focus on her. Bea magnetizes my attention every time she appears onstage. "Cosette!" She turns to the audience in thought, reflecting on all she's endured since the last time she and young Cosette were together. She wears the hardship and longing for a different life in each gesture and expression.

Even when Cosette sings "A Heart Full of Love" with Marius, it's Bea's counterpoint vocals that arrest my focus. I don't know how anyone in the audience can take their eyes off her.

As the characters prepare for revolution, they sing "One Day More," and Bea funnels all of Éponine's emotions into a current straight to my heart. She rises from the ground and cries out *What a life I might have known*—and all the love, longing, and regret of Éponine blast through me. The moment clouds my eyes with tears.

I used to long for Bea that way. I felt so isolated by my love for her. But here I am now, watching this radiant girl who loves me back, whose love soothes all the lonely days that came before. It's a happy ending Éponine never got, and one I'm still trying to prove to myself that I deserve, that I can trust.

If Éponine's longing got me misty, her death scene in Marius's arms under the rattle of stage rain has me bawling. I try to get it together as the play ends and the curtain falls, wiping my tears on the sleeve of Bea's jacket. The cast members all bound back onstage as the audience rises to their feet in applause.

Joy beams from her like a beacon. She takes her costars' hands and bows, and when their hands release at the end of the ovation, she hops right off the edge of the stage to greet me.

"Are those tears?" Bea touches my cheek.

"No." I sniffle.

"Did I give you *feelings*?"

I hand her the cluster of dahlias. "Maybe? Okay, yes. Don't make a big deal out of it."

"I made you *cry*!" she sings.

"I'm not the only one! Mr. Frederich was full-body sobbing behind me. And—you were totally radiant," I say. "I had no idea you could do that."

Bea grins into her bouquet. "Acting hopelessly straight for Spencer for two full hours? Neither did I." We both laugh.

"It means a lot to me that you came," she says, glancing down at my button-up shirt. "Um, I was promised a puffy-paint public acknowlededgment of your love for me."

I bring my hand to the waist of her torn-up costume. My heartbeat booms through me like the thunder of students leaving their auditorium seats. "Can I kiss you instead?" I ask her.

Bea answers by wrapping her arms around my neck, flower bouquet and all. Her face is dewy from the lights and marked with stage-makeup dirt and lipstick. I touch my nose to hers, a gentle hello.

I know people are watching—students and teachers and staff. We don't have the cover of darkness that bolstered me with bravery on the night of Winter Formal. It's bright stage lights and full view now. Maybe we'll get in trouble. Maybe we'll get hassled at school on Monday.

But I kiss her anyway, and the crowd falls away. It's just Bea and me reclaiming our place here, and soaring on the celebration of it, like we've burst confetti poppers inside of us. I forget everything else when her lips find mine. For the first time at Holy Trinity, I feel untouchable.

HolyHorror Group Chat

Mitra: congrats everyone!! You all were amazing!

Max: we did it!

Cara: thanks, I don't know, I feel like I was flat on In My Life

Cara: I'll keep working on it

Ellie: girl don't be so hard on yourself! You were flawless

Bea: did anyone else hear Young Cosette fart in the middle of Castle on a Cloud

Cara: hear or smell? Because . . . yes

Ellie: not the type of *cloud* we were expecting

Max: ewwww stop

Mitra: all of that will be forgotten on opening night

Mitra: you're gonna knock their socks off!

Bea: aww thank you Mitra!

Max: Spencer and Jack didn't pummel each other during intermission

Max: so all in all I'd call that a win

Bea: Cara, did you see your mom up in the front?

Cara: EVERYONE saw her

Cara: she was standing up the whole time snapping pics

Ellie: you know I love Mrs. Liu but you better remind her there is NO flash photography once we open!

Ellie: I'm not above kicking her out!

Mitra: guys she was being precious, leave her alone

Mitra: I could hear her singing along with you to In My Life

Bea: I think our cast bonding party paid off BTW

Max: nothing like facing down Godzilla and Darth Vader side by side to get the team working together

Bea: how are we gonna celebrate after the play is over?

Ellie: will there be a Cast Party Round Two?

Cara: on it!

Everything

BEA CLUTCHES HER dahlias all the way home. I drive Gary so she can sprawl across the reclined passenger seat with her feet up on the dashboard.

"I knew you were something else," I tell Bea when we pull up to her parents' empty drive. "But I didn't see that coming. I'm so proud of you. And proud to be with you."

She turns against her seat to look at me, her hand tucked under her face. "I don't know the last time someone told me they were proud of me."

"Yeah?"

"My parents haven't been proud of me since I was, like, seven years old. Back when I still took piano lessons and went to Sunday school."

When Bea talks about her parents, she almost always adds a punch line. Laughing about their absence is easier for her than the alternative. This time, she lets her words hang humorless in the space between us.

At home, I know Bea feels somehow disconnected and stifled at the same time. I didn't know she never felt worthy. I can't imagine what that's like. My dad finds new reasons to be proud of me every day. Even my mom has made it clear that she's proud of who I've become, and we've only been in contact again for the past couple months.

I reach across the emergency brake and wriggle my hand into hers. "Hey. Everything you do makes me proud."

"I like hearing that." She pauses with her hand tight around mine. "Turns out they can't come to the play."

"What?" My stomach plummets. "But they got their tickets already. And . . . they promised you."

"My mom got roped into speaking at some corporate retreat in Santa Fe, or San Antonio, or . . . I don't know. And my dad's tagging along."

The post-performance low seems to have stripped away her usual stoicism. She closes her eyes when she speaks again. "I wanted them to be there. Just this one time."

I wish I could change this for her. Make her see that she deserves every ounce of love and care that she isn't getting from them. Bea's parents have no idea how amazing their daughter is, or how much they've missed out on.

I curl my hand around the back of her neck, brushing my fingers through her soft hair. "I'm sorry." It's not enough, but I say it anyway. "I'll be there, okay? Cheering you on. I promise."

Bea squints at me. "Thanks, Mitra." She kisses my palm.

When we leave the car, we step into her dark house and head straight up to her room. Bea springs onto the bed and waves me over to her. I lie beside her and she burrows her body into mine, tangling our legs together. She takes off her glasses, and underneath her freckles are just starting to darken from spring sun.

"Don't go home tonight," she says. "Please?"

There's an edge to her voice, like a craving, like she can't hold me tight enough.

I catch her mouth with mine, running my tongue across her

bottom lip until she hums in response. She tips deeper into the kiss with me, into my arms, and I let myself be swallowed in her soft sheets and skin and smell. When I taste the skin at her neck, she's salty and smooth and a little bit floral.

There are so many things I want to experience with Bea. I've loved savoring the before-sex energy with her, basking in all those butterflies together. But imagining what's ahead of us makes me realize something: "I want everything with you."

Bea kisses the soft spot below my ear. "Yeah?"

Her fingers work to undo the buttons from my collar downward. All the invisible nerve endings in my skin flicker awake when I shed my shirt.

I reach up for her earrings, unhooking the warm metal clasps one by one. She laughs when I lift up the hem of her cotton shirtdress, tickling her knees. When I pull the dress over her head, she tackles me back into her sheets. I trap her cross necklace in my hand and guide her in for another kiss.

She moves down to unfasten the button of my jeans, and I let myself lie completely still beneath her. "I might not know what I'm doing," I say.

"Like I do?" She chuckles as she tugs off my pants.

Without my jeans, I revel in that extra sense again: our skin creating its own combined magic. When she slides her leg in between mine, it feels like we were made to fit together.

I press my lips to her forehead, then look at her. "What do you want?" I breathe. "What would you like?"

She answers by unclasping her patterned bra and slipping off her underwear, and I follow suit.

I will never get used to the sight of her. Something in my brain whirs back to the very first words we wrote in our never-ending poem, the beginning of everything: *you're the thunderclap and the flash of bright light.* Bea has lightning humming inside her.

"I haven't done this before," I tell her.

"I know."

"But I want this with you. I'm ready."

She won't stop smiling at me. "Me too. And—I haven't either."

"Seriously?"

Bea brushes the hair from my eyelashes. "You think I would've had the kind of self-restraint necessary to keep something like that from you?" She laughs. "Trust me, you would've heard about it."

So we'll be figuring this out together. I kiss Bea's lips, brush my nose along her jaw, discovering each part of her bit by bit. She pulls me on top of her and my hair spills over her collarbone. Then she takes my face in her hands, leading me into a kiss that lights our way forward.

Us

Me: ready for everything
I've never done, toes at the
brink of a bridge I can't even
see the span of, but your
hand links in mine and

You: touch and taste and
breathe and laugh, all
senses alight in the path
you travel over me and

You: prayer burst alive
under my fingers, poem
forming from your freckles,
words rise from your skin
and land into my mouth
ready to be spoken and

I: used to sleep beside you
with fists balled and eyes wide
terrified, blocking out
the promise of falling deep
but now I swim in surrender

And us: basking in every
gift we discovered, heartbeats bubbling over the
brim of our joy like magic
too wild to be bottled
inside us

The Morning After

Mitra: so guess what

Bea: what??

Mitra: my girlfriend and I had sex!!

Bea: hot damn!

Mitra: first time

Bea: and how was it?

Mitra: . . .

Bea: . . . ??

Mitra: AMAZING

Mitra: just wanted to gush to my best friend about it

Bea: TELL ME EVERYTHING!!

Picture Perfect

IN THE MORNING, I wake up to Bea's hand twitching on my stomach while she sleeps, and my phone chiming three times in succession:

> **Jaleh:** Hi Mitra joon!
>
> **Jaleh:** Azar is planning to come over in
> a couple hours to spend the weekend. I
> thought I'd ask if you'd like to come with her
> this time?
>
> **Jaleh:** Your choice. Love you. Mom

I bring my thumbnail between my teeth, staring down at my mom's words. *Your choice.* One worried bumblebee buzzes around my lungs.

I might get scared, and I could get hurt. I could regret saying yes. The easiest thing would be to stay home with Dad. I could do that. And I could miss my chance to see Mom showing me, again and again, that I can trust her now.

Bea drops me off outside the Crossroads house an hour later. I'm sure Azar will sense the glow about me, but she must be so thrown off by my willingness to join her at Mom's for the weekend that she misses my *I HAD SEX!* vibes.

Azar and I walk to Mom's apartment together. I bring a backpack with a change of clothes and my toothbrush and an old collection of Naomi Shihab Nye poems as my security blanket. When we slip out of our shoes and pass the hamsa into her home, we find Mom wearing sweatpants and no makeup. Her curls are tied back with a folded green bandanna. Every time I've seen her in the past few months it's felt like a high-pressure Official Occasion, but today she looks just like herself, and that comforts me. A few dishes line the sink and there's a hot waffle iron on the stovetop. On the couch, she's propped a book open on a blanket and pillow.

"Girls!" Mom pulls us into a double hug. Azar and I have four cheeks between us, and she kisses them all. We grab plates and meet her at the stove. "What do you want to do today?"

"I have some photo editing and design stuff I want to do," Azar says, flopping a waffle onto her plate. "Wanna do an arts and crafts slash *Making a Murderer* marathon again?"

"I don't think Mitra likes these crime shows as much as you do, Aziz," Mom says.

That's one thing that hasn't changed about me in the past five years. I'm surprised Mom remembers.

We finish dishing up and take the toppings—whipped cream, syrup, strawberries—to the bar counter to eat.

"We could do that new miniseries on archaeology," Azar says. She's really throwing me a bone if she's suggesting a science documentary.

"Also, I need a couple more subjects for the series I'm working on." Azar looks at Mom and me pointedly as she stabs a strawberry. When we don't say anything, she sighs. "I'm talking about you two. You're the subjects."

"I don't know." I cut a square out of my waffle.

"What's the project?" Mom asks.

"It's kind of a math-inspired thing." When I raise my eyebrows, Azar smirks at me. "I know. But I was looking at these geometric tiles on some of Dad's old picture frames from Iran, and it got me thinking that it would be cool to do some tessellation designs. Like, doing a family photo series with stuff inspired by ancient Iranian tile patterns."

"I think that sounds inventive," Mom says. "Count me in."

The last time I had my photo taken in Azar's presence was before Winter Formal, and she mimed a robot dance behind Dad just to mock me. Not a great look. But after last night, I think I'd say yes to everyone and anything right now.

"You get three minutes of photographing," I tell her. "And I get to see your art in progress this time."

That makes her grin around her waffle bite. "Deal."

We finish devouring our breakfast, and then Azar queues up the TV with an episode about digging for Ice Age mammoth fossils. She pulls out her tablet to do some digital drawing over a profile shot she took of Gigi. I take a seat on the small sofa next to Mom, who has pulled out a plastic tub of beads and wire.

"Want to make jewelry with me while we watch?" Mom offers. "I learned a few basic skills in treatment. Maybe you could make something for Bea?"

I sift my hand over the little compartments of beads. There are plenty of colors Bea would like. "Sure."

"Have you heard anything from Reed yet?" Mom asks when Azar is in the bathroom.

"Nothing yet."

I haven't told anyone about my desperate prayers to the admissions gods when Bea and I were waiting on our UW acceptance emails. I've been handed the thing I wanted—a new world to explore with Bea, and four years to revel in it—but still, my mind draws up flashes of me in the shelter of trees outside Eliot Hall, or leaning on my elbows deep in discussion with the Poetics of Resistance and Resilience class. That pebble of doubt keeps rattling around my stomach.

At this point, I just want the universe to force the choice for me. Give me an uncomplicated future at UW, like Bea and I had planned.

My mom saw the sparks of excitement in me when we visited Reed. "Something will come soon, I hope," she says, patting my knee. "That reminds me. I dug this up for you after we got home from Portland."

She lifts the open book from the sofa cushions and hands it to me. It's thin and the purple cover peels back at the corner, chipping a bit of the title: *Saffron Dreams* by Jaleh Vakhshoori.

I skim my fingers over the crackled cover. There are so many things my mom and I don't know about each other. Sometimes it feels like too many unknowns to recover from. But I'm holding a book built on her vision—everything inside filtered through her eyes, her mind, her hands.

"Thanks, Mom." I set the book beside my old Naomi Shihab Nye collection, vowing to read it later tonight.

In the evening, we walk to the shopping center across the highway to get Ezell's fried chicken to go, and we take it to a bench in Highland Park. It's a bright April day and the wildflowers at the edge of the park are starting to bloom. As we munch on chicken tenders, kernel corn, and dinner rolls, we watch a group of elementary school girls playing a pickup game of softball in the field.

"Okay." When we finish, Azar wipes her greasy fingers on a napkin and pulls out her phone. "This is good lighting." She beckons us to the wooden boardwalk over the marshy trench of the creek. "Mom first."

I stand back with Azar and watch her give directions. "Look at me. Okay, now look out into the distance. But serve some attitude while you're at it. Great. You're doing great. Now I want you to look at me as if you're contemplating the meaning of life." Mom obliges all of Azar's requests. When Azar looks down to swipe through her shots, my mom crosses her eyes at me.

So many demands, she mouths. But I think she likes being bossed around by my sister.

"Now the two of you together." Azar points at me.

Jaleh watches me. "Let your sister decide," she says quietly to Azar. "Maybe she wants to do the picture alone."

The framed photo of the three of us in Mom's apartment flickers through my mind—us with sticky smiles on our hot Sacramento porch, giddy from watermelon. I was only six or seven at the time.

It's a nice memory, but that isn't us anymore.

I join my mom at her spot on the boardwalk alongside the creek. She loops her arm around my shoulders. For the thirty seconds that Azar spends taking pictures, I let myself relax into my mom's side.

When Azar is satisfied with her six billion photos, I pull her toward the playground. It's nearly sunset now and the park has cleared out. Azar does a few cartwheels in the damp grass before dragging me to the twisty slide.

"Come on!" She goads me all the way up the ladder. "*One time* down the spiral slide isn't going to kill you."

"What if someone sees me? They could send me back to middle school, or revoke my driver's license or something."

She huffs at me. "Nobody's here."

I haven't seen her this energetic since we were little kids, and that fact alone has me clambering up the ladder behind her.

I wonder if she's feeling what I'm feeling: the sturdy force of the three of us Esfahani women, reunited.

At night, after Azar has given us all pedicures, she and I head into the small second bedroom. A twin bed lines each wall, but her side of the room is littered with pictures and books and unfolded laundry. My bed has never been slept in. I slip under the covers and look up to find one photo right beside me, taped to the wall. Azar and me grin at the camera, arm in arm with matching lunch boxes on back-to-school day. We must've been eight and six years old, and we both have missing teeth in our smiles.

Azar catches me looking at the photo. "I found it in Mom's stuff. Thought your side of the room needed some decoration."

"Thanks, Aziz."

I used to be so afraid of reeling moments like those out of the water of my memory. All of them carried the stain of Jaleh's addiction—even the sweet ones. This time, I don't shove down the image and all its thorny emotions. Instead, I let myself sink into the memory.

Saffron Dreams

DIASPORA

by Jaleh Vakhshoori

This man and I mourn for our twin homes lost
a desert apart, caravanserai highways running
the distance between our buried hearts. How
can a human survive so long with this vital
organ unspooled outside the body? Only post-
cards from our parents, photos of my growing
sister spinning in the red rock citadel where I
took my first steps—only dried barberries and
rock sugar wrapped like jewels in his mother's
luggage can become capillaries from the land
we've lost. This man cups his hand for mint and
watermelon seeds, plants them in California earth
and sings them ballads of lost love in our
native tongue—*So they'll know where they
come from.* We water and tend them like
children. A great grief tethers us together,
but so do those seedlings, so does this dream.

Admissions Gods

I WAKE UP to a knock at the door, and for a minute I can't remember where I am. Then my eyes land on the back-to-school photo and Mom's voice trails in from behind the door.

"Mitra joon, are you awake?"

Azar groans from the bed next to me.

I pad over to the door in my bare feet and pj's. Mom greets me with a cup of chai. "Baba's here," she says. "He has something for you."

None of this makes sense in my sleep-clogged brain. "What time is it?"

"Eight thirty," Dad calls from the kitchen counter where he's pouring himself a steaming glass. "I waited as long as I could."

"What's going on?" I join them at the counter and stir milk into my chai, bracing myself for chaos. I don't know why my dad showed up here at eight on a Sunday morning, but it can't be good. Some irrational part of my brain says: I shouldn't have spent the night here. I screwed up the normal order of life between me and my dad, and now something bad has happened.

"I forgot to check the mail yesterday," Dad pants, giving me a hurried kiss on each cheek. "Something came for you. I found it this morning. Thought you should have it right away." He pulls a crumpled envelope out from the inner pocket of his raincoat. It's a little bit toasty. I wonder if he ran all the way here.

The envelope is emblazoned with the red insignia of Reed College.

Mom's and Dad's eyes grow as wide as cookies rising in the oven.

"Well?" He pushes the envelope into my hands. "I didn't open it yet." He seems pleased by his self-restraint. *Thanks for not committing a federal crime, Dad.* "I saved it for you to do the honors."

All the sleep-induced haziness vacuums straight out of my mind when I see the insignia. I wasn't prepared for this today. I wanted to have time to think, time to listen to the warring voices in my brain before the letter arrived.

I fluff the letter in my hands, unsure of what to make of it. It's not a big envelope. That's a bad sign. But it's not totally flat and tiny, either.

"Give me a minute to wake up," I say. I take my chai to the sofa, drawing in a long sip while the two of them pretend to wait patiently. Their anticipation penetrates my silence.

I run my thumb under the seal of the envelope and my parents lean forward in their seats. A fist clenches in the top of my chest. This letter could start with *regretfully* or *unfortunately*. Everything I dreamed up on Reed's campus—that good thing my mom and I envisioned together—could disappear in this instant. And that should be a comfort, because then I'd know for sure that I'm meant to go to UW with Bea. A no from Reed just means a clear, uncomplicated future. But it still feels like a loss.

"Okay." I pull out the letter, my hand shaking.

"What does it say?" My dad shouts before I even unfold the papers.

"Dear Mitra," I read. "Congratulations! I am pleased to offer you admission to Reed College . . ." That's as far as I get before the pride and relief crowd out any free space in my airway.

"Woo-hoo!" my dad screams, leaping into the air. Mom ululates a high-pitched trill of excitement.

That draws Azar out of the bedroom with a blanket still wrapped around her. Her hair tumbles out of a sloppy morning bun. "Who died?" she grumbles. It's a fair assumption. The last time we heard Mom ululate was probably at a wedding or funeral.

"You want to tell her?" Dad asks me with his eyes still glowing.

"I got into Reed." Saying those words makes my stomach slip 'n' slide around inside me.

Azar turns her blanket into a cape and tackles me on the sofa. "Congrats, sis!"

I wrestle out of her cuddle and look at the other two papers included in the envelope. One of them is an award letter. With financial aid and work-study and an academic scholarship, the award covers most of my tuition, room, and board. Something warm wells up in my eyes.

"Let me see," Dad says, taking the papers from my fist while I try to collect myself. "Mitra, there's a handwritten note in here." He reads it aloud to me while I hold my head in my hands.

> Mitra,
>
> I hope you'll consider becoming a Reedie next year.
> We could use voices like yours in our community of
> learners, and it would be a pleasure to welcome you into
> my class in the creative writing major program. Keep
> sharing your stories of resilience and resistance. They're
> in your blood.
>
> Warmly,
> David Gutierrez

"We are so, so proud of you." Mom squeezes my shoulder.

I don't know what to tell my parents. Through the surges of excitement and relief, panic takes root. I'm not ready. I'm not ready to remake the decision Bea thinks we've already made. I don't want to say no to that hopeful voice in my head just yet. Not now—when everything I imagined at Reed has just become possible.

The blanket can't keep up with my tears. "Do you have that Holy Trinity contacts list?" I ask my dad.

"I have it saved in here," he says, pulling his phone out of his pocket. "Why?"

"I want to call my teacher."

Ex-Nun Stuff

Mitra: hi, um, is this Ms. Acosta?

Ms. Acosta: this is her.

Mitra: hi. it's Mitra. from your class at Holy Trinity.

Mitra: is it a good time to talk? or are you busy with . . . ex-nun stuff right now?

Ms. Acosta: hi, Mitra! no, I'm doing the crossword. I'm glad you called.

Mitra: oh. just because it's Sunday, you know. I wasn't sure.

Ms. Acosta: I attend the ten a.m. services on Sundays. and the secret, ex-nun meetings are in the evening.

Mitra: oh. haha. okay.

Ms. Acosta: what are you calling about?

Mitra: my dad brought the mail over. There was a letter from Reed in it.

Ms. Acosta: yeah?

Mitra: I just wanted to tell you I got in.

Ms. Acosta: oh, congratulations, Mitra! I suspected you would.

Mitra: I got a handwritten letter from Professor Gutierrez too. He wants me in the creative writing program.

Ms. Acosta: how wonderful! I hope you have something planned to celebrate.

Ms. Acosta: you have a lot to be proud of, Mitra. that's quite an accomplishment.

Mitra: thanks. well, I just wanted to say thanks for everything you did to help me. this wouldn't have happened without you.

Ms. Acosta: I doubt that. but I'm glad to be in your corner.

Ms. Acosta: have you decided what you'll do next year?

Mitra: um . . . no. not yet.

Smarter Than the Smartest Nerds

AFTER CHAI WITH Mom, Dad lets me borrow the car to go see Bea. "You need to celebrate," he says.

I pull up to her driveway and Bea sprints out of the house barefoot, screaming my name. She jumps into my arms when I step out of the car. In her blue- and green-striped knit dress, she's soft like a favorite sweater. I bury my face in the crook of her neck where she smells like rosemary and coconut curl balm.

"You did it!" she cries into my ear. "My girlfriend. Smarter than the smartest nerds. You got into the school that made *Ms. Acosta.*"

There's not an ounce of worry about my Reed acceptance in Bea's voice, and that twists my guilt even tighter. "How'd you know?" I ask.

"Azar texted." That little stinker. "Get in Gary," Bea demands. "I'm taking you out." She runs back to the house for her car keys.

"Shoes!" I shout after her.

Bea drives us to Molly Moon's ice cream parlor by Downtown Park. I buy her a salty caramel scoop with a waffle cone, and she gets me a sweet cream sundae with strawberry sauce. "My girlfriend got into one of the most rigorous colleges on the West Coast," Bea tells the cashier with a goatee. "Give her extra sprinkles."

We take our treats to a bench in the sprawling circular park. There's always something happening here, and today a string band has staked out a spot in the center of the giant green, a woman plucking an upright bass beside a pair of men playing violin and guitar. An audience of ducks flaps their way from the waterfall fountain toward the band. It reminds me of the geese at Reed.

"I kind of can't believe we made it," I tell Bea. "We're going to college."

We've been dreaming of getting out of Holy Trinity for so long, but it never felt like a future I could wrap my fingers around until now. Escaping together was the goal. I never thought much about what would come after; college was a twinkly fantasy we never fully fleshed out. What am I supposed to dream about now?

"If you hadn't transferred in, I definitely would've gotten kicked out of Holy Trinity," Bea says, licking the melted caramel from her knuckles. "And college would've been a reach."

"What?"

"If I didn't have you to vent to, I would've been airing my grievances about Holy Trinity directly to *every single* teacher I had. I don't think they would've kept me around long."

I let Bea steal a bite of my strawberry sauce. "They wouldn't have expelled you for that," I say. "And you're brilliant. You'd be getting offers from all kinds of colleges whether or not I was around."

She pokes me with the plastic spoon. "Remember when I wanted to boycott all my Religion assignments freshman year? It would've destroyed my GPA. You talked me into at least doing the bare minimum to pass the class."

Bea watches me from behind the glint of her glasses. "You kept me in check, Mitra. You're sensible in every way I'm not. Plus, you were my motivation to come to class every day." She chuckles and shakes her head at me. "Even when you didn't know it. You're the reason I put up with that place."

A warmth spreads across my skin, and underneath it, little pinpricks of doubt. She needs me just as much as I need her. I can't imagine being apart from her next year.

"Do I even need to say it?" I ask. "Without you, I'd be eating lunch alone in the chapel every day. Hiding. And writing sad, angsty poems all by myself."

She rests her head on my shoulder, nestling into the waves of my hair. "But we found each other."

That's the miracle. In all of the millions of realities in which I never would have met Bea, somehow I had the luck to land in this one.

College next year still blurs with unknowns. I feel like Gibran's prophet on the shore, watching my ship come in, but dread spikes through me because I don't know where the ship is headed. I don't know what will happen once I step on board. And once I do, I can't go back to shore again.

When we've finished our ice cream, I take Bea's hand and we walk a gravel loop around the circumference of the park. She swings our clasped hands between us like a pendulum keeping time with our steps. Oak trees strung with lanterns shade our way, migrating light filtering through their leaves. The rosebushes boast deep pink buds, and kids flock around the rim of the waterfall fountain. We've been here a thousand times together, but it's starting to hit me that we won't come here a thousand times more.

I think I'm finally starting to see the whole scope of love: that it can't exist without loss. I couldn't love Bea the way I do now without losing what we used to be to each other. Loving my mom meant that I was—I am—chased by the grief of her addiction. And I can't have one of the futures I've dreamed up without turning down the other.

Questions storm my head, so I focus on what I do know.

"We got here together," I say, squeezing her hand. It's the strongest comfort I can summon: Whatever comes next, we'll figure it out together too.

That thought opens like a blossom inside me. Everything I've been afraid of—college, the unknowns of next year, even things with my mom—I've imagined myself navigating alone. But I'm not alone.

I don't have to have all the answers. Bea will be walking beside me through it all.

Mitra & Bea

Another veil lifts between
our hearts, the final borderline
dissolves and I see all of you

welcoming me into the eagle-sky span of your
arms and somehow you in your wholeness
can embrace every messy wild inch of me

and I learn what it means
to know you, caught in those
webs between your fingers

caught in spindled spiderweb of our traded
breaths, you become some enchanter stretching
time 'til there's enough for us to swim in

and we surface from the water
changed, if your kiss split me open
now you've sealed me whole

stepping forward into a forest of question marks
with this indomitable strength seeded between our
clasped hands: we know how to find our way together

Family Dinner

AFTER SCHOOL THE next Friday, Azar transforms the kitchen into her private laboratory. I stand at the mouth of the kitchen watching her preside over a pan of spitting oil with an old apron tied around her waist.

"What are you doing?"

"Cooking," she says. "Don't distract me."

"You can't talk and cook at the same time?"

Azar fastens a nozzle onto a bottle of batter and I inch closer, watching her drizzle circles of a yogurt and cornstarch mixture into the pan. Her swirly florets puff up the instant they hit the oil.

"First time making zoolbia alone," she says. "Don't want to mess up." The doughy flowers deepen to a golden brown and she holds her breath, flipping them onto their uncooked bellies with chopsticks.

"I can help." I join her at the stove and she hands over the bottle. "What's the occasion?"

Azar glances at me while she fishes a flower of hot-fried batter from the pan. "Mom's coming to dinner." She dunks the floret in a bath of saffron syrup, the hot pastry perfuming the air with saffron. "She showed me how to make these a couple weeks ago, but I've never done them solo."

"Coming to dinner *here*?" I freehand my first zoolbia flower, trying to make it as symmetrical and elegant as Azar's. But she's had practice, and my work doesn't have the same finesse. My swirls come out looking like a preschooler's drawing. "With Dad?"

Azar looks unfazed, but I feel like we just agreed to host peace talks between two conflicted territories.

"What time?" *Les Misérables* opens tonight at eight, and I have big plans to camp out in the front row of the theater with a bouquet of sunflowers for Bea. With her parents bailing, I want to roll into the auditorium with three times the amount of supportive energy of one normal human. I've never been to any kind of sporting event, but I'm trying to summon the thespian-equivalent enthusiasm of one of those face-painted, shirtless guys at football games. All I'm missing is a foam finger.

"Yup, it was Dad's idea. He said six o'clock, so you can still make the musical." Azar can't hide the satisfaction on her face. And some of it must be from her immaculate zoolbia, but I think some of it stems from the knowledge that our parents will be eating under the same roof together again.

I know my parents have been talking regularly since Mom moved to Bellevue, mostly to coordinate our schedules or make polite conversation during drop-off and pickup. They've had a few cups of chai together, but they're Iranian, so that's like a basic level of civility to show each other. I figured most of their private conversations were an excuse to do a combo of bragging and complaining about me and Azar. But a family dinner?

I trade Azar the bottle for the chopsticks and wait a few seconds until my pastries deepen to a dark brown color before flipping them. It takes a lot of concentration to lift these dainty things from the oil, but I'm thrown off by the question on my tongue.

"Do you want them to get back together?" I ask.

I peek up at Azar while I drop my flower in the saffron syrup, but she doesn't raise her eyes from her handiwork.

"I don't really remember what they were like before Mom's addiction. But—" She squiggles her next flower. "They seem good together now. I think it would be nice. You know. If we were a family again."

She watches me as I prod the pastries in their saffron bath. "What about you?"

I remember what Mom and Dad were like before. I remember them in the kitchen together on the Nowruz before Mom's car accident. They weaved around each other with fistfuls of herbs and spices, Mom making ash-e reshteh and Dad grilling sumac-roasted fish. Mom would add more saffron to Dad's dishes when he wasn't looking, and Dad would stand over the pot of Mom's soup, inhaling the steam. Dad told us stories about the long noodles bringing good fortune for the next year while Mom sang half-remembered lyrics of folk songs.

But that was our family before, and that shattered once Mom started using. I think of Kahlil Gibran's quote: *Pain is the breaking of the shell that encloses your understanding.* I had an understanding of what my family was, and it crumbled under the foot of my mom's drug use. There is no resurrecting what's broken. There is no way to mend all the cracks in what used to be.

And maybe that's okay. If I clung too tight to that understanding of our old family, I'd miss out on what we're becoming now.

"I want them to be friendly," I tell Azar. "I want them to be on good terms. Like, stable."

I help Azar sift the zoolbia from the syrup and rest them on a cooling rack. I always thought these were too sweet for me, but they smell amazing, like hot Sacramento summers we spent on the water. Mom would wrap the pastries in plastic and feed them to us between swims. We'd get all sticky and rinse our hands off in the river. "Can I try one?"

Azar nods, and she grins when I pick one of her flowers. They're just prettier. The pastry crunches and softens on my tongue in a sweet puddle of saffron, rose, and lemon.

"They're perfect," I say. "Mom's going to love them."

Dad comes home at five and commandeers the kitchen, steaming up the house with the smell of lubia polo and baked salmon.

At ten after six, Dad sets out the polo and sabzi with the salmon, tenting it with tinfoil to keep it warm, because Mom hasn't arrived yet. Azar arranges the zoolbia on one of our fancy china plates. We wait at the table, mouths watering from the toasty spices wafting toward us.

"The fish will get cold," Dad says, planting his palms on the table. "Maybe we should start without her?"

"I'll text her," Azar says.

I'm annoyed at Mom for holding us up, but I also can't really blame her. It's a lot of pressure to come and sit down with the whole family again for the first time. When my dad made me go to the early Nowruz dinner at Mom's apartment, I wanted to hide out in his car for as long as possible. And at the end of the night, I left so fast I probably blasted a Looney Tunes-style outline of myself in the living room wall.

Azar's phone chimes. "She says she's running late."

"She lives only a few blocks away," Dad mutters. He keeps aligning his fork and spoon on the table.

"She was going to pick up apple cider to toast Mitra's college acceptance," Azar says. "Maybe she got held up at the grocery store."

We wait another ten minutes, munching on radishes and basil and mint leaves from the sabzi platter while trying not to disturb Dad's cool plate arrangement of herbs.

Dad asks Azar to check her phone again, but this time there's nothing.

"Nobody likes cold fish," Dad says. "We should start. She can join when she gets here."

My eyes slide from Dad to Azar, who clearly wants to wait a little longer. "I have to eat if I'm going to get to the theater early enough," I tell Azar. "Sorry."

Dad looks grumpy, and I feel bad for him. Underneath his scowl he's obviously disappointed, and probably worried about us too. He cut one of the radishes into a rose-shaped garnish, and it turned out beautifully. He never does that when it's dinner just for us. I wonder what he thought dinner tonight would mean.

I want to remind him: He and I might share that same internal sense of order and rules. You make plans, you show up on time. You say you're going to do something and then you do it. But even before her addiction, Mom was never like that. Her favorite word was *improvise*. There were days when I loved that about her—like the days she plucked us from school early to take us to Fairytale Town—and other days, like today, when I wished she could be reliable. But to invite her back in our lives, we have to make room for *all* of her.

Still, a kernel of worry clangs around my brain, a drumbeat that intensifies as the minutes drag on.

We dig into dinner, and I distract Azar from her disappointment by telling her about the latest backstage gossip I've heard from Bea about the musical.

Just as I'm finishing up my dinner and reaching for another zoolbia, Mom knocks at the door. I get up to let her in, and when I open the door, she's facing away toward the rain-slicked street.

"Did you walk here in the rain?" I ask. "You didn't bring your umbrella?"

"Forgot," she says.

Her voice stops me short.

"Mom?" I reach out for her shoulder and she turns to face me. Her curls are wet, some of them sticking to her forehead, and her rumpled slacks and blouse are spotted with water.

Under the porch light, Jaleh's eyes glare, unfocused. Her pupils circle around me like insects looking for a place to land.

All these little gears in my head start churning into motion.

"Where were you?" My knees wobble under me. It's taken all of three seconds for the hope to drain from my body. Blood courses hot behind my eyes and inside my chest.

Somewhere behind me, a chair scoots back from the table, and I pray that it's Dad. But Azar's footsteps sound their way toward me. I block the door with my body, hoping to keep Azar inside. I don't want her to see Jaleh like this.

"I had a meeting that ran late. Let me in, joon, it's raining." Jaleh's words melt into each other like the puddles at her feet.

"You're slurring," I say softly.

"I'm not feeling myself," Jaleh says. "I have a headache."

A bitter laugh escapes my lips. *I've heard that one before,* I want to scream at her. I've heard them all before.

My stomach clenches around my dinner: the fish Dad seasoned the way Mom likes it, the zoolbia Azar swirled into perfect rosebuds for her. They both poured their wishful love into every dish.

And I did too.

I hoped she could be different. On our trip to Reed, I saw the mom I remembered: the one who wanted only good things for me. The one who was loving and present and wise. I welcomed her in, believing that she would stay. I trusted her. But this other mom was nipping at her heels the whole time.

I can feel Azar standing behind me now.

"What's going on?" she asks, trying to fit into the doorway with me.

"Just, go sit down for a second, Azar," I say.

"Aziz!" Jaleh shouts. "Your sister won't let me in."

Azar freezes just behind me in the doorway at the sound of Jaleh's voice. I thought she was too young to remember this mom, but some unconscious memory locks Azar's body into stillness. Her eyes cut into mine, and when her hand brushes my arm I'm hit with a wall of crushing disappointment.

We both know. Our mother is nowhere to be found.

I step back from the door to take Azar's hand. Devastation ripples across her face, and she's nine years old again. Jaleh is yelling at Azar for spilling cereal, and Mom stomps in the scattered cereal bits, grinding them to dust.

"Dad," I call from the doorway, tears catching up to my voice before I can stop them.

He stands up from the dinner table and halts there, and we share a look that tells him everything he needs to know.

I let Jaleh in and then pull Dad aside in the hallway. "What are we going to do?"

He sighs, rubbing his beard. His eyes haven't left Jaleh and Azar. "What we always do," he says.

Clean Up

We fall back into old patterns
like muscle memory, a circuit
of nerves I hoped time would
prune away, but here they are
at the ready—like tendons taut
poised for impending terror I
thought I'd shed. He'll make up
a bed for her, call the sponsor,
shuttle her to a meeting for the
refrain ready at her tongue: *Hi
my name is Jaleh I'm an addict*
and I've memorized my own
role: mold myself into a shield
for my sister, *Azar I'm here, I
have you,* bandaging each
bruised part of her heart, but I
can't undo anything already
done, I can only sweep these
broken pieces we're left with.

What We Always Do

EVERY FEELING INSIDE me folds tight so I can move through the motions on autopilot. Dad ushers Jaleh to the car, and then I meet him on the front porch where the awning shelters us from rainfall. "There's a meeting down south that starts in thirty minutes," he says. "They can help connect us to an inpatient treatment program."

"Want me to come with?" I'm dressed up in my best jeans and an olive collared shirt and tie for Bea's opening night. My oxfords are waiting by the front door with the bundle of sunflowers and the bracelet I made her at Jaleh's, but I don't have socks on. I can't remember where I left the low-cut socks that go with these shoes. I have to find them. I have to find them and I have to go with my dad.

"No," he says as I scramble to undo my tie. I'm way overdressed for rehab. "I can handle this. You're supposed to be at the play tonight. You should go."

"What?" He's not making sense. I don't see how something like the play could even be on his radar after the chaos Mom just dropped.

Dad brushes the raindrops from his hair. "You've taken care of so many things you shouldn't have had to." His voice carries a current of sadness that could wash me away if I let it. "I let you take on too much when you were younger. That's why you resisted when she came back into our lives. Because you got hurt back then. I should have protected you more." He straightens my tie and brushes his thumb over my chin. "Go to the play. Be a teenager. Everything will be okay."

My throat clenches to a knot, blocking out all the words I'd like to tell him. Jaleh's face illuminates in the fogged-up car window when Dad opens the driver's-side door. She's watching me, and I wish she would just turn away. It's not my mother looking back at me. It's the woman I hate, taunting me with my mother's face. Even through the dark and distance and the shield of the car window, I can't stand to look at her.

Inside the house, Azar sits balled up on the couch, her knees and arms curled inward. She's stretched her sweatshirt sleeves to the tips of her fingers and buried her chin into the collar, hot tears dribbling into the fabric. She's as small and hidden as she can be.

I can't leave my sister. I won't leave her alone tonight.

I need to text Bea and tell her why I can't make it to the play tonight, but I don't want to dump this disaster on her seventeen minutes before the curtain lifts. I'll write her as soon as the show ends and explain everything. Maybe by then I'll have the words to make sense of what's happened here, and to make up for abandoning Bea on opening night.

I sit down beside Azar and latch my hand to her knee. Her eyelids pinch tight around her tears when I do.

"Just say it," she whimpers. She sounds bitter.

"Say what?" The china plate of zoolbia still rests on the dining room table. She put so much care into her flower pastries. And she looked so proud.

"You were right. You said this would happen." She tunnels her face into the fleece of her sweatshirt.

I reach my arm around her and bring her head to rest on my shoulder. "I didn't want to be right," I whisper.

No part of me feels righteous about this. Azar just wanted to have a mom again. She was brave enough to hope that she wouldn't be hurt this time.

Those lines from Hafez's poem clang around the cave of my chest.

My weary heart eternal silence keeps—
I know not who has slipped into my heart;
Though I am silent, one within me weeps.

I can feel it now. Without noticing, without ever really making the choice, I let my mom slip into my heart again.

Anger stampedes through my veins. Jaleh lulled me into trusting her again with promises that she had changed, with speeches about how sorry she was. She knew just how to make me feel small and hopeful again. She knew to offer Azar exactly what she'd longed for, and then wrench it away.

I hate Jaleh for doing this to me and Azar. And Hafez, for stinging me with his unwelcome lessons. But I'm the one who knew this would happen, and I stepped on the land mine anyway.

Azar rests her head in my lap, her black Jaleh hair tumbling out from her sweatshirt. She holds tight to my knee. "What are we gonna do?" she asks.

Through my tears, I reach for my phone and pull up Azar's favorite Robyn songs, the ones I used to blast for her in our Sacramento bedroom to drown out Jaleh's shouting. They're too upbeat for tonight, but I want the hopeful rhythms to wrap her in a hug. I don't have the right words for Azar in this moment. Maybe I never know the right things to say to her when it comes to our mom. But Robyn's lyrics fill in for me.

Little star, I got you. I got you, you'll be okay. You'll be okay.

We stay curled together like that in the wash of music, and then we cry ourselves to sleep.

After-Party

I WAKE UP to the sound of the front door unlocking. Azar is still asleep, now spread across the other end of the couch with a blanket draped over her. Dad plods quietly through the house toward us until he notices my open eyes.

"How's Mom?" I blink the haze from my eyes, but I can't clear the thicket of disorientation surrounding me.

He settles onto the sliver of couch not occupied by Azar and me. "The counselor at the meeting found us a treatment center not too far away that had an opening for your mother. She agreed to check herself in." He runs a hand down his sagging face. "It's a four-week program. With family days. If you and Azar want to consider joining her. That's up to you."

The soft hall light blares in my eyes. My brain pulses and throbs from inside my skull. "I can't think about that yet." I sit up and try to ground myself. "What time is it?"

"Ten thirty."

Shit.

"You didn't go to the musical," Dad says.

"I couldn't leave Aziz."

"You're a good sister."

Maybe that's true, but I failed at being a good girlfriend tonight. The play should've ended a while ago, and I passed out before texting Bea. I dig around for my phone and check the screen, but there's nothing from her. She's probably mad at me. I promised I would be there for her, and I let her down. I hope she knows I wouldn't have missed her debut for anything less devastating than what happened tonight.

I wipe the salt from my eyes and shake the sleep from my head, looking at Dad and Azar beside me.

We were a family of three for a long time. It was easy to overlook the beauty in what we made together. But I see it now. This is the love story that never got its poem.

Dad retrieves his keys from his pocket. "I meant what I said before. You need to be a teenager. Go and find Bea. I'll stay with Azar."

Aziz turns over in her sleep beside me. I don't want her to wake up and find me gone. After everything that happened tonight, I want her to know she still has a family she can count on. But I need to show up for Bea tonight.

"Love you," I tell Dad, taking the keys. My oxfords are still by the door next to the slightly wilted bouquet of sunflowers. I rush into my shoes and jacket and sprint for the car. I've missed the play, but I can still make the after-party.

On the drive, the disaster-response autopilot of earlier in the night completely powers down. I'm alone now. No problems left to solve, and no one to take care of anymore. Each breath forces me to feel the rawness inside me. It's like I've been scraped of all skin. My protective barrier is gone, and nothing stands between me and the wildfire of feelings. All I know is that I need Bea.

I want to fall into her arms. She doesn't need to know what happened to work her magic on me. Just being there with her and feeling her steady embrace around me will make me feel safe again.

The after-party is at Spencer's house. *House* might be an understatement for the sprawling estate his parents own in Clyde Hill. With the tennis court and pool and guest studio and gazebo out back, they might just qualify for their own zip code. I've never been invited to Spencer's house before, so I was picturing a low-key party like what the HolyHorror crew used to have at Cara's on Halloween, with her parents hanging out in the dining room the whole night. But there are dozens of cars already parked in the private roundabout in front of the house when I arrive, and the thunder of a stereo system buzzes my car windows.

I push my way into the dark house with the bouquet in my hand, the bass beat throbbing louder than my headache. The living room and kitchen are packed with people. I didn't think drama kids would party this hard, but I guess musical theater takes all kinds. Sweat and breath and alcohol thicken the air.

"Mitra!" Max shouts, and I follow their flailing hands to a window-framed breakfast nook in the kitchen. "You made it!" Max, Ellie, and Jessica are crowded onto the L-shaped bench in the window with some of the tech crew and chorus singers. Max has their arm draped around Jessica, and they're both grinning. No Bea.

"Where were you?" Ellie asks.

I scan the room, but I don't see Bea anywhere. "Is she mad?" I swallow.

"You missed opening night." It comes out in a wobbly song, and my eyes adjust enough to make out the red lightning bolt painted down Ellie's face in stage makeup. She has to be pretty drunk before she gives herself a Ziggy Stardust makeover. Then I realize *everyone's* faces are streaked with paint. There are more than a few penises on the prop master's cheek.

"Cara said she was a wreck backstage. But she still pulled it together before she went on. Aw, you brought her flowers!" Ellie slurs, her eyes wheeling to the bouquet in my fist. Her slippery words sound just like my mother's. I promised Bea I'd be there for her, and I failed. My stomach twists around my dinner.

"Flowers fix everything. She'll forgive you," Ellie says.

"Where is she?" It's too hot in here. The bass presses in on me, and everything smells like hard liquor. Everyone around me is glazed-eyed and stumbling. All I can see are Jaleh's shiny pupils spinning.

"You okay, Mitra?" Max might be the only person who's not wasted. Their cheeks shine pink and they have rays of yellow makeup streaking from their eyes. "Where were you?"

I grip the flowers so tight that my knuckles ache. Maybe the after-party was a bad idea. "I got held up," I say. "I just want to find Bea."

Out the window, the gazebo glimmers with thousands of white lights lacing its dome. I can almost make out Bea's cluster of curls under the lights. "Be right back."

"Wait." Max stands up, but I'm already halfway out the glass door. A few couples have paired off in the backyard, making out on the patio sofa and giggling to each other under the bistro lights on the terrace. I sneak my way around them, trying not to ruin their romantic moments as I trek toward the gazebo.

The music and the hot air lift out here, and that release of pressure makes my breath start to shake. I haven't even reached Bea yet when water rises to my eyes. She'll hold me, and she'll help me hold this pain. My tears blur all the lights and stars together. Through the distortion, I find the gazebo. Bea stands brilliant under the glow in her blue mini dress, her head tossed back in a laugh. She's not alone.

Cara, in her green romper and heels, hooks her hand around Bea's.

". . . you *would*," Bea chuckles to Cara.

"Just, come here," Cara says, pulling Bea into her arms. They lock into a tight hug. I watch them holding each other like that, swaying a little together under the gazebo lights, water sparking fresh in my eyes.

When Bea steps back from the embrace, she turns toward the house and her eyes land right on me.

Stomach acid spears a hot poker up my throat. I want to have words for what I just witnessed, but the only one that comes out of me is "Bea." Emotion chokes out my voice.

I expect her to look contrite or surprised or *something,* but she just stares at me with her flat glare. Her mouth opens and her hands knot to fists at her side. She doesn't say anything.

We stand there in stunned silence. Then she turns her back to me and walks out of the gazebo and into the garden, leaving me behind.

Cara's eyes flit from me to Bea and back again. When I don't budge, she follows Bea into the dark expanse of the backyard.

I turn and sprint toward the house, the sunflowers falling from my grip. When I reach the car, my whole body shakes with tears, my sobs drowned out by the waves of cheers and music inside the house. The realization hits me over and over.

I've lost my mother and my girlfriend in one night.

What You Counted and Carefully Saved

I knew, I knew, I knew.
Better to hold nothing, save
nothing, lose nothing, than feel
this cracked-wide, scooped-out
empty once everything's gone.

She's Gone

I PEEL INTO our dark driveway and cut the headlights, burrowing my fingers into my eyelids.

She's gone.

I don't even know who I'm grieving, and it doesn't matter. The words resound in my mind again and again. *She's gone. She's gone.*

It's too deep a pain to let myself feel, like I'm letting someone worm their fingers into the chambers of my heart.

When I step outside, I seal all that devastation away in the car and lock it behind me. Only anger burns through me now. It grips tighter as I climb the stairs to the front door. The house is empty and dim but for one hall light stretching shadows from the furniture. I'm alone and shaking. Anger is the strongest muscle in my body.

How could she. She made me feel safe with her, and all my defenses softened. I believed I could trust her with every part of me. I fought *so* hard to trust her. She knows me better than anyone, and so she knows just how to hurt me. And I gave her that power. I let her in. I handed over everything she'd need to obliterate me, and I did it willingly.

I should have known. I've been through it before.

This sick part of me feels vindicated. I *did* know. From the beginning, I knew Cara had a hold on Bea. All those nights I stayed up with Bea while she sobbed post-breakup, it was obvious she still loved Cara. And maybe she'd always love Cara on some level. My mistake was imagining that my love for Bea could change that.

Just like I imagined my mom's love for me could change her addiction.

I let them hurt me. I opened my heart, and opened myself up to this pain.

The muscle of my anger mounts, clamping around every inch of me until it feels like I'm exploding.

I snatch my dad's copy of Hafez's *Divān* from the bookshelf and flip through it. *Just give me an answer,* I'm screaming inside. *Tell me what to do.* But he's silent tonight. His poems land flat before my eyes, and they may as well be written in their original Farsi. I'm so far beyond listening for his wisdom at this point. I toss the *Divān* aside.

On the next shelf of the bookcase, all fourteen volumes of The Book line up side by side. I yank out the current volume and careen through the pages, fuming.

All these promises Bea made. All of these hopes I fooled myself into believing. All of it, documented here.

Each line of poetry pierces its barbed corners into me, flooded in our love. I can flip back far enough in our never-ending poem to the time before I knew what it felt like to be loved by her, but I can't unwrite all these pages of our love story.

We agreed years ago: No rewriting. No tearing out pages. No apologizing.

But Bea already broke our rules. When I jam my eyes shut around my rage, her silhouette in Cara's arms carves itself into the darkness.

So maybe the rules mean nothing now.

I land on a section of the never-ending poem I wrote last year after Sadeh. A spark blazes through my anger.

Shatter hope to kindling.
Mine the fault lines of those best laid plans.
Perfect timber to toss into the fire.

The words strike a match in me.

Perfect Tinder

Burn: the first page, first
book, first smile—watch them
all consumed in a quick ball
of flame. Dry bark and twigs
and pages of false promises
all spark the same, churning
smoke upward like charred
prayers. If I burn your words,
did they ever exist? Maybe
they were wisps of bitter black
smoke from the moment you
inked them. We both know
how to destroy things we once
loved, swallow all the dreams of
our younger selves in one swoop—
crackle, spark, embers shoot up
like distress flares in the aftermath of our collision. Every word.
Every promise. Every *I love you*
snowed in gray ash now, as coals
drain of their gleam. Only last-gasp,
flickers of our never-ending thing.

After

I WATCH THE embers fade. All that bright red chaos mutes to dull black and gray. My anger dwindles along with the heat and color. I wait for satisfaction to flood in—some wave of relief to wash me clean. It doesn't come. With all the anger wrung from my body, I'm just empty.

Leaving the ashes behind, I trudge upstairs to my bedroom with soot still marking my hands.

I drift through some space between asleep and awake all night, my mind trumpeting back to me everything I lost. *Mom relapsed. Bea is with Cara. You destroyed the safe place you spent years building.* I wake up more hollow than the night before.

Everything in this room harbors pieces of Bea: photos of us at the bay and dressed up on Halloween, the strip of rooftop where we'd read and sun-soak in summer, the friendship bracelet she wove me in eighth grade that I wore until it broke, and then repurposed into a bookmark. She's everywhere. My life is unrecognizable without her. Like it was once unrecognizable without Jaleh.

Torched

"MITRA?" AZAR'S FINGERS drum on my bedroom door. I haven't talked to her since we cried ourselves to sleep on the couch last night.

"I need a minute."

"Okay. But . . . Bea's here." Azar pauses. "I texted her. It's eleven and you haven't even come out of your room. I wanted to make sure you're okay." She sighs through my closed door. "I didn't tell her anything," she says in a low voice.

I'm not ready to tell Azar about what went down between Bea and me last night. "I don't really want to see anyone right now," I say.

"Mitra." Azar waits me out. "Come on."

I pull in air through my nose and hold it inside my chest until it stings. "Fine. She can come in."

Bea steps in and closes the door behind her. I ball up the sheets in my fist and pull them up over my sleep shirt, like somehow the sheets will protect me from the twisting knife of this conversation.

She stands at the foot of my bed in leggings and a long-sleeve shirt, her face bare except for her glasses and a trace of eyeliner from last night's stage makeup. Her curls have doubled their typical volume, which means she probably didn't sleep either. She doesn't sit down on the bed with me.

"What happened to you last night?" Her voice comes out low and hoarse. "Why didn't you come to the play?"

I've spent enough time with Bea to register the various tones of her anger. And right now, she's pissed. That just ratchets up my own fury.

"Well, it looks like you and Cara had fun without me." Each word from my mouth is tied up so tight that it might combust.

"What's that supposed to mean?"

Normally I can't look at her when I'm saying hard things, but this morning my eyes bore into hers. "Stop. Don't lie to me anymore. I can't believe you would do that to me." Betrayal injects itself into my voice, jagging my words. "And then you wouldn't even acknowledge me, or say it to my face when I got there? You just torched five *years* in one night. All of it, gone—just like that. But you're not the only one who can burn things down."

Bea's body tenses. "What are you saying?"

"I burned The Book last night." Spite drips from my voice until I don't even recognize it anymore. "All of them."

That breaks Bea out of her frozen stance. Her jaw slackens and her eyes jump with her voice. "You *what*?" she yells. "What the fuck, Mitra?" Her eyes well up, and a sob storms under her words. "Why would you do that?"

The pain in her voice knocks me back, my fists unfurling. I thought she'd feel guilty. I thought this blow would land as hard as the image of her in Cara's arms struck me last night. But she looks betrayed and furious.

"Because I saw you. Together."

Beads of water spill from her eyes. "I didn't kiss Cara!" she shouts. "We *talked*. She apologized for how she ended things on Halloween. Jesus, she said she was *happy* for us. And she was trying to cheer me up because she knew how sad I was that you didn't show! At least *she* was there for me."

Blood thunders in my ears. "You were holding each other."

"We *hugged*."

"But you saw me and just walked away."

"Yeah. I was pissed about you not showing up, and I didn't want to talk to you. Not everything is about you, Mitra! Cara and I were having a conversation about *us*. It was, like, closure. A goodbye to our time together, to the play, to senior year. We were moving on from everything that's happened. That's all. I would never cheat on you."

Bea slumps to the corner of the bed, her gaze falling to her hands. "What, do you really think so little of me?" She takes off her glasses and presses her thermal sleeve into her eyes. "You think I would do that to you? You said you trusted me."

Adrenaline thrums in my arteries. My body's still responding to the threat I thought I saw. But it doesn't really matter if she and Cara didn't kiss last night. I saw how they acted around each other—it's only a matter of time. Eventually, the people you love will let you down.

"I lied," I say.

"God, Mitra. That's fucked up." Bea shakes her head. "I've been patient with you and your worries for five years. And you couldn't even be there for me for *one night* because you were so threatened by the idea of seeing me with Cara."

My jaw locks tighter with each of her words.

Bea's face reddens as she cries. "You promised me you'd be there last night. You knew how much it mattered to me. And then you burn five years of our poetry—our *history*—just because you saw me hugging Cara? How could you do that?"

She runs her hands down the hot tears on her face. "The Book meant something to me," she whispers. "I thought it meant something to you too."

The memory of last night's fire clings to me like camp smoke. I knew as soon as I lit the match that there would be no going back, but I thought I would feel better—or feel *something*—after burning The Book.

She latches her hands to her knees. "You need to deal with your shit because it's going to ruin us." Bea unfolds her glasses and slides them back onto the bridge of her nose. "You're so in your head all the time that you don't even *see* me anymore. You just project all your fears onto me and then expect me to live up to it." She runs her shirtsleeve under her eyes. "You keep holding yourself back. If you never let yourself actually trust someone, you're going to keep sabotaging every good thing you have."

Heat zings up my cheeks. My empty stomach tumbles inside out. Is that really what Bea has thought of me all this time?

"I didn't miss the play because I was jealous." My voice frays. "I missed it because my mom relapsed."

All the fury scrubs free from Bea's face, replaced by shock. She scoots toward me on the bed and reaches her hands for my knees. "Oh my god, Mitra. I had no idea."

I shake off her hands and draw my legs tight to my chest. "You would've known if you had bothered to speak to me when I got to Spencer's house. I tried to show up for you. I didn't give you the benefit of the doubt with Cara last night, but you didn't give it to me, either. I'm always there for you."

"I'm so sorry about your mom."

She's trying to be kind and gentle now, but the impact of her words still ricochets through my veins like venom. She thinks I'm some cowardly, terrified kid, running around and sabotaging everything with my anxiety.

She sees all the shameful things I've ever tried to hide inside me. Worst of all, she thinks I don't even see her clearly.

"Yeah." I bring my chin to my knees and keep my eyes down. I'm done looking at her. "Well, I'm sorry I've been such a burden on you all these years. If you really think I'm that fucked up, you should just go."

I listen to her weight shift on the comforter beside me. "Mitra." The shadow of her arm passes through my field of vision on the blankets, reaching for me, but she doesn't touch me again. I stay bolted tight. I learned long ago to fold into myself, like origami. It's a skill I perfected over almost five years at Holy Trinity, making all my angles small and crisp and quiet. But now it's like I've compacted to sharp metal edges. Too prickly for Bea to touch.

She hesitates a moment more, and when she exhales, I feel her body lift from the bed. Her old loafers with the Pegasus outsoles trudge away from me. I won't lift my gaze. The bedroom door clicks when she opens it, and she closes it so softly that I barely catch the sound.

She's gone. This time, for good.

Confession

BEA'S ABSENCE BREAKS a spell in me. The one that kept me curled up and quiet. My arms and legs unfold and I jump out of bed, and then I'm tearing at everything around me. Knocking the framed photo of Bea and me off my dresser, trashing the friendship bracelet, ripping down a picture I printed out of my mom at the Canyon. My arms flail and my voice rages out of me in sobs.

She's gone. Burning at the edges of my anger is a loss too big to name. Bea broke my heart, and so did my mom.

But I broke my own heart too.

I thought burning The Book would prove I didn't need Bea. Or that I could hurt her just as much as she'd hurt me. I wanted revenge and a clean break all in one strike.

And I got it.

Quiet Emptiness

IN THE RUINS of my room, the *Divān* lays undisturbed on my bed-side table. I haven't reached for it. Hafez answers questions; he's for hopeful and optimistic people. People who have something to wish for. I don't deserve answers, and I torched all hope.

Instead, I hear Father Mitchell's voice. I usually tried to pay attention in Masses, because maybe there were poems waiting to be found in the hymns, and because the Bible readings seemed to me like the Catholic version of divination: lots of reading obscure passages and hoping to be moved by a divine spirit, hoping to come away with wisdom. I thought that I could skate through Catholic school that way—like a visitor or an anthropologist, listening in without absorbing all the stuff about guilt and fear and sin. But here in the quiet emptiness, one of the passages from Father Mitchell's liturgies burrows deep into my shame.

Romans 9:20-22

But who are you, a human being, to talk back to God? Shall what is formed say to Him who formed it, "Why did You make me like this?"

Does not the potter have the right to make from the same lump of clay one vessel for special purposes and some for common use?

What if God, although choosing to show His wrath and make His power known, bore with great patience the vessels of His wrath, prepared for destruction?

If I'm made of stardust, some cosmic swirl of ash, then why would the universe make someone as flawed as me?

Why am I like this? Does God even know?

What if some vessels really *were* made only for wrath and destruction?

Is that what my mother is?

Is that what I am?

Wednesday

Jaleh: Mitra joon, I just got my phone privileges back.

Jaleh: I know words are not enough, but I'm so very sorry. I know I hurt you and your sister again.

Jaleh: I love you.

Jaleh: I'm working very hard to get better. I don't expect you to visit, but if you'd ever like to, family days are on Saturdays.

Sister

I FAKE SICK on Monday morning. My dad doesn't really buy my weak cough or vague groaning, but he lets me stay home from school anyway. Azar is suspicious of me. She pokes my lymph nodes with her finger and cups her hand on my forehead. "You feel normal to me," she says. When I shrug her off, she takes my shoulder in her hand and looks me head-on.

"Mitra. You can't skip school every time you have an emotion."

I don't have any walls left to keep Azar at bay. And after what we went through with our mom on Friday night, I don't want that distance from her anyway. "Something happened with Bea."

Something. I remember when that word lassoed all this unnamable magic between Bea and me.

After I tell Azar about what happened, she stops hassling me to go to school with her. Instead, she wrings me tight in her arms.

When I return to Holy Trinity on Tuesday, I learn what it feels like to be invisible again. I move through the day on autopilot, like some generator has kicked on inside me, preserving only the basic functions. Walk, breathe, sit quietly in class. Eat lunch. Eyes down. I spend more time memorizing the pattern in my tartan skirt than anything else.

Bea won't look at me, let alone talk to me, so I give up on raising my eyes to hers at all. She's not wearing her Pegasus loafers. Her new shoes are black and shiny and unmarred by my art.

Poetry seminar is the hardest. The room is too small to insulate myself. She fidgets all through class, sitting next to Max and Cara. Max tries to bridge the distance between us during writing activities, asking if I want to be their partner and offering their commentary on the readings. But I don't talk anymore, and eventually, Max gives up.

Sometimes I indulge my misery by imagining what Bea would say to me if we were still speaking. But even in my imagination, I can't escape what I've done. She opens her mouth to speak and all the words I've burned away come spilling out.

So instead, I revisit memory reels from the time before. Back when I hadn't ruined everything. Back when the never-ending poem was our most precious escape. Taking Popsicles to Lake Sammamish on the last day of school, staining pages of The Book with bright red drops of melted ice. The summer night we went to Inspiration Playground after all the kids had left, running under the spray fountains until we were drenched. The sound of Bea's cackle every time I screamed and grabbed her hand during our Catholic horror movie marathon. Lying sleepless beside her in bed that whole night.

In my fog, I can't see myself clearly anymore. But I know things must be pretty bad for Azar to join me for lunch in the chapel. Her first time eating under the eyes of the saints and statues on Tuesday has her squirming and uncomfortable, but by the next day she's lounging on the pews with me, chewing her sandwich with her mouth open while she talks.

"You're right," she says around her mouthful. "It is kind of peaceful in here."

I don't have a lot to say to her these days, but Azar knows how to fill the silence.

"This would be a killer place for a sleepover. Lots of space for sleeping bags, and we could project movies on that giant wall behind the altar. Plus, perfect acoustics for karaoke."

I open my bag of chips and offer it to her. Azar feels around in the bag until she's selected the perfect potato chip. Her bites echo through the church. When she finishes the chips, she casts her eyes sideways at me.

"When are you two gonna start talking again?" She says it softly, like she's waiting for me to snap.

Azar knows Bea and I had a nuclear meltdown, but I didn't tell her the details. And it's not that I don't trust my sister. It's that I'm too ashamed to tell her. How can I even name what I did? I took away every poem-gift Bea ever gave me. Soured every loving word she wrote. We inhabited this whole beautiful world together inside The Book, and I incinerated it.

I pull my lip between my teeth. "Have you been talking to Bea?"

I can't believe I'm sinking so low as to try to buy information from my little sister with potato chips, but here we are.

"Nope." She licks the salt from her fingers.

I sharpen my eyes on her, not buying it. She and Bea used to text almost every day. I can't believe they haven't at least hashed out their feelings about some new unsolved mystery show, or traded astrology memes.

"Seriously!" she says. "We haven't talked since, like, the day you two had your blowup." Azar pulls the red hair tie from her hair, scrunching her dark curls. "Why do you think I'm in this creepy church with you eating lunch? I chose my side."

My heart flickers to life for the first time in days. "But you know me. You said these things are usually my fault."

"So?" She swats my arm. "You're still my sister."

I drop my head to her shoulder, trying to freeze time around those words.

After a minute, Azar's breathing changes and she starts picking at her nails. "Hey. I have to ask you something."

I lift my head and watch her eyes circle the stained glass window above the altar.

"I want to go visit Mom this Saturday. And I want you to come with me."

Adrenaline zips up my chest, prepping me for the catastrophe hidden in her words. I have to hold the *no, no, no* from jumping off my tongue.

She watches me hesitating. "You're mad at her," she says. "I get it. So am I."

"It's not just about being mad at her." My fingernails dig into the edge of the pew. "I don't want to keep giving her the power to hurt us again."

Azar leans against the backrest of the bench, her black locks flowing over the wood. "I know there's things I don't remember," she says. "And you do."

I don't say anything. I lean back beside her, staring up at the vaulted ceiling of the chapel.

"I didn't want to think about what happened before," she says. "I just wanted to start over with her. Forgive. But maybe it's important that we don't just forget."

Aziz turns to face me. "I need you for that."

I take a breath and track all the tiny expressions flowing across

Azar's face. Somehow, she holds hope and disappointment in her skin all at once.

"You believed that she could change," I say. "You've always been good at being hopeful. I need you for that."

Azar's face lifts with a small smile.

She wants me there by her side. And for the past few days, she's shown up for me exactly when I needed her. There are so many disasters I can't fix right now, but I can do this.

"Okay," I say. "I'll go with you."

The Other Deepest Thing

MS. ACOSTA ASKS me to stay after poetry seminar on Thursday. She may be nearing eighty, but she can still see well enough to tell that I'm basically a ghost. My hair hangs in unbrushed clumps and my eyes rim with puffy crescent moons. I haven't raised my hand in class all week.

"Mitra," she says, patting the armchair next to her. I slump down and stare out at the bay. "Something weighing on you?"

I don't know how to answer.

She rides out the silence with me. "I know it's almost college decision-making time," she offers.

I bite my thumbnail and try to think of something to tell her. "It's not that. Just personal stuff."

She nods and waits, and for a moment the only sounds are Ms. Acosta's exhales and the tick-tock of the classroom's clock.

"Just . . . relationship stuff." I can already feel my throat constricting. "And family."

"I see."

I want to ask Ms. Acosta, *Do you know why I am the way I am?* But instead I say, "You were a nun."

"I was."

"So you probably read a lot of the Bible?"

She chuckles and folds her hands into the lap of her black slacks. "That is a big part of the life."

"You remember Father Mitchell's reading the other day, about some vessels being made by God for good, and some being made for his wrath?" I glance over at her.

"Romans, 9:22," she says with her eyes closed.

"Yeah. Do you think it's true?"

Ms. Acosta's eyebrows lift above her reading glasses. "How do you mean?"

Salt water stings in the corners of my eyes. Can I even ask her what I want to ask? Why did my mom relapse, and why did I think she wouldn't this time? Why did I ruin every good thing I ever had with Bea?

"Do you think some people were just made for destruction?"

Ms. Acosta purses her lips. "Humans can be destructive. But God is still patient with us." She focuses her eyes on me. "Are you patient with yourself?"

I can't answer that.

Ms. Acosta sees the sheen of water blurring my eyes. "Am I right, Mitra, in thinking you're not Catholic?"

A quick breath of laughter escapes me. "What gave me away?"

She smiles and takes a moment to think, and we both watch a sailboat ripple across the bay. "I could expand on the significance of that particular passage with you. But I don't know if that's what you're really looking for." She sets her hands on her knees. "The Bible is one source of wisdom that Catholics turn to. You're a poet. There are other wise words we can consult with."

Ms. Acosta stands and skims her bookshelf for a thin paperback. "Do you remember the poem I read at the start of our seminar?"

"It was one of Naomi Shihab Nye's," I say. "She's my favorite."

"So maybe she's a meaningful teacher for you to turn to in this moment." Ms. Acosta licks her fingertip and flips through the paperback to dog-ear a page. "Here." She hands me the book. "Take this home and give the poem another read. See what you make of it."

I take the book to my bedroom after school and sit in the middle of all my unmade blankets and open to the page with "Kindness."

> Before you know what kindness really is
> you must lose things,
> feel the future dissolve in a moment
> like salt in a weakened broth.
> What you held in your hand,
> what you counted and carefully saved,
> all this must go so you know
> how desolate the landscape can be
> between the regions of kindness.

I've read this poem a few times before. I know it already, and still somehow the ending of the poem reaches under my ribs to grip my lungs and clutch my heart.

> Before you know kindness as the deepest thing inside,
> you must know sorrow as the other deepest thing.
> You must wake up with sorrow.
> You must speak to it till your voice
> catches the thread of all sorrows

and you see the size of the cloth.

Then it is only kindness that makes sense anymore,

only kindness that ties your shoes

and sends you out into the day to gaze at bread,

only kindness that raises its head

from the crowd of the world to say

It is I you have been looking for,

and then goes with you everywhere

like a shadow or a friend.

Water splatters the pages of Ms. Acosta's book.

I've spent so much of my life trying to avoid pain and sorrow. I thought that if I didn't hold or save anything, I could protect myself from the devastation of loss. Loss was the worst thing I could ever imagine.

And now it's happened. Just like it did years ago.

The Size of the Cloth

AFTER MS. ACOSTA'S assignment to consult Naomi Shihab Nye for advice, I pull other texts from the Ancestor's Shelf. I reread Hafez's thirteenth poem, and my mother's favorite Rumi quote, and then I revisit *The Prophet*'s guidance on pain.

> *Your pain is the breaking of the shell*
> *that encloses your understanding.*
> *Even as the stone of the fruit must break,*
> *that its heart may stand in the sun, so must*
> *you know pain.*
> *And could you keep your heart in wonder*
> *at the daily miracles of your life, your*
> *pain would not seem less wondrous than your*
> *joy;*
> *And you would accept the seasons of your*
> *heart, even as you have always accepted*
> *the seasons that pass over your fields.*
> *And you would watch with serenity*
> *through the winters of your grief.*

My shell has crumbled to dust. I know that. Out here without the protection of that shell, emotions abrade my skin with the force of a sandstorm. But maybe the pain has cracked me open. Maybe I'm finally ready for a new understanding.

I walk into poetry class on Friday with my eyes clear of the fog that obscured me this week. I want to do what Gibran said: accept the seasons of my heart.

There's an empty seat between Lilith and Max, and I settle in for the lesson. "Hi," I whisper to Max while Ms. Acosta pulls down a projection screen. She's showing us clips from the National Poetry Slam competition today.

Max perks up at my greeting, and I place my hand over theirs, squeezing.

"You're back," they say, brushing the side of their head against mine.

While the poetry slam performers draw the focus of the class, I look around the room. I always thought Bea and I were alone at Holy Trinity, two sore-thumb outcasts in a perfect Catholic crowd. But it was never just us. This seminar is proof of that. If I had really seen them, maybe I would have noticed sooner: Lilith and her goth doctrine of nonjudgment; Rashad, the Quiz Bowl champion, with his nerdy love of iambic pentameter; Tala, my old volleyball partner, writing her freaky fantasy poems about elves. I could've had more allies here if I had reached out for them.

Maybe Bea was right. I *did* hold myself back in some ways. If I can't open up to the people here, or let down my guard enough to trust someone like Bea, what makes me think college will be any different? My worries will follow me into whichever future I choose.

I glance over at Bea, seated in a green armchair on the other side of Max. I'd bristled when she told me I stopped seeing her—that I only projected my worries and expectations onto her. This morning, I try to look at her through newborn eyes. Not as my girlfriend or best friend or some prize on a pedestal, but as a girl in white knee-high socks and a rumpled red skirt, one suspender sliding down the shoulder of her white Peter Pan blouse. She's wearing matte red lipstick and no eye makeup today, dark shadows lining her eyes. Her focus strays from the slam poets as she chews on the end of her pencil.

Beside her, Cara outlines notes on a blank sheet of paper. When a new performer takes the stage she taps Bea's shoulder, pointing to the projection screen and mouthing something.

I used to take a moment like this and let it rocket me up that roller coaster Max described at 8-Bit. *Cara is flirting with Bea. She's trying to get back together with her. Maybe Bea still loves her.*

Today my mind takes a different tack. Maybe Cara isn't some femme fatale out to ruin my relationship. Maybe she's just a person living her own messy life, like me.

When I look back at Bea, her eyes snag on mine for a second. Before she can pull them away toward the screen, I register a flash of the sadness in her eyes. That glimpse of her grief sticks a thumb right into my bruised heart.

Seeing Bea and Cara hugging on opening night felt like a fishhook piercing my heart, dragging it down my body on an invisible line. I didn't think I could contain any more pain that night. Not after finding my mother at my doorstep, high and no longer herself. They both hurt me. But I hurt Bea too. And I hurt myself.

I remember Naomi Shihab Nye's words in "Kindness":

Before you know kindness as the deepest thing inside,
you must know sorrow as the other deepest thing.

I do know sorrow now. I wake up with sorrow. I wake up having lost my mother, my best friend, my girlfriend, and the poetry that made me come to life. The future I saw, the past as I knew.

But I also wake up with my mother's sorrow. I feel the aching shame in the hesitant texts she sends from treatment. And I wake up with Bea's sorrow. Her faint smiles at school are rare now, and they never reach her eyes.

I finally see the size of the cloth.

If Bea and my mother feel one drop of the sorrow I'm feeling now, then I know they deserve all the kindness I can offer them.

And maybe I'm worthy of the same.

Family Day

DAD DRIVES AZAR and me to the treatment center on Saturday morning. "I'm not coming in today," he tells us, kissing our foreheads. "But I'll be waiting right here if you need me."

The building is big, like a high school or a community center, but it's landscaped with ferns and a rock garden. Rainwater collects in the rocks and trickles along a path of native plants. A family with three kids sits on a bench under a Japanese maple drinking punch out of plastic cups. Azar takes my hand before we even reach the front door.

"We can leave anytime you want," I tell her.

"I know."

A welcome sign greets us at the front desk, and we follow others to a rec room that looks kind of like a living room built for five families. Couches, tables, and chairs span the linoleum floor, and a few board games are laid out across the tables. Small clusters of families gather around the furniture. The big room reverberates with conversations—some lively, some hushed.

Jaleh sits next to a gas fireplace in an armchair that looks like a faded version of the one in her apartment. Her hair is down today, curls loose and framing her face. She has a trace of black eyeliner ringing her eyes, but otherwise she's gone without makeup, like she did that Saturday morning we spent at her apartment making waffles. When she sees us arm in arm across the rec room she shoots to her feet, a smile transforming her tired face.

Her smile breaks me. The expression isn't restricted to her lips; it spreads everywhere. It sparks through her curls and up her eyebrows and down to the tips of her fingers. But the thing that pierces me most is that it clarifies her eyes. They're not spinning and blurred and foreign anymore. They're hers. It's my mother looking back at me.

I'm crying before we even reach her. I should be embarrassed, shedding tears in front of dozens of strangers, but I'm too raw to care.

"I didn't know if you'd really come," Mom says. Azar and I drop hands and fit ourselves into her open arms. Even in this sterilized place, she's retained that jasmine honey *mom* smell. She presses a palm to each of our heads and holds us in her embrace.

We settle into the cushy chairs beside her. Mom sits with her hands on her knees, her face swirling with sadness and gratitude at the same time. "How are you girls?" she asks.

Azar won't tolerate small talk today. "What happened?" she says, her voice eroding from emotion. "Why did you start using again?"

Mom nods as she formulates her words. "I wish your baba and I had talked to you both more about what was happening when you were younger," she says. "So you could have understood. But— sometimes there is no *why* with addiction. It is a disease that makes the brain believe there is nothing more important than drugs."

Water rims our mom's eyes. "Not even the people you love most in the whole world. It feels like you will not survive without it. I had been doing well for a long time, but sometimes stressful events or big changes—like moving to Washington or struggling with things at work—they can trigger the addiction again."

"Was it too much pressure?" Azar wipes the tears from her face. "Having us in your life again?"

My memory of that overheard conversation between Mom and Dad at the treatment center years ago steps forward. *I can't be a mom right now,* she'd whispered to my dad. *It's too much.* In the eight years since I heard those words, I believed she'd chosen in that moment to stop being our mother. I didn't realize that the disease of addiction made it so that she couldn't be.

Mom leans forward and takes Azar's hand in hers. "This was not your fault," she says to both of us. "They have a saying here for the children of addicts: You didn't cause it, you can't cure it, you can't control it. It is not on you. But—I think I put a lot of pressure on myself when I moved here. I wanted things to be perfect when I came back into your lives. I wanted you to see that I had it all under control, that I was completely better.

"And you know what?" She huffs a little laugh. "I'm not perfect. I should have asked for support. I should have told Baba that I was struggling. The truth is that I let you down, and let myself down."

Her admission tugs at all the nerves under my skin. I know what it feels like to lose myself, and to disappoint the people I love most.

Ever since she started using, I've split Jaleh in two: Every good and loving memory was *Mom,* and the addiction, the stranger who stepped into our lives like a cyclone, was *not-Mom.* I don't know how to bring these warring mothers together in my mind. It's hard to stomach that she is just one person, both deeply flawed and deeply loving. Like me.

I didn't want to love my mom because I didn't want her to hurt me again. But the very fact of my hurting means I've loved her all along. It's just like Bea said that afternoon when she helped me divine answers from Hafez: My mom didn't slip into my heart; she was already there. I spent five years convincing myself I didn't love her or need her, but I do. I'm exhausted from pretending otherwise.

Accepting that I love my mom, and accepting that she hurt me, means I have to really see her too. She is not perfect. She could relapse again, and I can't change that.

"I'm sorry I expected you to be perfect," I say. "I'm not."

The rest of the words I can't bear to say out loud: *I hurt someone I love, and I did it on purpose. I'm far from the person I want to be right now.*

My breath turns choppy like storm water, and my shoulders tremble. Azar and Mom watch me with warm eyes.

"Joon," Mom says. "What's wrong?"

"I screwed up." My voice doesn't sound like mine. It's high and jaggy over my tears. "I ruined things with Bea."

Mom cups my cheek in her hand. "What happened?"

"I saw her hugging her ex, and I thought she was cheating on me. But she wasn't. But I got so angry and jealous and thought she was going to break up with me. And I burned all of our books. The poetry we've been writing for five years. I ruined all of it."

Azar sucks in a breath, and Mom clucks her tongue at me.

"There's something wrong with me." I smear my tears around my face. "Every time things are good with her, I get insecure and I just screw everything up. She does everything right, and I still don't know how to trust her. I don't know how to be her girlfriend. I'm not a good person."

I curl tight into the chair and let my tears saturate the knees of my jeans. I make a little cave of myself, a place filled only with my steamy breath and sniffles.

An arm reaches around me, and then another, making me lift my head from my knees.

"You are a good person, Mitra," my mother says. "I'm so sorry." She lowers her chin to her chest and presses her eyes closed, kissing the top of my head. "It was my job to teach you differently. You should have learned that the world is a safe place for you. That you can trust the people who care for you."

She brushes her thumb over my chin and Azar's temple. "I broke your trust. I'm so sorry I taught you to be afraid. To not trust even the people who love you very much."

Mom swipes a finger under her eyes, looking out across the rec center floor. "You know that I'm here to recover, to heal. It's hard work, and I have to keep at it, but it's worth doing. Maybe there is healing work that needs to be done for you too, huh?" She squeezes my hand. "It's hard, but you need to learn to trust people again. You know that Bea is worth the effort."

Azar grabs me a tissue from one of the end tables and I blot all the smudged tears and snot from my face. I try to soften myself around Mom's words. If she had spoken them on Nowruz, I would've thrown a fistful of sabzi at her and ran out the door. I didn't want any advice from my mother. But at this point I can't muster the will to get angry or defensive at her. I have no sharp points left inside me. I'm just dust and ash and howling wind inside.

She's right. And I have nothing left to lose.

Maybe I am like my mother. But we're not only destined for destruction. My mother is just a flawed human who has hurt the people she loves. I know what it feels like to do unforgivable things. If my mother can raise her head and carry on, and work everyday to show Azar and me that she's trying to change, then I can do the same.

I am more than the things I've ruined.

I lean into my mom's shoulder and she skims her fingers through my hair until our locks are indistinguishable.

Maybe I won't ever fully trust my mother to stay sober again. But I can love her.

Azar pats my knee, and the three of us sit like that for a while, quiet in each other's presence. Then Azar asks Mom about rehab— *How's the food? What crafts are you making?* and Jaleh shows us her latest beading project, a set of bracelets for Azar and me. Aziz pulls a tiny Tupperware container out of her purse and hands it to Mom.

"They're a week old," she says. "They're probably really stale and gross."

Mom pops open the Tupperware and unwraps two sticky zoolbia roses. If they are stale, Mom doesn't say anything. She savors every bite with a smile, licking her saffron-syrup fingers after she finishes.

At the end of Family Day, Azar and I promise to come back and visit Mom again next weekend. We find flyers at the reception desk for a support group for teens coping with parents' addictions, starting in twenty minutes. Azar freaks out about the fact that the flyer promises pizza and doughnuts at every meeting.

"Can we stay for this, though? Seriously?" Azar says when I tease her about her pizza obsession.

"You want to?" I scan the flyer again. It has a lot of clip art on it.

"Yeah."

I glance over at Mom, who is checking her schedule for the rest of the day. She told us she does therapy *every day* here, like hours and hours of it. Individual therapy, group therapy, art therapy, occupational therapy. There's even family therapy, if we choose to join. She wasn't exaggerating when she said she's working hard.

"Okay. I'll text Dad that we'll be a little longer," I say. Azar fills out our information on the sign-up sheet.

If Mom is doing all that work, I can go to this support group. She's right. I have my own healing work to do.

As we say goodbye to Mom, I remember that I have something for her too. "Wait."

I dig through my shoulder bag and find her note card, now even more tattered than when she gave it to me. "Thanks for letting me borrow this, Mom," I say. "I thought you might like to put it up in your room."

The note card may be crumpled, but her handwriting hasn't faded a bit. Rumi's words shine.

Love nourishes and mends.
Love opens the clenched body,
lets the soul breathe.

Hope

It's strong medicine, forgiveness
lodging in the river of every shameful
thing I've done—let it dissolve inside
me, build someone ready to love her

Foreword

DAD LENDS ME the car on Tuesday to drive to school while he car-pools to work. At the end of the day Azar and I turn onto Eighth Street, headed toward Crossroads, but I'm not ready to go home yet. I search for Azar's eyes at a red light.

"Want to keep driving around?" I ask her. She nods and leans back in her seat.

I don't know where I'm going. I drive Azar from Lake Sammamish to Lake Washington, up through Bridle Trails, down along the Cougar Mountain Wildland. The whole span of our world here in Washington. I loop us from lake to lake and back to the beginning again, but it doesn't feel aimless. We're knitting something together as we go.

Azar doesn't speak for the better part of the first hour. But on our second circuit hugging the coast of Lake Sammamish, she turns to me, wedging one foot up on the seat.

"It's going to be weird without having you here next year."

"It's going to be weird for me too," I say. "I still have no idea what I'm going to do."

I keep following the boulevard, and this time around I remember what's coming next: the trailheads on the right, then the resort, and then the highway.

"I thought you had it all mapped out," she says. "Like you do with *everything*."

"Not anymore." I watch the trees blur out the window. "But maybe that's not a bad thing. Maybe I could stand to be a little more like you."

She stares at me when we thread under the highway. "What do you mean?"

I flex my fingers on the steering wheel as the road transforms, shedding its stoplights as it arcs through the woods. "Open," I say.

Out of the corner of my eye, I catch Azar smiling.

When we head north toward downtown again, Azar makes us stop for coffee at the drive-through. "So." She cradles the iced cup in her hands. "How are you going to get her back?"

I don't know if Bea will ever look at me the same way again. Going back feels impossible. But I know what I have to do if we ever want to move forward.

Azar and I stop at the art supply store and she leaves me alone in the paper section. I feel my way along the spines of every note-book and sketchbook I can reach until I find it: a blank book bound in espresso-colored leather. It's handmade and heavy, the cover soft under my fingers. Thick card-stock pages fill the inside. The book smells like glue and singed string and Bea's thrifted Royal jacket.

It's not like our old volumes of the never-ending poem, and I don't want it to be. I wanted to find something sturdy this time. Lasting. Something that won't give into the flames. When we get home, I fold the book open to the first page and begin writing.

Dear Bea,

Do you remember how the never-ending poem started?
You've asked me that a million times, and I always gave you the
same answer. It was that paper scrap. It was your wild thirteen-year-
old boredom in homeroom, and your mischief, and my fright and
newness, and some connection we saw coming but couldn't name
yet. And all of that is true. But it's also not the whole story. Do you
remember how it started, really?

It started with your trust. You plucked me from the crowd of good
Catholic kids. You trusted me with your words. And I trusted you
with mine.

We made a world and we made rules for that world. Honesty, always.
Tell the truth even when it's hard. Even when it feels impossible.

I broke that rule for years. But I'm ready to be honest with you now.

When we left Sacramento—when we left my mom—I thought I had
left the pain and the hurt behind too. I thought cutting my mom out
of our lives meant I had cut away all of her: the good memories and
the terror, the moments that still burn to touch, the ones that plunge
me back into my twelve-year-old skin. What it felt like to have a
mom, what it felt like to lose one. I wanted to wash all of that away.

Somewhere, back in the mess of everything that happened with my mom, I learned to stop counting on other people. I learned to stay safe by trusting only myself. I loved you from a safe distance; I never dreamed you could love me the way I loved you. But then you did. Only, the more you loved me, the more terrified I felt.

You and I have spent years together yanking at the seams of words, finding ways to make them fit the weight of our experiences. And we also know that sometimes words just can't hold it all. I am so, so very sorry. And I know those words are nowhere near enough.

But my love for you is the truest, most trustworthy thing in my life. I know that, even when I know nothing else. I will do everything it takes to earn back your trust, little by little, if you'll let me.

I remember how the poem started. I remember, I remember. If you remember too, meet me in the chapel before school tomorrow.

Love,
Mitra

Heart

ON TUESDAY NIGHT, I borrow the car to drive to Bea's house. Her mom's Tesla is parked in the driveway, so I pull up behind it and sit for a minute, listening to my breath. Of all the days her parents could be home. I just hope Bea is downstairs, and that she cares enough to answer the door.

When I've steadied myself, I walk to the front stoop and lay the leather-bound book on top of the welcome mat with a note with Bea's name.

I have the hardest time leaving the book there. It's like setting my heart on the cold doorstep, turning my back, hoping it doesn't get trampled.

I ring the doorbell and turn back to the car. The front door opens as I drive away, but I don't wait to see who answers.

The Wait

I TAKE THE bus to Holy Trinity an hour before school starts on Wednesday, and I'm ready at the door when a clergywoman first opens the chapel. She's silver-haired and dressed in a long skirt and red turtleneck. She smiles at me, a little startled to find me lining up at the church entrance like I'm waiting for a holiday doorbuster sale at Target. She lets me in, presumably to pray, and then disappears into the back offices.

I plant myself on the front pew and watch morning light move its way through the panes of stained glass overhead. Student footsteps and voices lift outside, and then they die away. I reach into my backpack for the one comfort I brought: Hafez's *Divān*.

I'm not reading to divine answers today. Bea has probably already made her decision, whatever that may be. I just want Hafez's love and despair and delight to flow over me. If I'm really going to let the light in, I have to make room for all of it—the highs and the heartaches too. I'm trying to hold tight to what Kahlil Gibran said: my pain is no less wondrous than my joy.

I start with the first poem in the *Divān* and journey my way through the book. It's hard not to hear my heartbeat begging the question on every page: Will Bea come and find me? Does she still believe I'm more than the destruction I've caused? I breathe into the questions, and I keep reading.

The morning bell rings with no sign of Bea. She's made her choice, but I'm not ready to let go. First period comes and goes. So do a few clergy people, and so does Father Mitchell. He smiles and nods at me but doesn't disturb me. Even though it's clear I'm not praying the rosary or reading the Bible or looking pious in any way. I keep waiting for him to kick me out or force me to go to class. Instead, he lets me read in peace. I had no idea Father Mitchell could be so chill. He must be able to tell I'm working through something important.

When I finish the last ghazal, I start at the beginning again.

I lose track of how many bells have interrupted my reading. I must've missed a few classes by now. But the lunch bell announces itself in its own way, trailed by the rush of student voices toward the plaza and the cafeteria.

The creak of the front door to the chapel sets my heart running, and I have to remind my body that it won't be Bea. Azar knew I was going to try to make things right with Bea this morning. If someone's here at lunch, that means Azar knows I failed.

Footsteps tap forward down the aisle, cut by the clap of the door closing behind them. I draw a breath into my lungs and hold it there, letting grief shiver through me. Facing Azar means I have to admit to myself that Bea has given up on me.

I set the *Divān* face down on the pew and turn toward the sound of footsteps. They aren't my sister's.

Adrenaline zips through me, kicking me out of my stillness. *She's here.*

Bea treks down the aisle toward me in her Pegasus loafers, the leather-bound book hugged into the fold of her blazer. For the first time in a week, her earthy eyes stay on mine.

I leap up from the pew, knocking over the *Divān*. "I'm so sorry," I start.

It's absurd. In my letter, I wrote all about how those words can't do the work I need them to do. It's like my mom once said. Only I can live out that apology in the way I show up for Bea, for our relationship, every day from here on out. Still, my desperate voice shouts the words across the church at her. They echo back to me when they bounce off the high ceiling.

Bea lifts a hand to stop me. I hold my tongue until she meets me at the front pew, and we both sit cross-legged on the bench, facing each other. No more hiding.

I missed her freckles and her runaway curls. I missed the way her glasses cast light to brighten eyes. I missed the twist of her mouth when she's thinking. I missed looking at her.

I listen to Bea inhale and exhale. I listen to the whoosh of my heartbeat in my ears and throat and fingertips.

"Thank you for sharing this with me." She raises the book in her hand. "I knew you and your mom had a tough relationship, I just . . . I don't think I understood before."

"You couldn't know when *I* didn't really understand," I say.

A crease forms in the space between Bea's eyebrows. She opens her hand and extends it to me hesitantly. After more than a week without her touch, this one point of contact thunders through my insides.

"You've been through a lot," she says. "Maybe more than I can ever really know. But all I need is for you to let me in, and you did."

Tears well in my eyes again. *God is patient,* Ms. Acosta said.

"Does this mean you can forgive me?" I coil my hand tighter into hers.

A little grin lifts the corners of her mouth, and she nods.

She brings her hands to my shoulders, runs them up the back of my neck to sleep in the darkness of my hair. She touches her nose to mine, and then her lips. Her kiss bursts stained glass glitter behind my eyelids. I bring everything—the dredged-up parts of me, everything I lost, everything I want—into the kiss. It's the most honest and trusting thing I can offer.

Kissing Bea feels like coming home. The warmth and comfort of her mouth surround me. I pitch deeper, clawing the boundaries of what a kiss can be, transforming it into its own never-ending thing. Her hands come alive in my hair.

Here, I think. Here is what Rumi promised me. We are nourished and mended. We are broken open, pure gold.

Unwritten

WHEN WE BREAK apart, I keep my fingers curled with hers. I don't want to let go now that she's in my arms again.

"I have something for you," Bea says, kissing the salty curve of my cheek. "It was supposed to be your graduation present, but I kinda feel like now is the right time." She reaches into her backpack and pulls out a square package wrapped in rainbow newsprint from *Seattle Gay News*. I unwrap the newspaper carefully and fold it up, tucking it into the hymnal rack for some future freshman to find. Inside the newsprint wrapping is a blue picture frame, and inside the frame lies a crumpled old paper scrap.

> They say you're the new girl
> but they should know better . . .

"We can't get those original books back," she says. Both of us take a breath under the weight of that knowledge, and I squeeze her hand. "But we'll always have this, to remember how it all started."

We didn't know it that day almost five years ago, when we hid this note in the pleats of our skirts and scribbled rhymes when Ms. Byrne wasn't watching. These words were the seeds that would build an entire universe.

"We'll never lose what we have," Bea promises. "You're not just some placeholder or consolation prize, Mitra. You're *it*." She chuckles a little on her exhale, as if bowled over by the magnitude of her own words. "There's no one like you. I know there's a lot of change coming. Things might look different, and we'll grow into different people along the way, but I'm serious about what we said when we started this thing: The never-ending poem is forever. That will never change."

I kiss Bea again, the both of us saying silent prayers for the kids we were when we wrote these first words together, and for the people we're becoming.

And I have to smile. Because maybe some of the never-ending poem is lost forever, but so much of it has yet to be written.

August

Mitra: still packing

Mitra: do you have my fancy pen?

Bea: I like that I already know what you're talking about

Bea: like you've talked about your "fancy pen" so much that it deserves its own name

Mitra: it's special

Mitra: it's fancy

Mitra: maybe I'll get a button-down shirt with a pocket just for the pen

Bea: so utilitarian of you!

Bea: you're going to become one of those rugged woodland queers at Reed, aren't you?

Bea: you're gonna start keeping ferns and pine cones and stuff in that pocket!

Mitra: don't distract me from the pen

Mitra: the Fancy Pen

Mitra: do you have it?

Bea: oh now it's a proper noun?

Bea: Mitra "FancyPen" Esfahani

Mitra: I know you wanted to keep something of mine to remind you of me when you're at UW

Mitra: but I thought we'd swap our favorite shirts or something

Mitra: not the pen

Mitra: anything but the pen!!

Bea: I'm not saying I have it

Bea: but if I did have it, you'd be getting handwritten letters AND never-ending poems from me in your fancy-pen ink

Bea: just sayin

Mitra: ok fine

Mitra: you can keep it

Mitra: I love you that much

Bea: !!!

September

"MADE SOMETHING FOR you," Azar says as we're all scooping our forks into Dad's steamy tomato omelette. It's a full Esfahani family brunch this morning: Mom walked over from her apartment as soon as I was awake and met us at the door with a plastic container of watermelon soaked in rosewater. Dad complained about us all still being in our pajamas, but Mom wouldn't hear it. *I don't want to miss a minute of time before Mitra leaves,* she said.

"You made *me* something?"

"For your dorm room." Azar pulls a piece of card stock out from under a book on the dining room table. "So you don't forget about us."

Printed on the card stock are four squares nested together like windowpanes, with each of our faces digitally painted in bold cut-outs of color. Behind us, geometric designs fit together in the style of ancient Persian tile: small chips of royal blue, yellow, and green, forming intricate flowers and stars. Above the quartet of our portraits, she's allowed bright turquoise tiles to bleed until they form a name: Esfahani.

"Aziz." I cup my hands around her creation. The portraits of Mom and me are digitally painted versions of the photos she took of us at Highland Park on our first full Saturday together.

I can't stand to leave Azar here in Bellevue while I take off to Reed. Anything could happen here with my mom, or at Holy Trinity, and

I want to be there for Azar through whatever. But I'm trying to do what my dad told me on the night Mom relapsed: I'm trying to finally be a teenager. Azar is stronger than I ever gave her credit for. We will always need each other, but she doesn't need me to be a protector anymore. She just needs a sister.

"Tell your roommate I'm coming to visit on weekends," she says. "I'll bring my own sleeping bag. There are showers at Reed, right? It's not *that* hippie of a place, is it?"

"How are you getting to Portland for these weekend visits?" Mom raises her eyebrows at Azar.

"She has her driver's license for one month and she's already planning road trips," Dad grumbles.

I devour the final bite of my toast with sour cherry jam and hop up from the table. "We gotta go if I'm going to say goodbye to Bea."

Bea and I have made a monument out of celebrating all our *lasts* this summer—last trip to Lake Sammamish, last movie at Crossroads, even a last trip to 8-Bit Arcade with Max, Ellie, and Cara—but this is our official, last goodbye.

"Did you finish loading up, Dad?"

He waves me over to the car to show off the Tetris-level job he did packing all my stuff into the back. I set Azar's art right on top, and when I close the hatchback, I'm encased in three sets of arms.

When we moved to Crossroads five years ago, I didn't think I'd ever have another four-way-Esfahani-family hug. When they happen now, they knock the wind out of me in the best way.

Dad drives me to Bea's house on our way out of Bellevue and parks the car just outside of her driveway. "Take your time," he tells me.

I've been running on adrenaline the past few days, whirling around in a tornado of clothes and suitcases and welcome emails from Reed, and all of that energy rinses out of me when I reach Bea's front porch. My heart roots itself in my throat and my eyes sting before she even opens the door.

She's wearing those goofy cat-print pajamas and an old pair of gold-rimmed glasses, sleepy-eyed and face clean of makeup, and her mouth opens to speak, but I dive into her arms before she can say anything.

"I love you." My voice threads its way through all the emotion. "You're my girl."

"No goodbyes, okay?" Bea says. "That would be like putting a period in the never-ending poem. And you promised me no terminal punctuation."

"Sacrilege," I say. "I would never."

Bea steps back from our hug and presses her forehead to mine. "Then what do we say instead?"

I kiss the tip of her nose, and she sweeps my wavy hair back behind my ear. "See you soon," I say. I'll probably be seeing her in two hours: I know we'll be texting and video chatting and calling each other all the time.

It won't be the same, and that's scary. But I'm trying to hold on to what I've learned in support group with Azar: Sometimes trust is about letting go. I can be my own person, and be all right in my own skin, and Bea will still be there when we come back together. I know she will be there when I need her. I know she'll love me, even when we're apart.

Bea takes off her glasses and nuzzles her face into my shirt collar, wiping away tears. "Here." She grabs something from an end table by the doorway and hands it to me: the new leather-bound book. "Your turn. But this better be in my mailbox within five to ten business days."

We both laugh as I wrap my arms around The Book. "I promise. Priority mail express."

She hugs me tight one more time, and I give her a kiss worth remembering. "Have fun at UW," I say. "Do amazing things."

"I love you," she says. "Don't forget."

My tears hit the binding of the book as I walk toward the car, toward everything ahead. I can hear Bea's sniffles behind me. It wrenches my heart to leave her. But there's lightness inside of me too. I know that ours is the realest kind of story: a story still unfolding. A never-ending thing.

Mitra & Bea

love this constant, steady
and true, defies even the
structure we built: words

like best friend/ girlfriend/ person can't name it
so I'll settle on everything and nestle into comfort
that the universe has language for indefinable love

like ours, turning struggle
into gold, watching us change
and then changing us in turn

that's our love—too vast for these words to tack
down, but we'll find a way to lift it up across
time and unknowns and even state lines

I've never rebuilt a sailing
ship before but here we are
restoring joy in all we touch

pointing our sails and traveling fresh-eyed
to some dazzling land as yet unnamed, hold
my hand and we'll find what we're made of

Acknowledgments

A MONTH OR so into the pandemic, a friend sent me a *New Yorker* cartoon of a person stranded in treacherous waters in a canoe, the sky unleashing lightning and rain overhead, ships capsizing in the distance, and what I can only assume were piranhas circling nearby. The caption read *This is it . . . the time to finish your novel.* "It's literally you!" my friend texted.

In truth, writing this book was a bright spot for me throughout the uncertainty of the pandemic. Through isolating times, I watched a dedicated and creative team come together to help me bring Mitra and Bea's story on to these pages. I am grateful to them—and to you—for engaging with this story. Book people are the best people.

All my gratitude goes to Quressa Robinson, my literary agent, for believing in the power of queer girls' stories—and believing in me—for years before this book even took shape.

Many thanks to editor Lanie Davis, without whom this story would not exist, for having the enthusiasm, patience, and insight to see Mitra and Bea through to their (never-) ending.

Epic thanks to Ellen Cormier, editor extraordinaire, for your super-smart wisdom and guidance, and for believing this story was worth sharing.

Thank you to the writers who lent their expansive worlds of words to Mitra and Bea (and me), influencing the writing of this book in many ways. My heartfelt thanks to Naomi Shihab Nye for your generosity: I couldn't have told Mitra's story without you. You are the embodiment of kindness.

To the powerhouses at Penguin Random House and its imprint Dial Books for Young Readers: publisher Jen Klonsky, editorial director Nancy Mercado, editorial assistant Squish Pruitt, copyeditor Regina Castillo, managing editor Tabitha Dulla, interior designer Cerise Steel, cover designer Kelley Brady, and associate director of publicity Liz Montoya Vaughan. Thanks also to Penguin's marketing team: Christina Colangelo, Bri Lockhart, Amber Reichert, Felicity Vallence, James Akinaka, and Shannon Spann.

Many thanks to the team at Alloy Entertainment, especially Sara Shandler and Josh Bank, for your hive-mind magic. To legal wizards Romy Golan and Matthew Bloomgarden for your expertise and dedication. To Kat Jagai, Laura Barbiea, and everyone else at Alloy who helped coordinate my first trip to New York. My visit to your offices is still one of my very favorite writing-related memories.

To Dana Kaye, Jordan Brown, Angela Melamud, Eleanor Imbody, and the whole crew at Kaye Publicity for advocating for this book, and for the generous gift of your Equity in Publishing Fund."

To the talented Beatriz Ramo, whose dreamy cover art brought Mitra and Bea into full color.

To the teams at Folio Literary Management and Nelson Literary Agency for your support.

To the poets on Mitra's Ancestor's Shelf, and on many a Haft Seen altar I've put together over the years: Hafez, Rumi, and Gibran. Thank you for delivering your divine intervention whenever it's needed most.

To my parents and stepparents, Behrooz, Heidi, Anne, and Walt, for encouraging my creativity (even when it was just picture books about snails), celebrating small successes, and showing me that what I have to say matters.

Special thanks to my big sister, Taraneh, for being a fiercely supportive reader and sibling. Thanks also to my sestra Emily for your encouragement.

To my spouse, Indhira: Much of this book was written with you asleep beside me on the couch. Thank you for being an adorable (and deep!) sleeper. I can't believe I get to spend my days with you. Thank you for believing in me, loving me, and being my greatest gratitude each day.

And to our dogs: Thank you for briefly letting me use my hands to do something other than petting you. I know you hated the interruption.

To Jess, for your eternal positive regard and wise mind: You're the best friend and chosen family I could wish for. Your cheerleading through every phase of writing and publishing this book kept me going.

To Emily: The universe conspired to make us friends by giving us the same house number, and putting us in that high school math class together, and then making us both queer. Mitra and Bea's neverending poem was inspired partly by the journal we began passing back and forth after graduation. Thanks for the lifelong friendship.

Thank you to my bibi jaan, Behjat, who taught me how to read between the lines of Hafez, and who showed me that poetry is in our blood, and it is an act of revolution.

To the teachers who went above and beyond, especially Kris

Johnson, who made me read my poetry in front of the whole class (I was terrified, and I learned that my voice was worth listening to!), and the late Jody Desclos, who taught me that I didn't need to be Catholic to be spiritual.

Finally, to the many resilient young people I've had the pleasure of knowing in my role as a therapist: May you believe your stories are worth telling.